WISHES AND WONDER

HIGHLAND HEATHER ROMANCING A SCOT:
CASTLE BRIDES

BOOK NINE

COLLETTE CAMERON®

Attn: Permissions Coordinator
Blue Rose Romance® **LLC**
info@collettecameronbooks.com
eBook ISBN: 978-1-966087-98-4
Print ISBN: 978-1-955259-92-7
collettecameronbooks.com

FREE BOOK!

JOIN MY EXCLUSIVE MAILING LIST
Collette Cameron Newsletter

AND GET A FREE EBOOK!

https://collettecameronbooks.com/freegift

Plus Sneak Peeks, Giveaways, Contests, Exclusive Content, and More... P.S. I promise only good stuff ~ **no** spam!

CONTENTS

Acknowledgments

A big thank you to Barbara Blanc and Kandi Torres for helping name my heroine! I hope you enjoy reading about the characters I named after you in *Seductive Surrender*. Thanks, too, to all of my Facebook friends who so graciously (and often hysterically) offered suggestions for southern expressions. I grinned more than once while typing them into the story.

~

DEDICATION

To Collette's Coquettes
An author never had a more devoted group of promotion
princesses.
Thank you, each and every one!

ONE

A deserted Highland Road

Twilight, September 1825

"Is he *dead*?"

Morbid fascination leached into Jeremiah's nine-year-old voice.

I hope to hellfire not.

Squatting beside the enormous, unconscious man sprawled flat as a fritter in the middle of the road, Gwendolyn tossed a harried glance over her shoulder.

The children shouldn't see this. They'd already experienced too much tragedy in their young lives.

Dangling over the coach's open window, his moss-colored eyes bright with curiosity, her nephew swiped his nose across his sleeve.

Not for the first time, either.

Dried snot trails adorning his sleeve wasn't the way she'd envisioned Suttford House's new master arriving to claim his birthright.

"He sure 'nuff looks like he's got both boots in the grave, Auntie Gwenny."

Gwendolyn considered the prostrate figure.

He did, indeed.

"Sugah, you're quite certain the gentleman hasn't already passed?" her maiden Aunt Barbara asked in her musical southern drawl.

Hovering beside Gwendolyn, Aunt Barbara turned down her mouth the merest bit as she skittered a timid glance over the gentleman in question.

"One way to know for certain." Gwendolyn stripped off her pigeon-gray, ecru lace-edged glove before touching her palm to the man's thick throat.

Sensation—tingling and scorching—ratcheted to her shoulder, across her chest, and then settled heavily in her breasts. She almost wrenched her hand away at the startling and unfamiliar jolt.

Good gracious. It's his sheer size. That's all. He's quite the largest man I've ever laid eyes upon.

Crimping her mouth into a purposeful line, she stiffened her resolve, firmly gripped her cavorting composure, and pressed her fingertips to his neck harder.

A sturdy pulse thrummed against the pads.

Thank heavens.

"Dead, *eh*?" This from Mr. Dodd, one of the bristly-faced leery, wholly unchivalrous coachman, loitering a carriage-length away. Some protector he'd proven to be, the spineless poltroon.

Gwendolyn shook her head, and a tendril sprang loose from the tidy knot at her nape. "No, he yet lives."

Oh, to be a man and be permitted to tell Mr. Dodd precisely what she thought of him. But southern belles did not curse. Ever. Instead, Gwendolyn assumed a well-rehearsed benign countenance and swore at him in her head as she tucked the strand back into place.

Craven ass.

Not as satisfying as delivering a tongue lashing, but sufficient to ease her annoyance a thimble's worth. It did nothing to appease her disquiet about this stranger, however.

Other than a few cuts and scrapes on his face, only the man's high forehead showed obvious signs of real injury, and those bumps and gashes didn't appear lethal. Difficult to be certain with head wounds, though.

Dried blood matted the ill-fated brute's longish midnight hair, and fresh scarlet rivulets trickled from his noble forehead, across a strong, patrician nose, and onto a stubble-covered left jaw. Bruised and battered cheeks tapered to swollen, split lips above a determined, cleft chin.

His puffy, damaged face made it hard to tell whether he was handsome, but given his chiseled features, she thought he might be passably attractive.

Not that it mattered a whit if he were as homely as a rotten potato.

She wasn't a frivolous young miss, easily cozened by sharply hewn features, slashing raven brows, and a square, black-whiskered covered jaw.

Much.

Pushing aside a stray curl teasing her forehead, she raked her practiced gaze over the architecture of his impressive form. He wasn't the first man she'd seen worse for wear after a sound thrashing.

The stable hands and her brothers, especially Markus, had returned home battered on more than one occasion, their bruised bodies recovering far swifter than their pummeled pride.

Except for that last tragic time when—

Tarnation.

Unbridled pain buffeted Gwendolyn's ribs, stalling her breath, and she balled her hands against the overwhelming desire to wail her grief.

Not now, Gwendolyn Nicolette Eleanor McClintock.

Attend to the matter at hand.

She drew in a shuddery breath.

Yes. Yes. The injured man.

Anything to distract herself from the awful, heartbreaking memories. Lips cinched from the effort to control her tears, she blinked rapidly to dispel the moisture pooling in her eyes and gave herself a severe mental shake.

As she considered the lines of the man's rugged face, she twisted her mouth in distress.

What other wounds might this poor scalawag have?

Was he a gentleman?

A nobleman?

His finely tailored black coat and buckskins—even dirt-smeared and torn—as well as his big—*very big*—once-shiny boots proclaimed him gentry.

Recently arrived from South Carolina, she wasn't familiar with attire worn by the locals, and they certainly weren't accustomed to hers. In fact, her practical split-skirt traveling ensemble had earned her more than one skewed brow and sideways smirk from the English and Scots, men and women alike.

For her part, she'd expected the Scots to be enshrouded in tartans from their calves to chins, all the while tooting bagpipes, quaffing whisky, and munching shortbread, clootie dumpling, and haggis.

Served her right for planting herself at Grandpapa Gawyn McClintock's knee and raptly listening to his wild—*and obviously exaggerated*—tales of his boyhood homeland whenever she had a chance as a child.

That dear man could certainly spin a fanciful yarn in his lilting brogue.

Trailing her troubled gaze over the insensate stranger, she released a silent sigh. Massively built, his hair unshorn, he resembled the wild, Highland warriors Grandpapa boasted of. All this fellow needed was a broadsword, a belted plaid, and a shield.

Once, long ago—*four wretched betrothals she'd rather desperately wanted to forget ago*—she might've appreciated such a fine masculine specimen.

No longer.

Nonetheless, she permitted herself another leisurely perusal of his extraordinary form.

You cannot deny he's unquestionably, quite pulse-stutteringly spectacular, Gwen.

Bah!

At her inane ruminations, she pinched her mouth into a tight line and narrowed her eyes in annoyance.

Enough moon-eyed musings.

Raising her orphaned niece and nephew to the best of her limited abilities was her only purpose nowadays. Even though it meant she must put aside her few remaining dreams. Seeing Jeremiah equipped to step into the role of a Scottish Lord of Parliament when he became of an age was paramount.

Whatever, precisely, a Lord of Parliament might be.

Something akin to a baron, according to Hubert Christie, the solicitor who'd contacted them all those weeks ago on behalf of Gerard McClintock's estate.

Gwendolyn still didn't quite understand all the title falderal, or how she'd manage to prepare her nephew for the elevated position. Still didn't quite understand how Jeremiah came to inherit the title either.

Grandpapa had been the youngest of four sons. What

were the chances his great-grandson would be the next in line to inherit?

Well, when Mr. Christie had written, he hadn't known of her brothers, Markus's or William's deaths. Nor Father's, either. Christie hadn't been altogether keen that a woman held Jeremiah's guardianship. In fact, his follow-up letters were quite peculiar, and he'd repeatedly asked if there were no other male heirs.

How very different things would've been if Papa and her brothers had yet lived.

Most of all, she still wasn't certain what she'd do when the children were raised and no longer needed her. Out of the question that she would remain in Scotland. The land was too wild and rugged, much like many of the untamed and unrefined people she'd encountered so far.

Homesickness, heavy and melancholic, already shrouded her. She missed the South's gentility, the sultry clime, the polite, considerate, slow-paced culture.

Though only September, she'd been nigh onto freezing her bum off from Scotland's permeating cold and damp, which seemed to increase with the elevation. She didn't even want to contemplate the discomforts of Scottish winters. First on her list was acquiring thick, woolen drawers and stockings, a heavy shawl, and two or three sturdier gowns—perhaps flannel-lined.

A slight breeze danced past, and she shivered, her skin puckering from waist to shoulders.

Add mittens and a snug cap to that list.

Drawing a steadying breath, she darted her aunt a swift glance.

Gwendolyn absolutely refused to become the nervous, self-conscious, trying-not-to-be-a-nuisance-lonely-tabby Aunt Barbara had transformed into over the years.

She'd find something to give her a focus or a purpose, by heavens.

"Miss McClintock, we canna delay much longer." Mr. Murray, their Scots guide, rubbed the back of his neck and shifted from foot to foot, his rheumy eyes and craggy countenance a muddle of impatience, guilty regret, and tension.

"We needs be gettin' on our way, or ye'll not reach Suttford House afore nightfall. The great house is a good six miles away yet." He levered a scuffed boot toe at the prone victim. "We can drag him off the road."

"Not exactly the epitome of compassion, are you, Mr. Murray?" Gwendolyn asked, disdain sharpening her question.

"He'll come 'round eventually." Murray's dubious tone contradicted his confident words.

Would he?

Two

A horse snorted, and Gwendolyn cocked her head as she shoved another escaped lock behind her ear.

She didn't have Aunt Barbara's tame tresses, but rather an abundance of ill-behaved ringlets with a penchant for escaping their pins at every opportunity.

Another equestrian breath sounded. That hadn't come from either of the patient teams.

Squinting, she peered into the pinewoods hugging the roadway. The dusk-deepened shadows revealed nothing unusual. And yet, she swore a horse shifted fretfully within the nebulous gloaming beyond.

Raised around horses her entire life, she knew the sounds of impatient horseflesh when she heard them.

Had the injured man tethered his mount in the woods?

Definitely the actions of an unsavory coon dog rather than an upstanding gentleman.

Botheration.

Her heart gave a queer little disappointed pang.

Tish tosh and sour lemonade.

She didn't give a ragman's scorn that he might be a black-guard after all.

At eight-and-twenty, her heart was resolutely, and-ever-so permanently and sensibly, on the shelf. Secured behind stout, closed, and triple-locked doors. The keys long since buried beneath trampled dreams, an equally pulverized heart, and the harsh, unavoidable realities of a spinster's lot in life.

"Likely a local. He looks to be a sturdy toff—" Mr. Dodd stammered to a halt, his ears turning crabapple red.

"*Ahem.*" Aunt Barbara made a disapproving sound and knitted her fine grayish-white brows over clear hazel eyes while delivering the driver a withering glare with aplomb only a southern belle was capable of rendering.

Quailing under her patrician scowl, he gulped and pulled his neck into his collar, rather like a gopher tortoise retreating into its shell.

Lacy black parasol properly angled to cover her lily-white skin, even though the sun was about to dip below the purplish-orange streaked horizon, Mama's petite sister shook her head. "Gwendolyn, darlin', we cannot possibly leave this unfortunate a-lyin' here. Why, it's unthinkable and utterly unchristian."

What to do?

Gwendolyn's compassion grappled with her common sense.

"Of course, we must take him with us," Aunt Barbara insisted. "Providence may have compelled us to travel to this Godless, uncivilized place where men parade about without draw—"

Her gaze swung to the chagrined drivers' none-too-clean trousers, and Gwendolyn subdued her involuntary smile.

A glimpse of a hair-dusted male buttock beneath a kilt their first day in Scotland had sent Aunt Barbara into a swoon, and now she scrutinized every Scot she saw as if attempting to determine whether he wore undergarments.

Rather made her appear a lecherous dame, peering at their nether regions with such intensity.

Several Scots had ogled her just as boldly, earning them an astringent, castrating stare from her sand-toned eyes.

"Well, never mind *that* unpleasantness." Her aunt made a brusque gesture. "As I was a-sayin'. I, by no means, left *my* Christian charity in America. We must take him with us."

"Ye should ken, folks at Suttford House dinna take kindly to bein' imposed upon. He winna be welcome." Jerking a grubby thumb at the fallen man, Mr. Murray's voice dropped to a barely audible mutter. "Ye winna, either."

"In all my born days, I've never heard such unprovoked impertinence from the lower orders!" Aunt Barbara huffed, her parasol dipping to a dangerous slant as if she might truly thwack him with the frilly accessory.

A first for her.

Her comportment beyond censure, Aunt Barbara was a genteel lady above all else. Her slip into indelicacy betrayed her stress.

Mr. Murray pulled on his earlobe, prudently avoiding the austere look she pinned him with, as sharply as a beetle tacked to a specimen board.

Worry curled Gwendolyn's middle tighter than a happy hog's tail. "I'm positive you're mistaken, sirrah. Why wouldn't Suttford House's heir be welcome?"

Truth to tell, she'd fretted about that very thing.

Each and every day since they learned of Jeremiah's new status. Each and every day since the plantation Grandpapa had built with his own hands had been sold, and they sailed to England, leaving behind everything any of them had ever known. And each day since arriving in Scotland and with every passing mile that brought them nearer Suttford House.

Despite all the smoldering qualms and misgivings, including Mr. Christie's not so subtle hints about his reservations regarding a female custodian, what choice had she but to plow forward into the unknown, dragging her small, reluctant, and wary retinue with her?

The one thing she'd done with utmost confidence had been to free the slaves. A gratified half-smile quirked her mouth upward at the corners.

Lance Eggleston's jaw had unhinged, practically banging his knees in disbelief when Gwendolyn handed her former betrothed the keys to Thistle Glen and announced the freed slaves had departed two days hence.

Adding a, "By the by, Lance, I permitted them to strip the house, barns, and stables bare before they left."

Lance's new, entirely lovely, peak-of-fashion French wife, had fairly gnashed her perfect, pearly teeth in vexation.

Her eyes sinking into irate slits and her cinched smile dimming, she'd cried, "*Non, vous n'oseriez pas!*"

But Gwendolyn *had* dared.

As Jeremey's guardian and executor of her father's will, she had the legal right to free them. Unlike her choice to uproot her family, she didn't doubt that decision. She rested easily each night, confident revenge hadn't motivated her decision, but rather the slaves' wellbeing had.

Besides, she'd never loved Lance beyond brotherly fondness. He was a comfortable, longtime friend she'd finally agreed to marry so as not to be a burden to her family, yet remain near them.

When Sabine had set her lacy, perfume-scented handkerchief for him, he'd been woefully ill-prepared for her heavy-lidded, exotic allure, petite blond beauty, and sultry French accent.

He'd tossed Gwendolyn aside faster than the contents of a sickroom chamber pot.

That had smarted more than a mite. Not being jilted, but how swiftly and effortlessly she'd been replaced in Lance's fickle regard.

Despite her stinging pride, she supposed she ought to be grateful. In the months since being rejected, she'd come to realize, she and Lance never would've suited. Nor would she have been free to escort Jeremiah to Suttford House, and nothing this side of heaven would've permitted her to send him without her.

Which brought Gwendolyn's rambling musings back to the point at hand.

Framing her lips between her forefinger and thumb, she regarded the scruffy Scot's wrinkle-scored face as he switched from one foot to the other.

"What makes you think we'll not be wanted, Mr. Murray?"

He hitched a bony shoulder while tormenting a rock on the dusty road with his boot. "Jist do. Tha's all."

She'd learned early on that though he, Mr. Dodd, and Mr. Todt—the other driver—grumbled aplenty beneath their breath and to one another, they avoided direct confrontation.

Wincing slightly, Gwendolyn folded to her knees.

Ah, much better.

Kandie, her old nurse, and now her lady's maid and also a nanny to the children, would scold her for soiling her traveling gown. However, unlike the unusual black and white crow balanced in a nearby pine keenly regarding them, Gwendolyn wasn't accustomed to perching for long periods, and her aching legs thanked her.

Her attention sank to the motionless man once more.

The longer he remained unconscious, the more concerned she became.

What if he *did* die?

What a horrid way to start their life in this foreign place.

Death and bereavement had driven them from America, and by peaches and pralines, Gwendolyn wasn't letting it ruin their new beginning in Scotland.

"Gwendolyn, Sugah...?" Cultured censure edged Aunt Barbara's verbal prod.

"Of course, we must help him, Aunt."

But to take a complete stranger into their coach? One that might very well be a varmint?

Scallywag? Criminal? Satan's spawn?

Gwendolyn must consider the children's safety, too.

Yet her ever diligent, absurdly fair conscience needled her.

The injured man's fresh wound could be laid squarely at Mr. Dodd's dusty feet. Well, his and Mr. Murray's.

Curse her sense of justice and responsibility. Couldn't she, just for once, be selfish?

Illogical? Impractical? Unreasonable?

No, not in this instance. Because instead of slowing when the Scot stumbled from the woods, clutching his ribs, Mr. Dodd had panicked and cracked his whip as he and Mr. Murray shouted the team onward.

The horses had plowed right into the befuddled chap.

A wonder he wasn't dead.

A smaller person would've been killed, for certain. Nevertheless, how were they to know the man was already injured and not in his cups or intent on robbing them?

Or worse?

Hadn't Mr. Murray warned her repeatedly that knights of the road frequented this stretch of desolate country of late? And this hapless fellow's battered face and disheveled appearance suggested he'd encountered them.

"If we leave him," Gwendolyn said, glancing up and down the roadway, "he might be set upon by ruffians again."

Mr. Todt, holding the lead horse's harness, patted the pistol and a wicked-looking blade tucked into his waistband below his considerable paunch. "Aye, even armed, I dinnae want to run into road agents."

Mr. Murray nodded. "Nae robberies for years, and in recent months a whole slew. Makes me nervous as a frog on a hot skillet, it does. The missus be beggin' me to find other work, but jobs are scarce."

Likely that explained the increase in highwaymen and robberies. Desperate men, especially those with a family, did all manner of things they wouldn't otherwise consider.

Nonetheless, the many layers of petticoats hidden beneath Kandie's gown contained more starch than either man's backbone.

Shutting her eyes, Gwendolyn pinched the bridge of her nose. Papa's loaded dueling pistols lay tucked in their walnut case inside the coach. She knew how to use them, and Murray and Dodd were also armed.

That was all very well and good, but what if the prone man before her *was* indeed a blackguard? A knave of the worst sort and had been injured while trying to rob another vehicle?

Cornbread muffins.

The gravity of their situation didn't escape her.

"Give him a good poke in the belly with your parasol, Aunt Barbara." Freckled nose crinkled, Jeremiah rested his chin on his elbows, obviously loving every minute of this unexpected adventure.

And have the mammoth suddenly awaken? I think not.

"I'm sure that's not necessary." Gwendolyn considered the second conveyance, a smaller tarp-covered wagon.

Perhaps—

"Let me see, Jeremiah. Stop hoggin' the window."

Five-year-old Julia had awoken.

Perfectly inconvenient timing.

"Move over, you big stink turd." Another mop of unruly, burnished hazelnut-hued hair—much browner than

Gwendolyn's fiery mane—thrust from the conveyance as Julia shoved her brother aside. Her green eyes, wide and wary, rounded as she breathed in awe, "Is *he* a heathen Scots?"

Aunt Barbara's misplaced influence again.

Poor, dear Aunt. She'd been most vocal in not wanting to leave America but had also refused to be parted from her only kin. Terrified the entire journey, no rational talk or repeated reassurance convinced her they wouldn't be ravished or murdered in their sleep.

Gwendolyn wiped her brow with the back of her gloveless hand. "Julia, we do not ever, *ever* say 'turd.'"

"You just said it." Sniggering, his pale sage-toned eyes practically capering in naughty glee, Jeremiah clapped his hand over his mouth.

Gwendolyn's severe look and sternly arched brow quelled his giggling.

Almost.

"And yes, Julia, I believe he's Scottish. His waistcoat's plaid." Was the royal blue and emerald green tartan his clan's pattern?

What the blue devil to do with him, though?

Her British drivers wouldn't know the plaid, but perhaps the Scottish guide would. She pointed at the waistcoat.

"Mr. Murray, do you recognize his tartan?"

THREE

"Nae, lass."

Pulling at his tam, Mr. Murray shook his grizzled head as Julia and Jeremiah continued to squabble and jostle each other in the window's small opening.

"Oft'n clans have multiple plaids, and I canna say I ken his. He might just be a cove who fancies a checked waistcoat."

"Kandie," Gwendolyn said, after searching the road in both directions again. "Please take the children for a short walk behind the conveyances. It's as good a time as any to see to their personal needs as well."

Heaven knew they could stand to stretch their little legs. Since leaving London's West Indie Docks nine days ago, they'd traveled from dawn to dusk, stopping only long enough during the day to change teams and to collect Mr. Murray after the first week of travel.

Gwendolyn, too, longed for physical exertion and couldn't wait to be done with the coach once and for all.

However, dawdling here was foolhardy.

"Yes'm, Miss Gwen." With some effort, the elderly Negress climbed from the conveyance. Grinning—Kandie always sported a broad smile upon her beautiful, time-creased face—she held her palms out beside her wide hips and wiggled her fingers. "Come on, young'uns."

Jeremiah and Julia promptly hopped from the coach and after grasping Kandie's hands, pulled her along, jumping up and down in their eagerness.

"Mercy me, slows down. Dis ol' body don' move so fast," Kandie chuckled good-naturedly. "Looky at that odd bird, chil'ren."

The crow cocked his head and marked their progress before turning his beady-eyed attention back to Gwendolyn.

What a peculiar bird.

A *whuffle* echoed again, but this time, a glorious black-as-night Friesian stallion cautiously advanced from the forest. Pawing the ground, he shook his great head, his raven mane and the reins hanging from his halter, flying about his neck.

Dodd and Murray beat a hasty retreat, and Aunt Barbara sensibly backed a safe distance away, too.

One hand resting on the Scot's slowly rising and falling chest, Gwendolyn remained immobile, mesmerized by the stunning creature.

Dropping her gaze so the horse wouldn't feel threatened, she studied him from the corner of her eye. He was every bit as massive and magnificent as his owner.

The stallion's nostrils flared as he nervously eyed her, then he dipped his large head and nuzzled the wounded man's neck.

No doubt as to whom the horse belonged, or that the creature loved him. That raised the man a notch higher in her estimation. A horse didn't show such devotion to an irascible scoundrel.

The crow cawed, and the stallion shook his head, almost as if they communicated with each other.

What utter drivel. Exhaustion and worry had her imagining fanciful things.

A moment later, the horse ever-so-gently nudged Gwendolyn's shoulder, and her heart leapt. She swore his big, chocolate eyes pleaded with her to help his master.

"I know, handsome boy," she murmured, wishing she dared to run a hand down his neck. Unwise, though. He didn't know her.

"Gentleman, have you any rope to spare?" She asked the question without taking her covert attention from the great beast. "We can bind the Scot, and settle him in the cart afterward. Make room by stowing some of the luggage inside the coach while I tend his head."

Aunt Barbara gave a dubious nod. "That will do, but we'll be awfully crowded then, Sugah."

"I'll ride the horse, and Jeremiah can sit behind me." Gwendolyn elevated a hand and let the horse sniff her. "Rope, Mr. Murray?"

"Aye, miss." He shuffled to the luggage wagon, jabbering heatedly to Todt and Dodd beneath his breath.

Were all Scots so insolent and disagreeable? Or was it because theirs was a party of women and children and the drivers thought to abuse their positions?

"Gwendolyn, I don't think the boy should get on that enormous creature. Kandie can hold Julia, and Jeremiah may sit between us. We'll be snug as caterpillars in cocoons, but at least the child will be safe." With that pronouncement, Aunt Barbara closed her parasol before gracefully stepping into the coach.

A low, muffled moan yanked Gwendolyn's attention to the man before her. Upon his pale cheeks, his black-as-sin, wickedly lush eyelashes quivered.

Her own auburn-tipped lashes paled in comparison.

A typical woman would be envious of the thick, sooty arcs edging his eyes.

Gwendolyn wasn't a typical woman.

She liked her red hair and her eyelashes' coppery ends. Her freckles smattering her nose and cheeks, not so much.

A grimace contorted his face, and he groaned again, rolling his head from side to side. His pain couldn't conceal the musical hum of his deep voice.

Bending near, she gingerly cupped his face on the unharmed side. She offered him a small, uncertain, yet reassuring smile. "Hush. Stop your thrashing. We're going to help you."

Gradually, as if the effort were monumentally difficult, he opened his eyelids, and Gwendolyn gasped as his gaze meshed with hers.

Mind-rattling, startling blue-green eyes, the color of a tropical ocean under a clear sky, held hers hostage.

A jolt of scorching electricity pelted to every pore, every nerve from knees to neck.

Even her nape hairs stood on end, twitching like an insect's antennas, as if in anticipation.

Expectation. Recognition.

Of what, she couldn't begin to venture.

"I didna ken angels had flames in their hair." A melodic brogue framed his thickly whispered words.

A shuddery sigh shook him as his eyelids fluttered closed once more. A rueful half-smile hitched his mouth.

"Och. *Shite*. I've died an' gone to hell."

~*~

Sluggishly clawing his way to alertness from the dense fug shrouding his wooly mind, Dugall swallowed against a guttural moan. He lifted his neck an inch and double-sided jagged swords speared his head and ribs.

Faugh!

A rhythmic, bone-jarring rocking had bile rising high and burning the back of his throat. His stomach growled and roiled as much from hunger as the eye-crossing, thundering ache hammering his skull.

Not dead then, but probably concussed.

How badly?

He took a quick mental inventory.

I'm Dugall Kester Hugh Ferguson of Craiglocky Keep.

I'm four-and-twenty years old, and the youngest child of Hugh and Giselle Ferguson.

My brother is Laird Ewan McTavish, and I'm his solicitor and steward.

And—

Bloody damned maggoty hell . . .

He'd been robbed on his way to Edinburgh.

Stupid as turnips, thieves.

Did they really think he'd carry Craiglocky's monthly receipts on his person? All they'd absconded with was a pocket watch, his dirk, and a few bank notes.

And he knew at least one of their names.

Bowie.

With Ewan's vast connections, they'd almost certainly be apprehended and count themselves lucky if only deported to Australia.

He'd bet his beloved stallion, Bran, he'd broken a knuckle or two—*likely all*—fighting off the three ambushing scunners last night.

Had they only used fists, Dugall might've prevailed, but they'd carried clubs and daggers, too. He'd readily dispatched one, but a blow to the back of his head ended his fight.

He dared to slit one swollen lid open and tentatively stretched his legs, seeking other injuries.

What the hell?

Eyes flying open, he jerked upright. At the abrupt movement, discordant agony speared his pounding skull again with the ferociousness of a battering ram.

Holy God in heaven.

Clutching his head lest it topple from his neck, he gulped against a crushing wave of nausea and blinked away the gray closing in, dusty black specks flitting before his eyes.

I willna pass out again.

Inhaling a restorative breath, he shut his eyes until the dervish in his head stopped spinning. His movements tentative and controlled, he again assessed his situation.

Stout rope secured his ankles and wrists, and he lay stuffed into the corner of a wagon loaded with several chests, boxes, burlap bags, and oddly shaped cloth-wrapped bundles. What looked like a carriage lap robe covered him from waist to calves.

Given his missing neckcloth, the robe and the padding behind him, someone had attempted to make him somewhat comfortable as the wagon bumped along, threatening to dislodge his head from his shoulder with each new divot in the road.

He lifted his bound hands and, jaw braced, gingerly touched his forehead. Encountering a bandage, he frowned.

Ach, his cravat.

The last thing he remembered after regaining consciousness and staggering from the forest was a coach and four barreling down on him.

Then nothing—until now.

He licked parched lips and closed his eyes for a long blink, willing the tormenting, brain piercing, thundering in his head to ease a jot.

God, what he wouldn't give for a drink of water. Or better yet, a tot or two of Ewan's superb whisky.

A sudden vision of coppery red hair framing a creamy, perfectly oval face from which glinted two turbulent bottle-green, umber lashed eyes, clambered to the forefront of his mind.

Ach, the ravishing ginger-haired angel.

He skewed his lips into a tiny arc—as much as he dared given his pummeled face.

No, angels abided in heaven, and haloes of shimmering red hair didn't frame their faces.

Did they?

But she'd been far too bonny to be a *deamhan*.

He'd dreamed he'd gone to hell, and that exquisite face had floated over him.

He could still smell her sweet, fresh essence. *Oranges and vanilla and flowers.* Could see the smattering of coppery freckles on her perfect little upturned, rather saucy nose, and her peach-tinted rosebud mouth bent compassionately. The flecks of gold simmering in her arresting eyes lit a receptive, spine-jolting spark deep in his chest.

Despite his sorry state, his cock pulsed.

A familiar snort sounded near his ear.

Och. Thank God. Bran.

He'd feared for his equestrian friend.

Dugall's relieved grin promptly transformed into a grimace as agony speared his face once more. He sucked in a raggedy breath. *Christ.* He might have to add a broken jaw and nose to his list of injuries.

"Ah, you're awake. Good. You've had us all quite worried."

Riding Bran, the red-haired vision patted the stallion's withers. Head slightly cocked—the black feather in her quaint impractical hat perched at a jaunty angle atop her glorious mass of red curls—she regarded him, her vivid green-eyed gaze curious but wary.

She possessed an unusual accent; like nothing he'd ever heard before. Soothing and lyrical, soft around the edges, and the slightest bit annoying in the manner it lengthened all of her words.

Like cold heather honey dripping from a spoon, sweet and syrupy, yet maddeningly unhurried.

"Your horse is magnificent. Truly one of the grandest I've ever seen, and my grandpapa raised Thoroughbreds."

Astonishment fueling him, Dugall summoned the strength to sit up straighter. Teeth clamped against the razing torture the movement caused, he raked his gaze over her shapely form.

Her beauty clobbered him like a sudden blow from a cudgel, and his nether region reacted with renewed enthusiasm.

Attempting to ignore the appendage's fervent pulsing, he focused his bleary vision on the exquisite creature straddling Bran.

Wait a hell-fired moment.

She rode Bran?

She actually *rode* Bran?

The temperamental, high-spirited stallion never allowed anyone to ride him except Dugall. Anyone stupid enough to try received a fierce bite or a well-placed kick.

Up until now.

How the devil had this supple nymph managed it?

Dugall's pained focus narrowed further.

And what the devil was she wearing?

Her slate-colored jacket looked similar to riding habits his sisters wore, though the dark blue braiding embellishing the front emphasized her full breasts straining against the fastenings.

Something he sure as Odin hadn't noticed about his sisters.

But unlike any skirt he'd seen before, her odd garment permitted her to ride astride.

Ending just above her ankles, the hem revealed the top of neat black half-boots and the merest, deliciously tantalizing peek of shapely azure stocking-covered calves.

His regard leisurely gravitated up the length of her impossibly, Amazonian long legs. Though her feet didn't quite reach the stirrups, she was still tall. Very tall.

Tall enough for me.

Four

Amusement jerked one side of Dugall's mouth.

Now *there* was an incongruous thought.

Probably dredged from the inane, nonsensical mental ramblings of an addled sot who'd been knocked soundly upon his nog and had yet to regain his full wits.

The woman's pretty bow-shaped mouth tilted upward, slightly higher on the left side, making the gesture all the more endearing. "We'll arrive at Suttford House soon."

Something akin to strain accented her high cheekbones, or a cacophony of lowing cattle, brass horns, and discharging cannons weren't ringing between his ears.

Once at Suttford House, then what?

Was he to remain constrained?

Not damned likely. Curiosity about her was the only thing that kept him from demanding his bonds be cut immediately.

"Just another mile or two, I've been told," she said with an upward tilt of her mouth and a quick downward flick of her expressive eyes, her auburn lashes casting shadows on her ivory cheeks.

The luster of her smile had him blinking like an inebriated

cull. Mayhap he'd injured his head far worse than he'd first suspected. Else why would he react so powerfully and unpredictably?

Blessed with a physique and countenance women found most appealing, he'd had his pick of lasses since his teens. None had him acting the jester within minutes of meeting, however.

She stroked Bran's neck affectionately and envy burned through Dugall.

"Truthfully, though I am keen to end our journey, I'd rather enjoy a longer jaunt on this impressive boy," she said. "I've missed riding more than I realized."

What *was* that accent? Where the devil was she from?

Wait.

He blinked to clear the lingering fog from his head.

Had she said Suttford Hall a minute ago?

Damn his eyes.

Nae good. Nae good at all.

Not only did longstanding enmity lay between the residents of Craiglocky Keep and Suttford House, but hell's very own spawn, Lloyd Hollingsworth, lived there.

Dugall hadn't laid eyes on him since they attended Edinburgh Law School together. However, the last time he'd seen Hollingsworth, Dugall had threatened to break his nose for trying to cheat an obviously new-to-her-profession light-skirt out of her coin.

Dugall had paid the girl a tidy sum to leave Edinburgh and start her life over somewhere.

He truly hoped she had.

And by God, a creature as exquisite as the one riding beside this wagon wouldn't be safe from Hollingsworth's advances. But how to tell her that when they'd only met, couldn't even be considered acquaintances?

Acquaintances . . . ?

He smothered a derisive laugh.

Prisoner was more apt, the ropes cutting into his wrists and ankles reminded him. As if she'd listen to advice from him in any event. He was a stranger. She'd no reason to take him at his word.

Bran nickered again, angling his big head toward Dugall.

"*Traitor. Reic mi a-mach airson paidhir de sleamhainn thighs straddling thu, a rinn sibh?*" Dugall murmured softly in Gaelic. The stallion enjoyed her slim thighs straddling him, lucky beast.

Face animated, joy darkened her eyes to the smoky, mystical shade of Wyre Woods just before dawn. "That was Gaelic you spoke just then, wasn't it? My grandpapa warbled a few phrases every now and again."

Och. Part Scots then. Her coloring hinted as such. Add intriguing and mysterious to her other tantalizing qualities.

Dugall loved solving puzzles and riddles. Particularly ones involving a lass with malachite shards glittering in her eyes and the sun's own fire ribboning her glorious cloud of hair.

"I only know a few words." She closed her eyes before testing the unfamiliar sounds on her tongue.

"*Granaidh, pòg, tapadh leat, mo muirnín* and *tha goal agam ort.*"

Her eyes popped open, and acute consternation flooded her features after she said the last phrases, "my darling" and "I love you."

Dugall scratched Bran's neck, seeking to distract her from her disquiet. "Aye. I was but reassurin' him. He's a braw laddie, but the attack last night frightened him. One cowardly knave cudgeled him, and he charged off. Which was why I was afoot when I tried to flag down yer coach."

Sodding lie, that.

Not the Bran running off bit, but the reassuring Bran codswallop. Dugall wasn't about to reveal he'd chastised the horse for succumbing to the temptation to have that goddess straddle him.

Plain and simple, Dugall envied the fortunate animal.

"I'm surprised to hear he fled, poor creature. He was probably terrified. He didn't leave your side the entire time you remained unconscious." The lass's lush mouth slid into an admiring smile, revealing a dimple in her right cheek Dugall hadn't noticed before. "I gave him his head, because he seemed so anxious to be near you."

"His name's Bran, and he's never let anyone else mount him before. You must have bewitched him."

Or her lovely thighs had. Dugall attempted a wink, but when his puffy eye refused to cooperate he settled for a wry twist of his mouth.

"Really?" A pleased flush mounted her cheeks as wonder filled her melodic, drawling voice. "Gracious me, then I'm truly honored, handsome boy."

She bent low, crooning in the stallion's ear.

The movement thrust her full breast near Dugall's head, and he could've no more torn his gaze from their plump splendidness, than scooped out his own eyes with a salt spoon.

Bran, the turncoat, pricked his ears and swiveled them toward her low murmuring.

Fickle beast.

Something very much like jealousy pelted against Dugall's chest.

Oh, for God's sake.

He was *not* envious of his blasted horse.

"Bran? What does it mean?" She chatted as if they'd just met and shared tea and shortbread biscuits together in Craiglocky's parlor instead of him essentially being held hostage.

"Raven. Because he's pitch black."

"Ah. It suits him." She veered her attention to the treetops. "Speaking of ravens. Do you see that black and white bird?"

She pointed to a hooded crow, and Dugall permitted a tiny, satisfied smile as he gingerly turned his head.

"That's a hooded crow."

"We don't have them in the part of America I'm from. Just all black ones."

Well, at least he had a partial answer to where she was from. "What part of America? My sister-in-law owns a shippin' company in Boston."

"South Carolina. Born and raised." His mysterious rescuer squinted at the treetops. "I believe the bird might be following us. At first, I thought it my imagination, but now I'm convinced the strange thing is actually matching our progress."

Dugall chuckled, and winced when his head strenuously objected to the minute movement by launching cracking pain from ear to ear. "She is. That's Coronis, and she's my pet. I rescued her as a nestlin' two years ago. She remembers, and now winna leave me. I suspect she thinks I'm her mither."

He whistled, and Coronis squawked an answer before swooping down to land beside him in the wagon. Issuing a grating coo, she cocked her head at the woman. "When she gets used to ye, I'll let ye feed her. She's a glutton for shortbread."

Twisting in the saddle to look at them more fully, the lass's mouth sagged slightly. "She's your pet? How utterly fascinating. I've never owned anything more exciting than a cat, though I've always wanted a pet squirrel." A chagrined smile curved her closed mouth. "Silly, I know."

Coronis set about grooming her feathers as if bouncing along in a wagon were an everyday occurrence for her.

The lass's self-conscious smile revealed her vulnerability. It caused a weird tightening behind Dugall's bruised ribs. He didn't want to ponder why. Instead, he raised his hands.

"Why am I bound?"

Her gaze skipped away for an instant, but she drew it back and met his perusal square on.

He liked that.

She wasn't afraid to be direct. She was brave, too.

Honesty in her gaze, she notched one well-shaped shoulder upward.

"A necessary precaution. I'm traveling with my young niece and nephew and had to assure their safety foremost. Although I did try to see to your comfort despite our inadequate supplies. I washed your face as best I could, too. You've a couple of cuts that require stitching." She tapped two fingers high on her forehead. "The one at your hairline's the worst, but you'll need to see the lot of them are thoroughly cleansed."

She'd wisely protected her wards and still considered a stranger's comfort. No shallow, insipid miss here. In fact, though by no means past her prime, a woman's gentle maturity and experience had replaced youth's first dewy bloom and naiveté.

A widow perhaps?

No telltale bulge graced her ring finger.

Auburn brows high on her smooth, creamy forehead, her attention strayed to the mound supporting his spine. "Might I ask who you are?"

The driver perked up and angled toward the wagon bed, his attention swerving between Dugall and the lass. The driver slowly lowered his left hand, pointedly revealing the weapons tucked at his middle, his meaning clear as Loch Arkaig in January.

Dugall inclined his head as much as he dared. "I'm Dugall

Ferguson, brother to Laird Ewan McTavish of Craiglocky Keep."

"Oh." Her gorgeous, bright green eyes rounded, and she nervously wet her lower lip with her adorable pink tongue.

The only part of his anatomy not bruised or sore lurched to attention.

Down, ye mangy mongrel. Now nae be the time.

"Hey, Murray?" The driver hollered to the coach trundling in front. "This cove says he's related to some fella named McTavish."

"McTavish, ye say?"

Dugall craned his neck to see who spoke. His ungrateful head rewarded him by kicking his brains from side to side again, much like a porcelain marble in a china teacup.

From the driver's seat, an elfin Scot wearing a shabby tam, scratched his bristly jaw and peered around the side of the coach before them.

"The McTavishes of Craiglocky Keep?"

FIVE

"The very same." Dugall met the lass's wary glance.

So Murray knew of Craiglocky, but had he knowledge of the Fergusons who lived there?

Murray cupped his ear. "What was that? Be he a McTavish clansman?"

The lass nodded, her delicate jaw taut and her slender backbone ramrod rigid. "Yes, that's what he said, Mr. Murray."

"Ye do have the build and coloring of the younger brother." Murray spat upon the ground and after wiping the back of his hand across his face, demanded, "What be the laird's name?"

God, must they have this conversation while the wagon yet juddered Dugall's spine? He feared he was about to heave his haggis. If he had anything in his hollow-as-a-beggar's-stomach to hurl.

Mouth gone grim, the lovely lass regarded him keenly. Almost apprehensively.

Nae. Nae *almost* about it. She *was* anxious.

"Ewan McTavish, also known by the English title Viscount Sethwick." Dugall quirked his mouth, and the lass's speaking, verdant eyes rounded even more before her dismayed gaze dropped to his bound hands.

Her expressive eyes gave away her every thought. She drew her winged brows together into a troubled frown.

Bran must've sensed her tension, because he lifted his head and pranced sideways.

"*Shh*, it's all right," she assured him, expertly bringing him back under her control.

Did she fear retaliation for plowing Dugall over, and then trussing him like a Hogmanay goose?

Had he been traveling with children and come upon a stranger in his questionable condition, he'd have done the same.

"Viscount, huh? Didna ken that," Murray replied. He shifted so that he sat sideways on the drivers' seat, his knobby-kneed legs bobbing like a marionette's as the coach bumped along.

"What be the McTavish cousins' names?"

What was this? A damned interrogation?

Dugall gritted his teeth and inhaled a long-suffering breath.

"Their names are Gregor and Alasdair. Their father, Ewan's uncle and second in command, is Duncan McTavish. Duncan's wife is named Kitta. My father, Hugh Ferguson, married Ewan's mother, Giselle, and I have three older sisters, Adaira, Isobel, and Seonaid. They're married to the Earl of Clarendon, the Earl of Ramsbury, and Monsieur le baron de Devaux-Rousset, respectively."

The woman's mouth slackened.

He stopped to inhale again before forging onward despite the relentless nausea plaguing him.

"Ewan and his wife, Yvette, have a son, Broderick, and twin daughters, Adreanna and Adelaide. They've two adopted children as well, Pedar and Iona.

"The butler's name is Fairchild.

"The cook is Sorcha.

"The bloody blacksmith is Niall.

"And the Keep's three boarhounds are named Tira, Arig, and Rona."

With an exhausted sigh, Dugall collapsed against the lumpy pile cushioning him.

"Satisfied?" he all but growled.

Her mouth forming a tempting 'O', the siren atop Bran nodded and blinked several times. Rather like a leery, befuddled bird.

"Mercy me," she murmured before presenting her profile.

He regarded her silhouette's elegantly curving contours, her lips now formed into a prim line.

Definitely apprehensive.

"Heard about yer sister marryin' that Frenchman. Me brother works in his silver mine. Good man, the Monsieur." The Scot released a cackling chuckle and punched the other driver's shoulder. "Dodd, ye plowed over McTavish's brother. And the laird be notorious for his black temper and for protectin' his family. Wanna ken what he did to the scunners who abducted his sister a few years back?"

Dodd shook his shaggy head and whined, "You told me to urge the team forward, Murray."

Blanching, Dugall's enticing warden swallowed, her expression growing more distressed with every hoof beat. "Mr. Todt, please cut Mr. Ferguson's ropes."

"Are you certain, Miss McClintock?" Misgiving scored the driver's skeptical face and lifted one corner of his mouth, exposing missing teeth.

"Yes. I believe we've more than enough proof Mr. Ferguson is who he says he is."

Her shoulders drooped the merest bit, and Dugall angled his head, considering her.

She was done in, though she did a valiant job of hiding her exhaustion. He admired her strength and hard-won composure.

"Raise your hands," Todt ordered.

With a few quick sawing motions, Dugall's restraints fell into his lap.

Todt passed Dugall the dirk. "You can cut your feet loose. I don't want the coach to get too far ahead."

Unaware the wagon had momentarily stopped, the laden coach lumbered onward.

"Thank you." Dugall accepted the knife, and once he'd removed the fetters constraining his ankles, proceeded to rub his sore wrists. "I'm thirsty. Is there water to be had?"

Without taking his attention from the road, Todt silently passed Dugall a flask.

Whisky. Better yet.

He took a long draught.

Miss McClintock fidgeted with the reins, casting Dugall little distraught glances every few moments.

A cheerful chap by nature, he didn't harbor grudges. Time to put her at ease.

"And may I inquire who you are and why you journey to Suttford House?" Dugall took care to not alarm her further by sounding accusatory. Or by letting his own burgeoning concern about her destination seep into his voice.

"Forgive me my deplorable manners, sir." Discomfiture tinged her cheeks pink and edged her wisp of a voice. "I'm Gwendolyn McClintock, and the coach carries my aunt, nanny, niece, and nephew. We left our plantation in South

Carolina because Jeremiah is the new Lord McClintock." She cut him an uncertain look. "Or should I say laird?"

Dugall bolted upright, gripping the wagon's rough side, and promptly drove a sliver into his third finger.

"Holy *shite!*"

"I beg your pardon?"

Miss McClintock elevated her pert nose, indignant jade sparks spewing from her eyes. The sun's last rays glinted off her incandescent curls, the fiery tendrils gleaming in the failing light.

Hell's bloody pealing bells.

Her nephew had inherited the entailment?

Dugall yanked the offending miniature wooden stake from his already abused flesh as he mentally scrambled for an excuse for his explosive outburst.

"Please excuse my vulgarity, Miss McClintock. Your news took me by surprise, and I reacted without my usual decorum."

Decorum his arse.

His plain speaking had landed him in suds more than once. He hadn't ever given a tinker's damn before, so why should it matter that this woman, a stranger, not think him an uncouth Highlander?

Ye aren't even speakin' with yer brogue, yer tryin' so hard to impress her, ye bloody, pretentious sod.

No hiding the truth from his exasperatingly intrusive and altogether too accurate conscience.

He offered what he hoped was his most polished, apologetic smile. However given his swollen mouth currently only obeyed his directives on one side, he probably more resembled one of the grotesque gargoyles adoring Paisley Abbey.

Not only did a Viking cadence beat inside his head in unison with the horses' clopping hooves, but at her casual announcement, genuine alarm riddled him.

She needed to know just how hostile an environment her little troupe was entering in a few short minutes.

And damnation, without a man to stand up to the worthless lot of parasites embedded like ticks on a sheep at Suttford, she'd need a general's finesse, daring, and cunning, as well as a strategic battle plan to survive a fortnight.

Nae, she needed a man—a Scot—at her side to guide her. At least at the onset until she could establish her position and take the reins herself.

"Miss McClintock, may I presume you haven't met any of yer nephew's extended relations which reside at Suttford?"

She shook her head, the feather cavorting with the motion.

"No. It was somewhat of an unexpected surprise." After a swift glance to the coach, she lowered her voice. "But the children's father and grandpapa died recently, and it seemed an opportune time to start over somewhere that offered us all a brighter future."

Bright as the Earl of Hell's black-as-soot waistcoat.

Dugall deliberated her genteel, composed features for a long moment. He hadn't missed the melancholia tinging her drawled 'all.'

What secrets did the alluring Miss Gwendolyn McClintock harbor?

Why wasn't she married?

A woman with her form and features surely had multiple offers. She was obviously cultured, of refined breeding, and she'd taken on the difficult role as proxy mother to her niece and nephew.

Mayhap this journey to Scotland was as much about escaping, or perhaps running away, as ushering in her nephew's birthright.

God's teeth, though.

She had no idea what was in store for them at Suttford.

Hollingsworth's suave manners and dastardly good looks

had snared many an unsuspecting lass before they realized his true character.

Dugall captured Miss McClintock's anxious gaze, trying to convey the urgency without sending her into a complete panic. She didn't seem the sort to dissolve in histrionics or topple over in a swoon.

In fact, he detected a strength in her, a commendable resolve and resilience. More to admire. Insipid, frail, helpless females abraded his normally easygoing nature.

He indulged in another tot of the surprisingly decent whisky. Two summers ago, he'd fleetingly considered starting a distillery, then dismissed the idea as too problematic and expensive. Tossing back another quaff, he sighed.

Whisky was the main ingredient in many a tonic. It had already taken the edge off his pain. Nonetheless, every part of his body thrummed with discomfort, including the wily appendage between his legs. Although, it ached for an entirely different reason than getting soundly thrashed.

"Miss McClintock, may I speak candidly?"

"Yes, please. It would help enormously to have an idea of what to expect from them. I'd just as soon not be the hen venturing into the foxes' den." A hopeful glint blossomed across her face.

Dugall's next words would wipe that radiance from her countenance.

He set the flask aside before flexing each finger, testing the digits to determine the extent of damage to his hands. "You can expect an unfriendly, likely a hostile and resentful reception. Not from the staff, but from the other residents."

"Other residents? Mr. Christie didn't mention anyone else lived there." Her slight smiled dimmed, and dismay replaced her earlier enthusiasm.

Remorse battered Dugall's ribs, but she must be prepared.

"After his wife and only daughter died more than a decade ago, McClintock was quite lonely."

Because the man was as foul as a cesspool to be near.

Her expression softened, her incredibly expressive eyes speaking as clearly as her words. "Go on, please."

"In recent years, he allowed"—*more likely he manipulated or guiled them into doing so*—"distant relations to take up residence at Suttford."

Old McClintock had reasons for everything he did, and none of them were charitable. Those living at Suttford likely had suffered at his hands. Now that the cur was dead, they no doubt felt entitled to the comforts the opulent house offered.

Relatives constantly underfoot. That was one of the things Dugall treasured the most about Craiglocky though. Occasionally annoying and meddling, but always loyal, affectionate, and good-intentioned. The weathered stones often rang with laughter and jovial conversation.

"Suttford's an enormous, convoluted place," he said. "Built over the course of a century, it's part rustic fortified towers and part elegant manor. I know I wouldn't want to bang around in that mausoleum with only servants to keep me company."

Truth to that. But he doubted loneliness truly motivated McClintock to harbor those living there.

Miss McClintock gave one measured nod, her acute focus on the carriage rumbling ahead of them. Did she worry about her wards' futures?

If she'd made the right decision relocating them here?

How could she not?

What was their tale anyway?

Her incongruous gaze flitted over him. "And you don't believe the people living at Suttford House will be pleased that an American has inherited?"

"It's more complicated and worrisome than that, I'm afraid."

Confident of her position, she arched a puritanical brow.

"How so? Jeremiah is the indisputable heir. If they prove contrary or incompatible, I shall simply advise them to remove themselves."

Had she ever tried to rid a sheep of a tick? The little well-fed buggers were as reluctant as hell to leave their comfy hosts. She'd find the same resistance at Suttford if she tried to rid the house of its imbedded pests. McClintock might've been a crotchety, controlling sot, but those under his roof were well fed and comfortable.

Dugall admired her pluck though. She didn't shy away from the unpleasantness.

While he cautiously probed his ribs for fractures, he debated how to alert her to Hollingsworth, finally settling on straightforwardness.

"There's a man living at Suttford House, Lloyd Hollingsworth. It's been assumed for five years or more, he'd inherit. Your nephew inheriting the entailment scotches Hollingsworth's schemes."

"Well, he'll just have to adjust." She pressed her mouth into a prim line. "What else can he do?"

Guid only kent.

Just what sort of treachery was Hollingsworth capable of? "I'll guarantee you, he'll do everything he can to try to force you to leave."

That worried Dugall as much as this very attractive woman sleeping beneath the same roof as the scunner. Aye, the sooner Hollingsworth was forced from the house, the better.

"We cannot leave. We've nothing, no one, to return to. Everything in America was sold." She drew her already straight backbone higher, ticked up her perfect little chin, and stubbornly shook her head.

By Odin, Miss Gwendolyn McClintock was a magnificent creature when riled.

"I didn't drag what remains of my family across an ocean and endure days of bone-cracking, teeth-chipping, skull-rattling overland travel to be turned away at the door." She delivered her speech with an Amazon's confidence. "We are in Scotland to stay."

Six

Dugall checked the admiring grin trying to kick up the corners of his mouth.

Miss McClintock gestured toward the cart angrily jostling his buttocks. "This wagon contains everything we own. I do have the monies from the plantation's sale, but those funds belong to the children."

Mouth grim, she squared her shoulders and jutted her chin higher yet, defiance radiating from her lithe form. "I shan't be dissuaded or bullied into leaving because of some *roué*. Our destiny lies at Suttford House."

Why didn't her tenacity surprise him?

"Then may I make a suggestion?"

Something deep inside Dugall clanged a raucous warning.

Be verra, verra certain, mon.

This wasn't a path easily, lightly, or rashly set upon, and the unforeseen consequences . . . Well, he didn't know what they might be, but there would be unexpected outcomes.

And expected ones, too.

Ewan and Father would be furious—would accuse him of conspiring with their worst nemesis.

Yet, the trusting woman gazing at him, a hint of optimism in her captivating eyes, held him in thrall. His intense and immediate attraction to her was as disarming as it was tempting. Never before had he, upon first meeting a woman, been prepared to cast aside his immediate plans and risk familial censure in order to personally assure her safety.

Nonetheless, he hadn't totally eschewed practicality for gallantry. *Or lust,* his confounded, much too on-point conscience mocked. "Ye need someone familiar with runnin' a large estate to act on yer behalf."

Her delicate brows scuttled to her coppery hairline. "A man, you mean? I oversaw our plantation for nearly a year. And before that, my father allowed me many duties normally relegated to males. I assure you, sirrah, I'm quite capable."

Och, he'd taken the wrong tact and offended her.

"Yer experience will definitely be helpful, but a Scottish estate with tenants is considerably different than a . . . What type of plantation did ye say yer family owned?"

"We bred and raised Arabian Thoroughbred race horses. Of course, they all had to be sold. Including my mare." Distinct wistfulness shadowed her words and her thin, fragile smile.

"My sister, Adaira, breeds enormous draft horses called Clydesdales," Dugall said, as he cautiously felt the tender flesh around his eye.

Interesting that both families had horse breeding in their backgrounds. Another commonality he could use to his advantage.

"Oh, I should love to see them." Renewed excitement danced in Miss McClintock's eyes, the color of Highland meadows in the spring at the moment.

"There are a few at Craiglocky still, but most have been moved to her husband's estate in England. Might I ask, did yer family own slaves?" Despicable practice and infinitely different than overseeing tenant farmers.

The line of her mouth flattened, and she gave a restrained nod. "A few. Mostly house servants and stable hands. I secretly freed them when my brother died. Every single one stayed on, by choice. Naturally I paid them wages. And before we sailed, I allowed them to take what they willed so that they had something to start over. Most decided to do so up North."

Exactly what he'd have done had he been in her situation. "I've been the steward for Craiglocky for three years, and because I was raised there, I ken the workin's of a vast entailment inside and out." Hand pressed to his chest, he angled forward in a partial bow. "I offer ye my experience and assistance."

Until he heard from the Diplomatic Corps, that was.

Dugall's suggestion was bold and impulsive.

Out of character. Unsettling. Risky.

Already, after a few minutes he'd made more of a commitment to her than any other woman. What was it about this odd-speaking lass that pulled at his senses? Made him hurl common prudence aside?

"How old are you?" She veered him a look from the corner of her expressive eyes.

Her question took him aback. Did she think him too young for such an undertaking?

"Four-and-twenty on my last birthday in June." The wagon lurched, ramming him against the side, and he winced.

Coronis cawed and flew off.

"And ye?" God strike him for an uncouth bore.

Something indecipherable momentarily flashed across her face. "Eight-and-twenty."

Only four years his senior.

Her avid feminine gaze examined him. "What of your commitments to your brother?"

Did this mean she considered his offer?

Something akin to relief blanketed Dugall, as a whorl of another unnamed emotion fluttered in his chest.

That he had a reason to remain near her, or that he might offer her his expertise as well as his protection?

Why did it have to be either, or?

Why couldn't it be both as well as an opportunity to explore this unique, fascinating woman?

"I've nae doubt Ewan will give me leave to assist until yer able to permanently hire a trustworthy steward."

He might not have if the old laird lived, but hopefully Ewan would see reason when it came to Miss McClintock and her nephew. They weren't part of the feud.

"Craiglocky lies three miles to the west. I'll send word and tell him of our intentions. Or better yet, ye can accompany me. We'll present our case together for me to act as Suttford's overseer for, let's say three months. He willna refuse for so short a period."

Guid willin'.

Best make it clear Dugall didn't intend to stay longer, no matter how alluring she might be. His trip to Edinburgh had been to post a letter to the Diplomatic Corps. He intended to follow in Ewan's footsteps and sought a position as a covert operative.

Hopefully, his offer to assist her wouldn't jeopardize his chances of being accepted, especially since Ewan's friend, the Earl of Ramsbury, wasn't War Secretary any longer.

Two fingers pressed to her mouth, her fine brows drawn together, Miss McClintock stared straight ahead. She cut him a sideways, speculative glance.

"Three months? Is that time enough, Mr. Ferguson?"

Odin's toes. Probably not. Dare he risk longer?

Hunching a shoulder, Dugall canted his head. "Mayhap

six at the most. I've applied for a coveted position, and if selected, must depart at once."

GWENDOLYN ALMOST GRINNED IN RELIEF, but it wouldn't do for him to think her too eager.

To know she had someone knowledgeable she could pose questions to, someone who had her and her family's interest at heart, eased her apprehension enormously.

She couldn't appear too enthusiastic or giddy. *Or desperate.*

Why she should trust this Dugall Ferguson, she hadn't the slightest notion. That he hadn't reacted unpleasantly upon awakening, stuffed in the back of a cart like a bag of cracked corn, wasn't reason enough alone to put her reliance in him.

But what choice had she?

Trundle up to Suttford and have the door slammed in their faces? Or worse, be chased off the property?

They were the outsiders. What was that term? Sassenachs? But that referred to the English, didn't it? That was one thing she shared with the Scots. No love for the English.

Honestly, she couldn't blame Suttford House's current residents for being a bit miffed or put upon.

Nonetheless, the law was on Gwendolyn's side.

Naturally, she possessed the documentation, proving Jeremiah's birthright, and for certain those at Suttford must be aware of the validity of his claim.

Still, the rag-mannered Scots she'd encountered so far possessed more forwardness and gall than an entire township of soft-spoken, deferential Southerners.

She rather admired the Highlanders' outspokenness and directness. No hidden meanings behind carefully chosen words.

No, bless your heart, when what the person really meant was your gown is so gawd-awful ugly, naked barn rats wouldn't make a nest of it if the temperature dipped below zero.

Not a timid woman by any means, Gwendolyn didn't know if she possessed the wherewithal to be outright demanding and rude if forced to advocate for Jeremiah at Suttford. She'd been raised to behave the opposite. Politeness at all costs.

However, an intimidating, large man such as Dugall Ferguson . . .?

Why, his size alone would have nearly every southern gentleman she knew shaking in his carefully polished boots and sweating into his fastidiously ironed and knotted neck-cloth and monogrammed handkerchief.

He knew best how to interact with his countrymen.

His mannerisms would take a bit of getting used to, none-theless. He'd already sworn in front of her. Something no man of her acquaintance in South Carolina would ever have done.

"That's not all, Miss McClintock."

She arched an incredulous brow and smothered the vulgarity tapping at her teeth. "Good heavenly days? There's more?"

Of course there was. Too much to hope anything about this adventure would be bump-free and easy-going.

"Aye, I'm afraid so." Mr. Ferguson rubbed his nape, picking his words with care. "Hollingsworth's a . . . He's no' a respectable sort when it comes to the lasses. I'd like to request a chamber near yers so I can dissuade any impropriety on his part."

Curdled cream.

That worry on top of everything else? What next?

And she'd intended to put Mr. Ferguson on the opposite side of the house. Where she'd be less inclined to run into him constantly. And ogle his magnificent maleness. Covertly, of course.

A southern lady would never be so indelicate as to openly admire a gentleman's form.

However, beneath her lashes, behind a fan, or gloved hand, stealing covert glimpses might be permitted as long as no one was privy to her ogling. *Except me.*

Gwendolyn didn't practice self-deception.

Dugall Ferguson stirred her in a way no man ever had. Not even her first two betrothed, whom she'd truly adored. Maybe it was her age. Knowing she edged toward the end of her childbearing years, and she'd never lain with a man, had her fabricating fanciful imaginings.

She was certain the man gazing at her expectantly could teach her a thing or two about bed sport. Even if he was four years her junior—*four and a half years*, she reminded herself sternly.

A man with his dashing, and slightly untamed looks, no doubt had *lots* of experience in that area. He was probably the epitome of masculine prowess in the bedchamber.

The notion disconcerted more than a little. More than it had any right to.

Marshalling her wayward musings, she threaded her fingers through Bran's coarse mane. "Why would you do all this for strangers? Foreigners not even from Scotland? Especially after my drivers ran you down?"

"Honestly? My honor winna permit me to let ye and yer family walk into that lions' den." His rich-timbred chuckle, a low melodious sound that curled around her senses, earned him a droll smile. "Actually, a pit of vipers is more apt."

"Isn't that doing it a bit brown? Surely they cannot be as awful as all that." She hoped fervently they weren't.

"Aye, perhaps a mite, but make no mistake. Ye need me. Need my familiarity of our ways. Need a man capable of protecting ye and the children. I doubt ye'll succeed without it, Gwenny lass."

The soft burr of his brogue pronouncing her name made her momentarily forget how inappropriate his addressing her thusly was.

She had a feeling he was a man used to doing as he pleased. That the standard for decorous behavior amongst these Highlanders would prove to be infinitely different than the rigid constraints the gentleman she'd been surrounded by her entire life had shown.

The notion thrilled more than it ought to.

Gwendolyn gave a slight nod, acknowledging the logic of his words even as she silently rebelled against them. In the distance, the evening sky illumined dual craggy, round towers. In minutes they'd arrive at Suttford House.

Her stomach flipped uncomfortably. She was as nervous as a longtail cat in a room full of rocking chairs.

She hadn't quite known what type of greeting to anticipate. But though she'd conjured all sorts of scenarios, a blatantly antagonistic one hadn't topped her list of possibilities.

"And what do you get if I accept your proposition, Mr. Ferguson? Until I examine Suttford's ledgers, I cannot make a promise of wages."

What if the estate were struggling or insolvent? Mr. Christie said he would discuss the financial details with her after they'd arrived. A trifle odd, that. She was to write him at her convenience once they'd settled in.

Mr. Ferguson considered her for a lengthy moment, his gorgeous eyes tender, yet acute.

"Why dinna we call it an act of charitable kindness? The same sort ye showed me by not leavin' me on the side of the road to die." Splaying his hands across his broad chest, he grinned as if he'd hit upon the perfect solution, flawed as broken glass though his reasoning was. "In fact, I owe ye. I'm duty-bound to reciprocate for yer benevolence in savin' my life."

What utter flim flam, and they both knew it. Besides, a mammoth brute like him wasn't cocking up his toes from a knock on his impressive nog.

"I don't think you were ever in danger of dying, Mr. Ferguson," she murmured, her tone smoother and dryer than chalk.

He gave her a cocky wink. "We'll never ken, will we?"

Angling halfway around, he grimaced and tapped Mr. Todt on the back. "Please stop. I shall ride the rest of the way."

"And how do you presume I finish the journey?" She slanted her head toward the cart lumbering to a halt. "In that? I believe a more dignified entrance is required."

First impressions were important, and she'd not arrive at their new home jostling about in a wagon bed like a cabbage. No one would take her seriously, much less respect her.

She had an obligation to Markus and his children, and despite the responsibility having been thrust upon her, nullifying any plans she might've had for her future, she'd not fail in the task.

Mr. Ferguson edged to the wagon's foot. His face had gained a bit of color, but no one with eyes could mistake his less than stalwart health at the moment.

"Why not ride in the coach?" he suggested, jabbing a pickle-sized thumb over his shoulder in the coach's direction.

He couldn't know, of course. "The coach is packed with people and the luggage we transferred to make room for you in the wagon."

"That's easily enough remedied." Dugall released a piercing whistle, and the coach shuddered to a stop, too. "Murray, Dodd. Help Todt here move everything back into this wagon. Miss McClintock will ride in the coach the remainder of the way."

Aunt Barbara poked her head out the coach's window. "Gwendolyn, Sugah? Why have we stopped? The chil'ren are asleep, and the Good Lord awillin', I'd prefer them to remain that way until we reach our destination."

And who could blame her?

Jeremiah and Julia were more spirited than a litter of kittens with an unattended knitting basket.

"We're almost to Suttford House, and I want to make a positive impression straightaway." Gwendolyn made to swing her leg over the horse's broad back then hesitated. She'd not present her raised bum for Mr. Ferguson's and the drivers' perusal. "Mr. Ferguson has recovered enough to ride, and I'll take my seat inside the coach once more."

Mouth pursed and her gaze dubious, Aunt Barbara regarded him. "Are you certain, sir? Should you pass out and tumble from that huge horse, I won't have my niece blamed because of your manly pride."

She clearly had wanted to say something less eloquent or complimentary.

"Your concern is appreciated, madam, but I assure you, I am quite recovered." He sounded every bit as lofty as the British lord who'd sailed from America with them.

Was Mr. Ferguson well enough to sit a horse, or did male bravado and overconfidence prompt him? Stupid, that. Men did a great many imprudent, irrational, absurd things for honor and pride.

Like fight idiotic duels they couldn't possibly triumph in.

Grief hammered her once more, and she crimped her mouth.

Not. Now.

Mr. Ferguson politely angled his head and gave Aunt

Barbara a partial, yet unmistakably dismissive bow before raising his damaged hands to assist Gwendolyn.

If she reacted the same way she had when she'd touched him earlier, she'd embarrass herself for certain. The first time, he'd been unaware of her powerful response, but now . . .

No, not wise at all.

"I'm perfectly capable of dismounting on my own." If he'd find something to do with himself for a few moments.

"I'm sure you are. However, Bran is unused to skirts, and I don't want him to become skittish and risk you taking a tumble." His gaze brushed her leg as it hugged the stallion's side.

Rags and ribbons.

Her pulse hummed faster than bees in gardenia bushes. "I fear bearing my weight would cause your damaged hands pain."

A charming smile kicked his mouth up on one side despite his facial injuries. "I doubt you weigh enough to cause me any great discomfort." He gave her a devilish wink. "I promise, lass, I can bear the burden for the few seconds it takes to assist you."

Why did everything he say seem so logical? She sounded like an ungrateful shrew for objecting. With a stiff nod, she laid her hands on his shoulders.

And there went that zing, galloping from her toes to her earlobes, and everywhere in between.

Oh my. Oh my.

What great, bunching muscles he had. Lord have mercy, what would he look like shirtless?

Her tummy quivered at the delicious concept.

He chuckled as if he knew exactly what she was thinking. Probably did. Men like him had no shortage of women drooling over them.

Biting the inside of her cheek, she stifled her automatic

gasp when he circled her waist with his powerful hands and slowly—*deliberately?*—brushed her along the length of his front as he lowered her to the ground.

His fingers flexed and spanned her waist for a moment longer than necessary. Had he felt the scorching current of desire sluicing her? How utterly mortifying.

She veered him a peek beneath her lashes.

A muscle ticked in his taut jaw, and carnal awareness deepened his hooded eyes.

Ah, he wasn't insusceptible either. The realization caused a sensation she'd long thought dormant to burrow dangerously deep in her middle. Deep enough it might take root.

And that would never do.

She'd been hurt enough for one lifetime. She'd never risk her heart again.

Seven

Summoning a stiff smile, Gwendolyn stepped away, and with her emotions tamped back to where they belonged, she strode to the coach.

The drivers made quick work of transferring her family's belongings, and in a few moments, had resumed their seats. Surprisingly, with no grumbling or outward signs of objection. It seemed having a brawny man about was a deterrent to their usual surliness.

Ten minutes later, they rounded a curve in the drive and Suttford House loomed before them. Mr. Ferguson hadn't exaggerated when he said the place was a monstrosity. Dual towers paralleled a grand house—three, four, no, five stories tall. And those were the ones above ground.

The front door gaped open, and a line of servants stood at attention while a handsome man near her age leaned insolently against the doorjamb.

Mr. Hollingsworth, no doubt.

Mr. Murray opened the carriage door as Mr. Ferguson dismounted.

Mr. Ferguson came forward and extended his hand to

assist first Gwendolyn, then Aunt Barbara, from the coach. Only then did he lift his raven head, his gaze colliding with the other man's insolent glare.

The Scot at the top of the stairs slowly straightened, disbelief stiffening his face into a death-sucking-a-sponge expression.

Mr. Ferguson gave a minute, terse nod. "Hollingsworth."

"Ferguson? What the devil are ye doin' here?" Hard, bitter lines scoring his cheeks, Hollingsworth scraped his caustic gaze over Mr. Ferguson.

No friend there.

The enmity between the men thrummed tangible and thick. Something else went on here or a pig's rump wasn't made of pork.

Mr. Ferguson had failed to mention he and Hollingsworth had a hostile history. At first opportunity, Mr. Ferguson would be explaining himself as well as what caused the antagonism.

"Take a tumble from yer horse?" Mr. Hollingsworth chuckled, as if he quite liked the idea.

"Not quite." Mr. Ferguson turned back to the coach to assist the others while the drivers and two footmen busied themselves unloading the wagon.

The children and Kandie exited the conveyance, and Hollingsworth's eyes sank into shrewd slits when they lit upon Jeremiah. Not angry exactly, but more assessing.

The child half-hid behind Kandie's ample hips, undoubtedly sensing the animosity speared in his direction.

Julia did the same, but not before sticking her tongue out at Mr. Hollingsworth, and then ducking behind Kandie once more.

"It's all right chil'ren," Kandie soothed, her usually jovial countenance furrowed and lips pursed as she nailed him with a *Y'all mess with my lil' uns, I'll squash you like a June bug* glare.

Envisioning her thwacking Hollingsworth with a rolled-up newssheet or rolling pin, Gwendolyn's lips twitched despite the tension permeating the air.

"You ain't got no call to be afeared, dumplin's," Kandie murmured gently while tucking her wards close to her side and giving Mr. Hollingsworth another of her narrowed, black-eyed juju scowls. "Some peoples jus' bent on bein' ugly."

Tread carefully, Mr. Hollingsworth. You don't want to stir that dear Negress's wrath.

Kandie's grandmother had practiced voodoo, and even though Kandie hummed or sang gospel tunes almost constantly, every now and again, when something strange or unexplained occurred, Gwendolyn wondered if the sweet servant didn't dabble in the dark art as well.

Giving the children one final dismissive look, Hollingsworth's attention gravitated to Gwendolyn. He examined her from her boots to her hair, then returning his perusal to her bosom. Acute interest gleamed in his eyes as an appreciative smile pulled his mouth to the side.

Unlike when Mr. Ferguson ran his gaze over her, this Scot's blatant approval did nothing for her woman's pride. In fact, she barely suppressed a shudder and balled her hands, fighting the urge to cross her arms over her chest.

Thank goodness, Mr. Ferguson had warned her about Mr. Hollingsworth and had offered to stay on at Suttford. Just knowing he'd be near brought a measure of reassurance.

Still, she'd sleep with a loaded pistol beneath her pillow and make certain her self-appointed protector did indeed have a chamber assigned near hers. Preferably right next door or across the corridor. At least until Hollingsworth had departed the premises.

Audacity in every step of his gleaming boots, Hollingsworth swaggered forward, his crooked smile causing the hair to raise to attention from her shoulders to wrists in a most unpleasant way.

If he thought her ripe for the plucking, he was slow as molasses at Christmas.

"Well, now," he murmured while grazing his fingertips along his jaw. "This be a most pleasant surprise, indeed. Nae one mentioned the wee ones' verra bonny governess be accompanyin' them."

Smoother than a hot knife through butter, he was. Bet he thought the sun came up just to hear him crow, too.

Gwendolyn hitched her chin higher. "You're mistaken, sirrah. I'm not their governess. I'm Gwendolyn McClintock, their aunt and guardian."

Momentary shock flitted over his attractive face, but he swiftly recovered himself before giving a neat, if somewhat mocking, bow. "My pardon. I'm Lloyd Hollingsworth, great-nephew to Gerard McClintock and Suttford House's bailiff."

Mr. Christie had made no mention of any such arrangement. But then, the solicitor had offered little information other than Jeremiah had inherited the title and estate and needed to present himself at Suttford House at his earliest convenience.

As he straightened, Mr. Hollingsworth spared Mr. Ferguson another animosity-filled glower. "Ye never answered my question, Ferguson. Why are ye here?"

Who was he to object to anyone accompanying her?

Time Mr. Hollingsworth was taken down a peg.

Gwendolyn accepted Mr. Ferguson's extended elbow, and delivered her most winsome smile. "Why, bless your heart. He's Suttford House's *new* steward."

"New steward?" Hollingsworth recoiled as if she'd dealt him a blow. He blinked slowly, his dumbfounded gaze vacillating between her and Mr. Ferguson. For an instant, he looked utterly lost and flummoxed, and a speck of compassion welled within her.

He probably viewed himself the victim, and she conceded to a certain extent he was. But only because he'd presumed and overstepped. His next words obliterated the morsel of pity.

"I canna countenance ye've made such a preposterous decision without givin' me an opportunity to prove myself, ye foolish colonial. Do ye think ye can take over, just like that?" He snapped his fingers. "I ken this estate." He swiped his arm through the air. "Ken its people, have seen to its management, and yet ye presume—"

"Mr. Hollingsworth, this is neither the time nor the place to hold such a discussion." Mindful of the children's rapt interest, she forced a cordial smile. "We're travel-weary and famished. I would be happy to meet with you once my family and I have settled in. Perhaps one day next week?"

She slid Mr. Ferguson a questioning glance, and at his slight confirming nod, continued. "You may have your say then. Think well on your arguments, for they determine whether you stay or leave Suttford."

"Ye'll not be rid of me so easily, as ye'll soon learn." Fury simmering in his umber eyes, his upper lip curled into a contemptuous sneer, Mr. Hollingsworth pivoted and rather than enter the house, stomped toward the stables.

"You intend to keep him on?" Mr. Ferguson murmured in her ear as he guided her to the servants.

Moisture beaded his upper lip and pain crinkled the corners of his arresting eyes. He needed to lie down before he tumbled over drunker than a sailor on leave.

She lifted her brows askance. "Likely not, but I think it only fair to give him an opportunity to present his case. His argument has some validity. If he stays, it won't be as the estate's overseer though. I am confident you're much more amenable to work with than Mr. Hollingsworth. There's something about him . . ."

"I think it's unwise and yer compassion is misplaced," Mr. Ferguson said, his attention focused on Hollingsworth's tall form stalking down the pathway. "He's wily and nae to be trusted."

Did Mr. Ferguson think her incapable of judging a person's character, or was he truly trying to be helpful? Or was there something else? Something he'd failed to mention?

Had she trusted too readily? Too desperately?

Probably.

Quite irksome for someone who prided themselves on their common sense.

Still, as much as she needed Mr. Ferguson's support and insight, if she were to manage Suttford house, he must allow her to make important decisions. That was the first step in earning the respect she must have to succeed.

She couldn't fail Jeremiah in this. His and Julia's futures depended on making a go of it in their new home. They'd nothing to go back to.

Gwendolyn stopped and faced Mr. Ferguson. "I'm confident you speak from experience. After all, you are acquainted with Hollingsworth, but try to put yourself in his place. He sees us as usurpers and probably didn't know Jeremiah existed until a few weeks ago. His whole world has been tilted bum over teacup."

As had hers.

Kandie had taken it upon herself to guide the bashful children to the waiting servants, and from the looks of the smiling and nodding staff, Jeremiah and Julia were well received.

"I confess, my first impression of him is not favorable." Eyes slightly squinted, she shifted her regard to Hollingsworth's stiff back for a moment. "However, I presume his actions these past months have been those of an heir, and from what I can see thus far," She let her gaze rove the area, admiring the neat lawn and drive, "he's done an admirable job overseeing the estate. I cannot conceive why our uncle didn't at least notify him of his bequeathment intentions beforehand though."

"I've nae doubt old McClintock had his reasons, and we dinna ken he didna forewarn Hollingsworth." Mr. Ferguson winked at Julia, clutching Kandie's calico skirt and regarding him warily.

She smiled and pressed her face into Kandie's thigh.

If he was Gerard McClintock's great-nephew, then Hollingsworth must be a distant cousin of Gwendolyn and the children. Were there other relations hereabouts, too?

Perhaps even children Jeremiah and Julia might become friends with? The notion was a thin, bright ray to belie Hollingsworth's less than affable welcome.

She drew in a deep breath while cutting the expectant, pleasant-faced staff a furtive glance.

"Enough of this chatter. We'll know more after interviewing Mr. Hollingsworth." In what capacity might she permit him to stay on, if she arrived at that unlikely decision? No sense fretting on it now, like a nervous hound protecting a bone. She put on a bright smile. "Now, let's meet the staff, shall we?"

Nearly an hour later, Gwendolyn finally reached her room. Following a cordial, if somewhat reticent greeting, from Lowry the butler and Mrs. Norris the bland-faced housekeeper. Then introductions to the sixteen other house staff whose names Gwendolyn couldn't begin to remember. And lastly after depositing her subdued nephew and niece in the nursery and Aunt Barbara in a lovely cream and rose hued bedchamber.

As Gwendolyn had boldly requested while climbing the impressive stone stairs to the upper floors, her bedchamber was beside Mr. Ferguson's, though she made it absolutely clear, there wasn't to be a connecting door.

Other than giving her one long blink, Mrs. Norris hadn't indicated anything unusual about the request. Gwendolyn squelched her unease when she contemplated what the housekeeper might think of the arrangement.

Gwendolyn might've tarnished her reputation in the attempt to prevent ruination.

Fortunate that a bedchamber had been available for him on such short notice, and Gwendolyn had made a point to compliment and thank the housekeeper for her foresight as well as for her cooperation.

So, too, did she rave about the superbly well-kept house—a model of tidiness and a devotion to detail. For every surface gleamed as if it had been polished that very day.

Probably had.

"The woodwork is magnificent, Mrs. Norris."

"It's my own special polish." Mrs. Norris nodded sagely as she sneaked a covert glance up and down the corridor. "Beeswax and vinegar," she murmured. "Those are the secret ingredients."

"Truly? Beeswax?" Gwendolyn strove to express an appropriate amount of awe without sounding disingenuous or condescending. "Thank you for taking me into your confidence. Perhaps one day, you could show me how to prepare the mixture?"

She loathed dusting and polishing furniture—housekeeping in general—but for the children's sakes, she'd pretend an interest.

"Perhaps." Mrs. Norris thawed a fraction and even offered the merest upward tilt of her full lips. The corners of her eyes pleated, revealing she smiled often.

Though why it should, that rather took Gwendolyn aback.

She'd believed the housekeeper a frosty sort. In the future, she'd would be more careful to refrain from forming an opinion at first meeting.

Except for where Mr. Hollingsworth was concerned. More than a little difficult to find something redemptive in his behavior thus far.

The housekeeper ran her astute gaze around the room, and apparently satisfied everything was as it ought to be, gave a brief nod.

"I'll check on yer bathwater, Miss McClintock. Though I expect it'll be at least a half an hour longer since we've so many baths to prepare at once. Cook's preparin' the evenin' meal as well." She checked the simple watch pinned to her bodice. "Dinner is served promptly at eight."

At the doorway, she paused. "Miss McClintock, ye should ken that though this wing meets my high standards, there are two suites of rooms in the other wing that are in disrepair." She pursed her lips, her disapproval tangible. "I fear they may harbor vermin, but the old laird wadna let me have them cleaned or made orderly."

"And you'd like to see that oversight remedied?" By vermin, did she mean mice? Rats? Some other manner of crawly creature?

Mrs. Norris gave a single stiff nod. "Aye, afore the whole place be infested. We've three cats roamin' the house, and they are left in that wing each mornin'. I also have the upstairs maid regularly place camphor and peppermint oil in the rest of the wing. The strong smells discourage unwanted visitors."

Mice and rats then. No surprise that a house this size with portions built a hundred years ago would have varmints scampering about.

"Mrs. Norris? What if, after I've become familiar with the running of the house and the children and I have established a routine, you and I inspect the chambers together and develop a plan?"

"That be more than acceptable, Miss." Mrs. Norris lifted a shoulder and sniffed. "A few more weeks willna make a difference. I've been here nearly forty years—the longest of any of the current staff—and they've no' been touched in all that time."

Gwendolyn suppressed a shudder and grimace.

Might be advisable to send a stalwart fellow or two with clubs in ahead of time.

"That's very curious, if you'll forgive me for saying so." Gwendolyn didn't want to get on the housekeeper's wrong side, but suites left in disarray for decades?

Decidedly peculiar.

"Aye, Miss. When I was retained, except for a cook, a valet, a single groom, and one maid, no other servants had been in the house for years." Head angled, her eyes mere slits, she pursed her lips and regarded Gwendolyn for a long considering moment, as if debating whether she could be trusted.

Gwendolyn would not probe. It would give the appearance of foraging for tattle. If and when the housekeeper felt comfortable enough to trust her, Mrs. Norris would tell her what she knew.

Mrs. Norris glanced over her shoulder to the door standing open, then edged nearer to Gwendolyn.

Secrets already?

"I dinna like gossip, and I dinna tell ye this to pass along rumors. But ye are the young master's guardian, and ye have the right to ken." Mrs. Norris drew in a deep breath and released it on a heavy sigh. "In a fit of rage, the old laird sacked the lot one night nearly fifty years ago. Every last staff member down to the gamekeeper and stable lads."

"My word. What on earth could've caused such wrath?"

Gerard McClintock was a cantankerous, temperamental creature, it seemed.

Mrs. Norris straightened the mantel clock, then rotated the lamp farther along the mantelpiece until the painted flowers on its base faced directly forward.

A stickler for detail.

Gwendolyn made a mental note. That might come in useful later.

"He kept a mistress here," Mrs. Norris said, her face pinched in censure. "One suite was hers, and the other his. She ran off one night. That be when he flew into a rage, sent everyone packin' 'cause someone helped her flee. Drugged him with laudanum, 'twas rumored."

A chill padded its icy feet down Gwendolyn's spinal column. "Flee? I don't understand."

With each additional thing she learned about her granduncle, Gwendolyn liked Gerard less.

"Sometimes circumstances, not choice, force women into situations they abhor. And when given a chance to escape, they seize it." Mrs. Norris fussed with a floral needlepoint armchair pillow. "That be what Heather Abernathy did."

"May I ask how you learned all of this if you weren't retained until much later?" Perhaps Mrs. Norris was mistaken, or perhaps, she was a gossipmonger.

"Naturally, the unjustly dismissed servants be angry and they grumbled. Word about strange goin's on always has a way of makin' the rounds, it do." The housekeeper lifted a shoulder. "The laird only hired me 'cause he was to wed. He wanted Suttford made presentable for his wife. After years of neglect, that took some doin', I dinna mind tellin' ye."

"I'm sure it did." What manner of other unpleasant things could Gwendolyn expect in her new home?

After Mrs. Norris departed, Gwendolyn released an audible sigh and shoved the heavy door to her bedchamber shut. She unpinned her hat, then unbuttoned her jacket and removed it. Honestly, she'd rather have a tray brought up, but she must make an appearance below to establish her position as mistress.

Yawning indelicately, not even bothering to cover her mouth, she stretched her arms over her head. She slowly turned in a circle, examining what was to be her chamber for the foreseeable future. A partially open door revealed a quaint adjacent sitting room, and she presumed the third door hid a bathing chamber.

Quite charming in shades of pale yellow, sage green, and peach, the room possessed an inviting and tranquil atmosphere. A feminine chamber with delicate cherrywood furniture, floral carpets covering the stone floors, pretty tatted doilies, and bric-a-brac displayed here and there.

She'd be comfortable here.

As comfortable as possible with the virile Dugall Ferguson next door.

Had such pains been taken for her arrival or had the room belonged to someone else? Something oddly disquieting about the latter. It made her feel all the more an intruder at Suttford.

Oh, to be able to climb atop the fluffy counterpane and close her eyes for a few moments. But Gwendolyn feared she would fall fast asleep and miss dinner altogether.

Trailing her fingertips across the large bed's thick coverlet, she yawned again. A far bigger bed than she'd slept in at Thistle Glen.

Everything about Scotland was bigger and bolder. More raw and natural. It intrigued as much as put her off. Peculiar, that—her indecisiveness. She generally knew her own mind.

She gave the array of ruffled and lace-edged pillows artfully arranged at the headboard a wry smile. She preferred simplicity, truth to tell, and the eight . . . ten . . . no, make that thirteen pillows adorning the bed would be stored away while she resided here.

For the next decade or more.

A decade.

She'd be—*Oh, my stars and garters*—almost forty. The same age Mama had been when she died.

That weird twinge that always started in Gwendolyn's chest and spread to her stomach, leaving her, not exactly sick, but wistful and empty, spasmed again.

Every time she contemplated her lonely future, the pang pealed like a cathedral's belfry, a clanging reminder of her lot in life.

The maiden aunt.

Gwendolyn sighed and flicked the tassle on one of the pillows. Enough dismal reflections.

She couldn't change what was. Only embrace what she could and make the most of the situation. Deliberately turning her back on her melancholy musings, she fished around for something less depressing to mull about.

How were the children settling in? She'd asked them to be placed in the same room for now. Too much change at their ages could be frightening.

The death of their grandpapa and father within weeks of one another, to start. Then Gwendolyn towing the lot across the Atlantic and to this rustic locale to start over. No matter how resilient Jeremiah and Julia might be, it was every bit as hard on the darlings as the adults whose lives had been uprooted.

Pressing two fingertips between her weary eyes, Gwendolyn closed them and drew in a long, fatigued breath.

Kandie was to see Jeremiah and Julia bathed and fed and then tucked into their beds with a promise that Gwendolyn would kiss them goodnight and read them their favorite fairy-tale, *Toads and Diamonds*, before going to dinner. The poor nanny had been half-asleep on her feet, too.

Most irregular that other than Hollingsworth, no one except servants had put in an appearance when their little troupe arrived. Where were all the other relatives Mr. Ferguson claimed lived here?

If anyone else did indeed reside at Suttford, she'd meet them at dinner in two hours. Unless they decided to dine in their chamber, either out of habit or in protest.

What to do about the other residents, if they even existed, she'd decide later.

While Gwendolyn waited for her bathwater, as well as the items she required to stitch and cleanse Mr. Ferguson's lacerations, she wandered to the double French-type windows opening onto a balcony.

She pushed the doors wide, and then gasped at the view.

Utterly lovely.

Momentarily awed at the unexpected beauty before her, wonderment rooted her in place.

Though dusk fully enveloped the Highlands now, in the distance, a rambling river separated two rolling green rows of hills. Lush meadows carpeted the foreground, and creamy fleeced sheep dotted one side of the river. What looked to be long-coated reddish-blond cattle milled about on the other side.

A dovecote as well as several stables, a carriage house, and four quaint stone, thatch-roofed cottages perched along the meadow's periphery. Golden light glowed in the curtained windows of each. Tomorrow, she'd take Jeremiah and Julia for a walk to explore the area and introduce themselves to the occupants.

Nearer the Keep, a tidy three-sided hedgerow enclosed a charming garden, complete with an arbor, several trees, a fountain, and at least two benches. From one of the trees an unfamiliar bird's call lifted to her.

Jeremiah had inherited a beautiful estate. No wonder Hollingsworth was so infuriated. Truthfully, she couldn't blame him. It did seem unfair that an American should claim Suttford when a Scot had lived right here all along.

However, she didn't make the laws and the entailment dictated who inherited. There wasn't aught she could do in any event.

Gwendolyn leaned her elbows on the balustrade, and breathed in the fresh air. It helped to clear her head and made her thinking sharper. She had a notion, invigorating as much as wearing, that she'd need her wits about her in the upcoming days.

Years.

A mild fragrance wafted past, and she closed her eyes and breathed in the pleasant scent.

"That be heather ye smell."

Eight

Gwendolyn whirled to her left.

Mr. Ferguson stood in the shadows, one knee cocked, his booted foot propped against the stones his broad shoulders rested upon.

Had he been watching her?

Noting his wet hair, she frowned. "You've bathed already?"

How? Mrs. Norris said the water would be at least half an hour.

"Aye." He shook his still damp head and swept his huge palm toward the river. "I made use of Suttford Bourne."

She knitted her brow. "Bourne? I thought it was a small river, and you risk infection if the livestock tainted the water."

Foolish man. With his open cuts and abrasions, his blood might become poisoned.

His rumbling chuckle drifted into the growing dusk, and a prickly sensation skittered across her flesh, making her shiver. "It *is* a river, lass. Scots have many names for waterways, and the water's sweet and pure in the pool I used. Too deep for cattle or sheep to venture into."

Rubbing her hands up and down her arms from elbow to shoulder, she shuddered. "That had to have been freezing."

"It was, but it helped with the swelling."

At the inflection in his voice, she gave him a piercing look. She wasn't altogether certain he referred to his bruised face. Flames licked her cheeks at her naughty conjecture, and her palms grew damp. She placed them behind her and leaned into the railing.

Did he feel the attraction between them as profoundly as she? Compelling and seductive, and she fretted, perhaps irresistible.

The angle at which he lounged against the house accented his size and strength. That sensual stirring she'd thought to never feel again bubbled upward for the umpteenth time since meeting him.

He proved a dangerous distraction. One she couldn't afford to indulge. Not only for propriety's sake—she must remain above reproach else risk losing the children's guardianship—but because she wouldn't survive more grief.

And Dugall Ferguson was a living, breathing, heartbreaking Adonis. She needed his expertise to help school her in the running of Suttford, but nothing else. She must make that clear.

Theirs was purely a business arrangement. Besides, he was younger than her by over four years. Scandalous even entertaining such an outrageous mismatch.

Ballocks to that, her conscience chided.

A rueful smile arcing her mouth, she faced the picturesque scene once more.

"It's very refreshing, Mr. Ferguson, and the view is spectacular."

"Aye, it is." The husky timbre of his voice forewarned her, yet as if compelled by some unseen, irresistible force, she still glanced over her shoulder.

Unwise and imprudent.

"And ye might as well call me Dugall, for I intend to say yer name at every opportunity, Gwendolyn. I like how it feels on my tongue."

And, God help her, she liked how it sounded. All warm and musical. And wholly natural.

Undisguised desire shone in his brilliant marine-colored gaze.

She'd never seen eyes that exact shade before. They assaulted her senses, weakened her ramparts, and though she'd only known him but hours, she feared she'd miss him horribly when he left in a few months.

A chorus of fear and pain and warning shrieked their denials. She couldn't—*mustn't*—allow herself to feel anything ever again.

So Gwendolyn pretended not to notice the smoldering in his eyes—and the answering warmth tunneling through her veins. Instead, she focused on the charming landscape. It really was quite entrancing.

Grandpa had claimed the same, always with a hint of wistfulness in his voice and a faraway look in his eyes. He'd never said why he'd chosen to leave Scotland, nor mentioned the family he'd left behind.

Gwendolyn had always assumed a desire to make his fortune in a land fraught with opportunity had motivated him. But perhaps a rift with his family had driven him to America.

He'd missed his homeland until the day he died, yet he'd never returned to Scotland. Not even for a visit.

Would it be the same for her?

Would she ever set foot in South Carolina again?

How long before they—*she*—stopped feeling like outsiders and this place became home?

Weeks? Months? Years? *Ever?*

Far too soon to even contemplate such a thing.

"Scotland possesses a rugged beauty I haven't truly appreciated until this moment," Gwendolyn said to distract herself from her doleful ruminations.

"Aye. She gets in yer blood. And once that happens, there's nae riddin' yerself of her power over ye."

She considered Dugall again.

Was he still talking about Scotland? It almost sounded like he meant something else entirely.

Weariness had her imagining things. She shook off her nonsensical, cackling-like-a-disgruntled-hen thoughts.

He pushed himself upright. "Gwendolyn—"

A knock sounded at her door.

"Come in," she called. "Mist—er, Dugall, that's probably the supplies I need to tend your face properly. Shall I come over there, or do you prefer to come here?"

Wasn't she God's own fool for insisting on stitching his face herself? But according to Mrs. Norris, the doctor was attending a birthing, and only one groom had any experience in sewing wounds. And that, only with animals.

Gwendolyn's neat stitches would scarcely leave a scar, and why that mattered, she refused to examine.

"Miss McClintock?" A dewy-faced maid, holding a basket, her forehead wrinkled in confusion, slowly turned around in the middle of the chamber. "I have the supplies ye asked for."

"I'm out here. Fenella, isn't it?" Gwendolyn stepped to the threshold. She'd remembered one name after all. "Just leave them on the table beside the fireplace. I'll see they're returned below when I've attended to Mr. Ferguson."

"Aye." After complying, the maid bobbed a curtsy and grinned. "The staff want ye to ken how happy we are ye and the new laird are here. He's a braw lad and his sister a bonny lassie."

"Yes, they are. And thank you for sharing those kind

words with me. It means a great deal." And it did. Winning over the servants was no small task.

Gwendolyn sliced a quick look to the other balcony before reentering her chamber.

Empty. Dugall had slipped away.

"Fenella, do others live at Suttford House?" Gwendolyn donned a crisp, white apron, then set about rolling her sleeves up before pouring water into the wash basin and thoroughly washing her hands. "I'd been told they do, but I saw no one when we arrived."

Rather rude, actually.

At once Fenella's countenance changed, and a carefully blank expression descended on her bubbly features. She speared the open door a hasty glance before clasping her hands before her pristine apron.

Ah, as telling as a dairy cow's full teats.

"Aye, Miss McClintock. Ye've met Mr. Hollingsworth."

"Yes, I did meet him." An experience as pleasant as hugging a mama gator protecting her eggs. "Anyone else?"

"There were others, but they left after the laird died, and Mr. Hollingsworth insisted they make themselves useful or find somewhere else to live. He said, dogs that dinna hunt dinna eat."

Fenella's tone and expression remained bland, but Gwendolyn detected a measure of approval in the servant's mien, nonetheless.

Either Hollingsworth wasn't as generous as his uncle, or those that left had been the parasites Dugall suggested they were. Then wasn't it to Hollingsworth's credit he'd booted them to the curb?

"So only Mr. Hollingsworth remains?"

Gwendolyn didn't really like putting the questions to Fenella. Nevertheless, servants usually had the right of it in a household this large, and knowledge was power.

"Nae. Now it just be Mrs. Agatha Whitworth and her daughter, Elspeth. They're cousins to the old laird. Mrs. Whitworth is blind. They're visitin' friends in Edinburgh and won't return for at least a fortnight." She glanced around guiltily, then lowered her voice. "Tattle has it Miss Elspeth be sweet on a young man there."

A tiny morsel of admiration for Hollingsworth sprouted. He'd permitted a blind relation to stay? He was a more complex man than Gwendolyn had first thought.

"There also be Miss Dolina. She be the old laird's sister. Sweet as clootie dumplin' but as deaf as a loaf of black bun and *aff* her *heid* a wee bit, too. She goes off by herself for hours on end, wanderin' the moors and bogs."

Eyes at once wide and luminous with contrition, Fenella slapped her hand over her mouth.

"Forgive me. I ought no' to have said that. I'm so sorry, Miss. Please excuse my impertinence." She wrung her hands in her apron. "I could lose me position, and I needs it so. Me mum be unwell, and I have three younger brothers. Da died two years ago."

Her lip trembled as she struggled to control her emotions.

"Never fear, Fenella. I admire honesty. As long as it's tempered with kindness and sincerity."

Carrying another candelabra, the towel she'd dried her hands with wrapped around the stem for sanitation purposes, Gwendolyn patted the maid's shoulder as she passed. She'd need plenty of light to suture by. "No one shall ever know what you've told me."

"I shall." Dugall stood at the entrance in all of his manly glory. He gave Fenella a conspiratorial wink. "Yer secret's safe with me as well, lass."

Poor befuddled girl, she gaped as if Zeus himself had descended from heaven and paid her a visitation. Not too far astray.

Even with his face bashed and battered, Dugall Ferguson was the closest thing to a mythical god Gwendolyn had ever laid eyes upon. Truth to tell, even though an on-the-shelf spinster, she was half-afraid to see what he looked like once he'd healed.

"Let's see to your face, shall we, Mr. Ferguson?" Lifting a whisky bottle from the basket, Gwendolyn indicated a nearby chair with a sweep of her hand.

She opened the top, and after pouring two fingers' worth into a bowl, set it aside before rubbing her hands with the spirit.

"Miss. Sir." Fenella bobbed another curtsy, but took her sweet time departing the chamber, casting Dugall bashful, calf-eyed glances the whole while.

He winked again, and scarlet blossomed across Fenella's round cheeks. Giggling, she finally exited, leaving the door open for propriety's sake.

Eyebrow cocked, and one hand wrapped in another cloth resting on her hip, Gwendolyn shook her head. "Do women always react like that around you?"

A good-natured grin quirked his mouth up on one side. He settled his oversized form into the chair, which squeaked in protest, and rested his forearms on the arms.

"And what would ye say if I said aye. All except ye?"

Except me? Why, I'd say you were an overly confident, cocky—

Gwendolyn wetted a soft cloth with whisky, and giving him a sugary smile, pressed the scrap to the worst of his cuts.

He bolted upright, almost smacking her chin with his head. His clean, masculine scent wafted upward, teasing and tempting.

She pleated her lips together to stifle the urge to lean nearer and sniff deeply. Did he have to smell so all-fired delicious?

Gwendolyn dampened the cloth a bit more. Lower lip captured between her teeth, she dabbed another ugly gash. She didn't truly want to cause him any more pain, but whisky was an excellent antiseptic, and after his dip in the river, she must be assured the cuts were thoroughly cleansed.

"Hell's bloody bells and ballocks," he hissed through his strong, white clenched teeth, his jaw muscles flexing rhythmically.

"*Tsk*," she clucked disapprovingly. "Such language." She lifted the cloth and peered beneath it. "I know it burns something awful, but it's the best way to sanitize the gashes."

"Mayhap, but I'll be bound ye did that on purpose, lass." His turquoise eyes bored into hers. "If'n I didna ken better, I'd say ye be jealous."

What utter drivel.

Old spinsterish maids didn't indulge in schoolgirl emotions. Most particularly where it concerned half-barbarian, uncouth younger gentlemen they'd only just met.

"Does your brogue always thicken when you're upset?" she asked, deliberately navigating her troublesome thoughts to safer territory.

"Nae. Only when sirens with flames in their hair and golden fairy dust in their green eyes pour whisky in my cuts." He grabbed the bottle and took a hefty swig.

Flames? Fairy dust?

None of her former betrothed had ever described her in terms that unhinged her knees and jaw simultaneously. Or singularly either.

Summoning her gumption, she waved the cloth she held at his hand, still encircling the green bottle. "That's meant for your wounds."

He winked and raised it once more. "If ye're goin' to ply me with a needle like a piece of fancy embroidery, I need to dull my senses."

She chuckled at the imagery.

"*Hmm*, I'm sure I can find a bit of puce or lavender thread if you really want your face to resemble needlework. I cannot guarantee the sutures will hold though. Do you have a stitch preference too? Back stitch? Chain stitch? Split stitch? I might even manage a French knot."

"Saucy, bonny wench." His Adam's apple bobbed as he swallowed another healthy draught before thrusting the brew at her, a challenge in his eyes. "Have ye sewn flesh afore?"

"Yes, a few times. I had the most stalwart stomach at Thistle Glen. As you can imagine with the raising and training of thoroughbreds, accidents occurred." She gently probed his cuts, checking to see which would heal well without sutures. "And my brothers had more than their fair share of scrapes, too."

"How many brothers did ye have?"

"Two. William, the eldest died in the War of 1812." The reason she couldn't abide the English. When he and another ten soldiers had been captured, the British had executed them for treason on the spot. "He wasn't married. And Markus— the children's father—died from an injury he received during a duel."

Run through by the husband of the woman he'd been dallying with.

Dugall made a sympathetic sound in the back of his throat. "Nae sisters? I have three older ones. I can tell ye they enjoyed bossin' me around."

"I had a twin, Marilyn. She died."

While eloping with my third fiancé.

"What happened to the wee ones' mither?"

His intense gaze caressed Gwendolyn's face, and she concentrated on folding the liquor-dampened cloth rather than meeting his eyes. She'd lost so many who were precious to her, and at times, anguish welled in her chest, threatening to overcome her.

She swallowed the lump that had formed in her throat and found her voice. "She passed from a fever, shortly after giving birth to Julia."

Compassion darkened his eyes to the deepest, most captivating, ocean blue, and he skimmed his fingers along her jawline.

"Ye've not had an easy time of it lass, have ye?"

Her breath stuttered at his unexpected understanding and empathy. Unanticipated wetness stung her eyes. No, she hadn't, but wallowing in self-pity was a waste of time and prevented one from seizing other opportunities that might arise.

"Everyone endures hardships—some more than others—and the plain truth is, life's not fair. There are many things we have no control over. How we respond to difficulties and trials is within our grasp."

Now she sounded like a preacher delivering a sermon. Nevertheless, the monologue gave her time to clear the dampness from her eyes. "Shall we get started?"

Dugall closed his eyelids and sighed. "All right. Have yer way with me."

Good gracious. If only she might.

When she remained silent and still, lower lip clamped between her teeth as she struggled to control the barrage of longing his innocent words caused, he cracked an eye open.

"Yer face be as pale as St. Andrew's arse, Gwenny."

Lord a'mercy. He'd given her a pet name already. The same one the children called her. And instead of being outraged and indignant, she was flattered.

Not that bit about being compared to a saint's posterior, however. No woman, breathing or dead, ever wanted her complexion compared to a man's bum.

Yes, yes. Perfect. Focus on the affront. His impudence. His crudeness.

"Did you truly just compare me to a man's behind? A poet you most certainly are not, Dugall Ferguson."

Actually, that line about flames in her hair and golden fairy dust—

Cease, Gwendolyn Nicolette Eleanor McClintock.

"And my given name—which, by the by I haven't given you leave to use—is Gwendolyn. Not Gwenny."

Sounded like a pet sheep's name, for pity's sake.

Or a hen.

Gwen the hen.

She couldn't quite check her groan at the absurdity.

Wasn't hen a Scottish term of endearment?

A cheerful grin, like a got-loose mule in a briar patch, curving his strong mouth, he picked up the whisky again.

Struggling for seriousness, she scolded, "You needn't look as happy as a dead pig in the sunshine."

He laughed, a deep throated burble that made her grin despite her determination not to let him affect her.

"Yer accent be tolerable, but yer colloquialisms . . ." Still chuckling, he shook his head, his raven mane brushing his collar. "They be God-awful."

"*My* accent is tolerable?" She poked his shoulder. "Your brogue is thick as cold bread pudding. And as for idioms, I think the pot doth call the kettle black. What was that expression you used earlier? 'Black as the Earl of Hell's waistcoat?'"

"Here." He thrust the bottle at her. "A swig will do ye good, I think."

"No." Gwendolyn gave one short shake of her head. "I don't drink heavy spirits. And besides," she swung the horse-tail hair before his face, "I'm fixin' to stitch your gashes, and I'll need steady hands to do my best work."

Touching him would frazzle her usual robust composure for sure. She needn't be tipsy from drink, too.

"Trust me, lass. One swallow of Scotch will take the edge off yer nerves, even if it be cheap swill." His eyes grew warm around the edges, and faith glimmered within them.

It would take a good deal more than a swallow to calm the source of her unease. All six-feet-five inches of it.

"I trust ye to do a neat job, and even if'n ye dinna," he lifted a broad shoulder, the movement pulling his shirt taut across his indecently wide chest, "it'll only give the other lads hereabouts a fair chance at the lasses."

What an insufferable, arrogant, charming scoundrel.

He dangled the bottle before her. "Unless yer afraid, that is?"

"Hardly." Afraid of a swig? Ridiculous.

Gwendolyn seized the neck and, inhaling, raised it to her mouth. She tipped the bottle and took a gulp.

Eyes watering, she gasped and choked as liquid fire raced from her throat to her stomach to pool in a molten puddle.

"Good heavenly days! You might've warned me." That wasn't Grandpapa's brandy, by Jove.

After setting the bottle aside, she swiped at her damp eyes. A pleasant feeling, rather like warm spice-laced peach preserves, spread outward from her middle.

"You wouldn't have dared if I had." He tilted his dark head, his gaze keen and probing, but tender, too. "Feelin' a bit braver now?"

"I'm always brave." Or tried to be.

"I vow ye are." Was that admiration in his gruff voice?

Gwendolyn set about threading the needle. He was right, drat him. She did feel a mite calmer.

"I shall try not to hurt you too much, but there's really no help for it. You have two cuts that require four or five stitches each and another pair that require at least two."

"I winna move an inch." Rather than close his eyes, he searched her face, then touched her jaw with his big-as-a-cigar pointer finger.

More warm preserves flowed languidly through her.

At this rate, he should worry she'd seduce him.

"I told ye, Gwenny. I trust ye."

Obstinate man. The sooner she stopped arguing with him, the sooner she'd be done and could distance herself from his much too alluring person. "Dugall, I'll have to . . . That is, I shall need to . . ." This proved harder than milking a steer. "In order to have the best angle to sew your gashes, I'll need to stand between your legs."

To Dugall's credit, though mirth and something much sultrier darkened his eyes and sharpened the planes of his face, he silently spread his legs.

Gwendolyn edged between his indecently marble-hard thighs, and with grim determination not to be distracted by the array of manly muscles so near her touch, set to her task.

Several minutes later, her poor lower lip having been clamped, chewed, and all around abused as she concentrated on suturing his lacerations, she snipped the last horse hair.

"There. Finished. Fifteen in all."

Dugall had closed his eyes about half way through the process, and she was most grateful. Having those penetrating orbs watching her, scant inches between their faces, his whisky-tainted breath warming her neck, proved wholly unnerving.

Every pore, every cell, every part of her—particularly the feminine parts, to her utter consternation—had noticed such things as his delicious manly scent, the firm, curving muscles she pressed against to reach his forehead, and the lips mere inches from hers.

She bent over him and carefully applied a bit of salve to each cut and scrape. "I'm sorry if I hurt you terribly."

He didn't move, and worry consumed her.

"Dugall?"

His preposterously thick eyelashes raised and his gaze trapped hers. Snared, incapable of moving, she didn't balk when his agile hands encircled her waist and pulled her onto his lap.

She didn't resist a jot when he lowered his head and claimed her mouth in a blazing kiss that made the whisky seem like cooled, sweetened cream.

And she didn't hesitate to wrap her arms around his sturdy neck and shoulders and eagerly offer up her lips like a woman starved, relishing his mouth upon hers as he skillfully devoured the tender flesh.

No, she readily surrendered.

His broad palms pressed into her back, urging her nearer as, kiss after hot kiss, he battered her ever weakening resolution to remain impervious.

He pulled away first and brushed her cheek with the knuckles of one hand. "Gwenny, I've wanted to do that since I awoke and saw ye hoverin' over me."

Dazed, her senses still reeling and her mouth tingling, she fought to bring her breathing and frolicking pulse under control.

"My heavenly days," she managed to whisper at last.

Not a one of my betrothed ever kissed me like that.

NINE

Betrothed? As in more than one? How many more?

The most irregular feeling coiled around Dugall's ribs. Not disappointment exactly, nor was it surprise. Bugger him if he could name the foreign, but wholly uncomfortable sensation.

He would bite his tongue in two before he pried, however. Something as intimate as a broken betrothal—*multiple broken betrothals*—needed to be shared voluntarily.

Her lips slightly parted, a few loose tendrils of Gwendolyn's vibrant hair coiling around her ears, and one hand clutching his shirtfront, she stared over his shoulder.

Finally, she cut him a wary glance. "Did I say that out loud?"

"Aye."

"Oh."

A fetching flush swept over her high cheekbones, making the freckles stand out. She released his shirt and inhaled deeply.

He would not probe, though curiosity danced an exuberant jig within his imagination. It was as obvious as his battered face that she'd not meant to divulge the information, and it disconcerted her that she had.

When she still didn't move, but continued to sit on his thigh, her countenance glowing and slightly stunned as only a woman thoroughly and satisfyingly kissed was wont to do, he gave her ribs a little squeeze and angled his head.

For someone who'd been betrothed more than once, she didn't seem all that skilled in the art of kissing. Just how experienced was she in other matters? He knew few couples who, once officially affianced, hadn't enjoyed life's more carnal delights.

Far too many early bairns confirmed that fact.

"The door be open, Gwendolyn. Anyone might pass by—"

She jumped to her feet, faster than a chicken after an insect.

"I . . ." She licked her lips, then with a slight shake of her head, set about straightening the medical basket, her chagrin palpable.

His face itched bloody awful, and the sutures pulled uncomfortably where she'd sewn his flesh together. The pain of the needle entering and exiting his skin hurt far less than breathing in her light floral fragrance as her knee or thigh intermittingly bumped into his pelvis.

That had been exquisite torture.

He knew few genteel women who possessed the stoicism to suture gashes. Other than Seonaid, his youngest sister, not a female in his family would've been capable.

Gwendolyn had been so intent on her mission, her pretty green eyes slightly narrowed in concentration, she hadn't noticed the gradual swelling of his groin.

Only by closing his eyes and conjuring every unpleasant thing he'd ever experienced, and imagining a few ghastly scenarios too, had he managed not to disgrace himself.

He'd either be for the river again tonight, or wait until the water turned cold before bathing. He'd be walking about with a cockstand for the foreseeable future. Normally, he might've accepted an eager lass's invitation to share a few blissful moments, but the notion held no appeal.

The only bonny woman he yearned to bed stood inches away and studiously avoided looking his direction. Which gave him more opportunity to study her form silhouetted by the blaze in the hearth.

Once she'd finished puttering with the basket and contents, and piled the soiled cloths into an untidy stack, she brushed her hands down her odd skirt's front. "Mr. Ferguson—"

"Dugall."

She flicked her long fingers dismissively.

"I oughtn't to have kissed you. I'm afraid having done so, I don't think the arrangement we discussed earlier would be wise after all." She met his glance squarely, though unease, or perhaps discouragement, rimmed the edges of her eyes.

He traced a fingertip along the armrest. "Why, because we enjoyed a kiss? We're adults. I wanted to kiss ye, and ye wanted to kiss me. There's no harm in that."

"You don't understand." Darting a leery glance to the doorway, she made to step away from him. "I must remain above reproach. I cannot risk losing guardianship of the children. Normally a male is appointed, and if anything untoward were to occur . . . Well, surely you understand how traumatic it would be for us all."

A valid concern, yet in his gut Dugall knew that was only part of the reason for her withdrawal into starched propriety. If ever a woman's blood sang with suppressed passion, it was Gwendolyn McClintock's.

He stood and grasped her elbow.

Her eyes widened, but she made no effort to pull away. So, she harbored a degree of trust for him, too.

"I do understand, and yer sacrifice is noble. But what do ye want as a woman, Gwenny? Are ye content to raise yer niece and nephew, or do ye want more? Because the woman I just kissed, wants more. She's starvin' for much, *much* more."

She did yank her arm away then.

"You overstep the bounds. You don't know me. That kiss was a mistake and mustn't happen again." Brushing wisps of coppery hair off her forehead, she pulled her auburn brows taut. "Which, as I said before, is why you cannot remain as Suttford's steward."

Dugall scraped a hand through his hair. "I canna in good conscience leave ye and the children at Hollingsworth's mercy. I give ye my word. I shan't attempt to kiss or touch ye again." He winked. "However, I winna hold ye to the same promise, lass. Feel free to seduce me at will."

Head canted as she considered him for a lengthy moment, her still-pinkened-from-his-kisses lips twitched, and she tapped her fingertips together.

"Purely a business relationship, Mr. Ferguson." She shook a finger at him. "No knavery or flirting. Is that understood?"

Och, back to Mr. Ferguson, is she? We'll see, my fiery American. We shall see.

He'd quite enjoy this challenge.

"Aye. But if ye ever want to talk to someone, my family tells me I'm a good listener."

Her expression closed as sharply and tightly as a snuffbox's lid. "Our discussions will concern the management of Suttford and nothing else. I'll not pry into your prior relationships, innumerable though they probably are, and you'll not enquire into mine. Understood?"

"Perfectly." His fanciest neckcloth was less stiff and starched than Gwendolyn at the moment.

She'd been wounded mightily. He'd stake Bran on it. But a woman like Gwendolyn was made to love. She might honestly have convinced herself she'd be content raising her niece and nephew, but she'd always feel like she'd missed out.

The trouble was, he wasn't the person to lure her from her self-imposed spinsterhood.

He had plans. Plans he'd carefully laid out for years. They didn't include forging a permanent relationship with a beautiful red-head, parenting her charges, and managing an estate larger than Craigcutty.

Now a delicious dalliance . . .

Prudent to change the subject before his thoughts became any more snarled.

"I'd like to ride over to Craiglocky tomorrow and apprise Ewan of the situation here." Dugall wandered to the door, and after glancing up and down the hallway, smiled at her. "Why don't ye come? Yer aunt, Kandie, and the children, too?"

It might help cool the tempers that were sure to rise when those at Craiglocky learned he'd collaborated with the enemy.

Indecision played upon Gwendolyn's features. "So soon after arriving here? I'm not sure that's wise. I planned on taking the children for a walk and exploring our new home."

Not an outright no as he'd anticipated. He pressed home his advantage. "There are children at the Keep near Jeremiah and Julia's ages, and I think yer aunt would find Ewan's Aunt Kitta very intriguin'. She's descended from a famous Viking earl."

"Ewan's aunt? Not yours?" Standing in the center of her chamber, exhaustion apparent in her rounded shoulders and the fine lines edging the corners of her face, she appeared quite forlorn.

Dugall folded his arms and leaned a shoulder against the door frame. "Aye. Kitta's married to Ewan's uncle. He was brother to my mither's first husband."

Part of the rancor between the two households stemmed from something that had occurred after Mither was widowed.

"From the list you rattled off earlier, you have quite a large family. I'd believed Aunt Barbara, the children, and I the only kin we had left, but now I suspect there might be a slew of relations we knew nothing of." A tiny frown knitted Gwendolyn's fine brows as she rolled her sleeves down. "Your family must be worried sick about you."

"I sent a missive to the castle right after we arrived. So what say ye about tomorrow, Gwenny?"

"Gwendolyn, you exasperating man."

Dugall wiggled his eyebrows and gave her his most beguiling smile. "We can ride and the others can go by carriage. I distinctly recall ye sayin' you'd enjoy a longer ridin' excursion."

She laughed, the musical echo floating around the chamber and coming to rest like a velvet mantle atop him.

"You remembered that, did you? What about your head?" She gestured to his face, concern pulling the corners of her mouth downward. "I'm not convinced it's wise for you to even be up and about, let alone atop a horse, truth be told."

"Unless I'm insensate, I'll not stay abed." Gently fingering the stitches, he hid a wince. "It aches, but not unbearably. Besides, the ride to Craiglocky takes less than an hour, and I must travel to the Keep. I need clothes and other essentials."

He glanced down at his tattered garments. "These are only fit for the rubbish bin now, I fear."

"You might save them for meaner tasks, so you don't risk ruining more." She removed her apron, and after draping it across a chair, swept to the fireplace.

"Say you'll join me," Dugall said. "It's a chance to meet your closest neighbors."

"Fine, we'll meet our new neighbors, but then it's to work

around here." She circled her hand in the air to indicate the house and grounds. "I cannot have Hollingsworth thinking I'm neglecting my duties. He's already running around like a blind dog in a meathouse."

Americans certainly had a colorful way of speaking.

Off-key warbling carried into the chamber. A moment later, Dugall stepped aside to permit a white-haired elfish woman, a faded plaid draped about her stooped shoulders, to toddle in.

Somewhere between sixty and eighty years of age, she shuffled to Gwendolyn. The pixie took Gwendolyn's hand and patted it as she peered up at her. "I'm yer Aunt Dolina, Gerard and Gawyn's sister. I ken when I awoke from my nap ye'd arrived. Ye have the look of Gawyn about ye. His hair and eyes."

Gwendolyn's dimple appeared with her genial smile. "Except for my hair color, I've been told I resemble my grand-mother when she was my age."

"Aye ye do, that's for certain. I can see them both in ye." Miss Dolina cocked her bird-like head, her gaze astute. She wasn't as frail as she first appeared, nor as old as Dugall had initially thought either.

"Venora was in line to inherit a title in her own right when she came of age, ye ken. She and I attended finishin' school together. For two years, she accompanied me home to cele-brate Hogmanay, stayin' a month each time." Staring into the roaring fire, Dolina sighed, the sound rather forlorn. "She was the sister I never had."

Gwendolyn exchanged a soft glance with Dugall. "That's very touching."

Miss Dolina didn't seem to hear her. "But when Gawyn came home from university that last time, they fell in love and eloped while everyone was at the Hogmanay celebration." Her face took on a faraway look. "Can you imagine that kind of love? Willin' to sacrifice everythin' to be together?"

"It sounds like such a romantic tale. You'll have to tell me all the details one day." Gwendolyn finished buttoning her cuffs and sent Dugall an almost shy glance.

Miss Dolina's expression pinched for a fleeting instant, so brief Dugall wasn't sure he hadn't imagined it.

The next moment, she gave a short shake of her cottony head. "I'm nae sure how romantic a story it is. Caused a terrible stir, it did. Some never recovered."

"Och, but the union produced our beautiful Gwendolyn, Julia, and Jeremiah," Dugall said, trying to lighten the mood.

A wide smile wreathed Miss Dolina's papery face as her faded tea-toned gaze swung between Dugall and Gwendolyn, as if noticing him at last. "That scamp, Lloyd. He didna' tell me ye were married, lass."

"Oh, heavens, we're not married," Gwendolyn rushed to assure her while spearing Dugall a contrite look.

Because she'd denied the charge so quickly, or because Miss Dolina had jumped to the wrong conclusion? Why did the former rankle rather more than the latter?

Gwendolyn's surprised start and the rush of color blooming across the delicate planes of her face would've been comical, except Hollingsworth chose that moment to saunter by.

Or had he been lurking nearby all along, eavesdropping?

From the stern look he impaled Dugall with, there wasn't a doubt he'd heard the elderly woman. And formed a wholly inaccurate assumption.

Damnation.

He probably thought Dugall had some sort of scheme up his sleeve, because that was exactly the type of thing Hollingsworth would've done.

Dolina chuckled a papery rasp, and shook her head. "Och, lass. I may be in my dotage and half-blind, but I ken when sparks fly between a man and woman. And fireworks to rival Vauxhall Gardens be goin' off in here when I entered."

TEN

The next afternoon, after having been introduced to the stable hands, grooms, gardeners, and drivers, Gwendolyn stood in the largest Suttford House stable and shook her head.

"I'm afraid I don't ride sidesaddle, Sam." She indicated her split skirt. "I ride astride. Would you please saddle me another horse?"

"Astride, Miss McClintock?" Sam's voice rose in incredulity as he scuttled Dugall a desperate glance. As if to confirm he'd heard the outlandish request.

Mounted on Bran, a slight smile tipped Dugall's mouth. He'd never hinted to her what he thought about her unorthodox riding practice or her heretical attire.

"Yes." Gwendolyn nodded, tapping her riding crop against her calf. "Since I was six years old. The only time I tried sidesaddle, I nearly broke my leg. Never again."

The flustered groomsman looked to Dugall once more.

He simply raised a sympathetic midnight brow.

No help there, my good fellow.

Sam scratched his head, hemmed and hawed, and finally

led the gelding bearing the sidesaddle away before saddling Marigold, a spirited, but gentle blond chestnut.

He kept casting Gwendolyn doubtful looks, as if she'd requested something entirely immoral.

Best he get used to it. This was how she rode.

Twenty minutes later, sitting atop the mare, as they followed the barouche carrying her family, Gwendolyn slid Dugall a sidewise contemplative glance.

He stared straight ahead, more reserved than she'd seen him in the . . . what? Twenty-some odd hours since they'd met?

My, it surely seemed a longer spell than that.

Last night, after Miss Dolina mistook him for Gwendolyn's husband, he'd exited Gwendolyn's chamber so swiftly, amusement had wrestled with annoyance in her breast ever since. All through last night's awkward dinner and this morning's stilted breakfast, too.

Both of which Hollingsworth most conspicuously skipped.

Fine froth he'd whipped himself into, it seemed.

Aunt Dolina had stirred Gwendolyn's curiosity about her grandparent's elopement. Could that have been why Grandpapa never spoke of his family?

Gwendolyn had invited Aunt Dolina to accompany them today, but after giving her an odd look her aunt admitted she already made plans for the day.

Aside from brief, polite responses to the questions she put to him, Dugall had little to say since they'd departed Suttford. For the duration of the ride to Craiglocky, she opted for silence rather than endure the strained conversation.

True, she didn't know him well—at all if she were totally candid—but one of the things she'd most appreciated about him from the onset, was their ability to easily converse.

How were they to work together, managing Suttford, if he

remained distant and uncommunicative? He was the one who insisted on staying on. Now because of an innocent remark by a dafty old woman who didn't have the sense God gave a goose, he dared have his feathers ruffled? Had gone all stoic and offended?

Why did men always do that?

Instead of communicate, retreat behind a barricade of sulky silence? By all the saints in heaven, did they expect women to read their pea-picking minds?

Gwendolyn had supposed him made of sterner, more gallant stuff than that. Or maybe, she wanted to believe that of Dugall.

Hadn't she learned her lesson about men yet?

Unfair. Your first two affianced were wonderful men. The second pair, however—

The barouche, its top down, rumbled before them, creaking every now and again from a particularly deep rut in the well-traveled road. Jeremiah or his sister repeatedly poked their burnished heads over the barouche's side before their saint of a nanny dutifully towed them back onto the seat beside her.

This time, when Jeremiah thrust his head out, he made a comical face and waved.

Gwendolyn waved back and Dugall also lifted a hand.

Unlike the children's father had most of their young lives, he didn't ignore the children or treat them like nuisances. She hated to speak ill of the dead, but since his wife had died, Markus had basically turned the rearing of his children over to Gwendolyn and Kandie while he drowned his sorrows in alcohol.

Gratitude welled within Gwendolyn that though something clearly vexed Dugall today, he still demonstrated kindness.

Jeremiah rested his head on his bent arm atop the

barouche's glistening ebony side. Rubbing his fingers along the shiny edge, his doleful features revealed the pensiveness that lay heavily on his thin shoulders.

He'd tried to be brave, but when she'd stopped in to kiss the children goodnight, she'd found him weeping into his pillow.

Not altogether considerate of Gwendolyn to bundle her family into a conveyance again so soon, either. Even with the vehicle's top lowered, the trip was a fairly short jaunt, and there'd been a promise of children to play with at Craiglocky.

That had been enough incentive to entice Jeremiah and Julia aboard the barouche. A glint had entered Aunt Barbara's eyes when Dugall mentioned luncheon with his French mother. Since breakfast, Aunt Barbara had gone about muttering French phrases beneath her breath.

Shifting in the saddle, Gwendolyn set her attention to the azure sky. Streaked with wispy clouds, it looked like a giant, chalky hand had brushed the heavens.

Circling above the treetops, her feathers gleaming in the stark afternoon sun, Coronis kept pace with them. She'd release a hoarse caw every so often to let them know she still followed.

The crow rather fascinated Gwendolyn, and she hoped to become friendly with the bird. Dugall claimed he could feed her by hand, and that she was partial to shortbread.

From beneath her lashes, she considered him again.

He rode with the ease of a man accustomed to long hours in the saddle. A man possessing callused hands and familiar with physical labor, too. Not soft, privileged gentlemen such as Benjamin Hampton or Lance Eggleston—fiancés three and four—had been.

As if sensing her perusal, Dugall slid her a swift, unreadable glance and offered an even briefer smile.

His indifference pricked far more than it ought. She'd

asked—no, demanded—precisely this distance between them. Theirs was a dispassionate, business association, nothing more. And his compliance ought to gratify rather than trouble.

Given her past, perhaps she'd become a mite overly-sensitive to men's rebuffs. Surely that explained her discomfiture.

Fiddle sticks and horse feathers.

She was embarrassed about her numerous troths, plain and simple. Any woman in her situation would've been.

Dugall had been keen to know more about her failed betrothals, but to his credit, hadn't pressed her.

Pride, self-preserving or misplaced, had kept her from telling him the whole of it. Rather degrading to have less carnal experience than a man over four years her junior.

Less? She snorted softly. How about none?

But then again, men had always abided by one set of rules while women were expected to adhere to a second, more severe and less fair list of protocols.

Her guardianship was proof of that. She'd been questioned repeatedly about the appointment, most stringently by Uncle Gerard's solicitor via numerous letters.

Honestly, why he was so bent on uncovering every detail of the guardianship, vexed. The situation was very simple. She was the children's closest remaining relative. On his deathbed, frail and barely able to hold the quill, Markus had scribbled one sentence naming her guardian. Then, weak as a too-soon-born kitten, he'd slashed his illegible signature. Barely legal, and easily contested.

It really stirred Gwendolyn's stew that anyone should presume her incompetent or incapable based solely on her gender.

She fretted, hopefully without reason, that a male relative might try to wrest the guardianship from her in order to control Suttford's lands and monies.

A crafty, greedy guardian—someone of Hollingsworth's caliber—could bankrupt the estate before Jeremiah was of age, which made it all the more important that Dugall remain for the interim at least.

If they could arrive at a comfortable accord. She wasn't so certain that could be accomplished now with the current awkwardness between them.

His kisses had been nothing short of divine. However, for the children's sake, she must control her baser urges. Must not surrender to desire.

One would expect such troublesome immoral tendencies and lascivious inclinations would've manifested sooner. Before this—before Dugall—she'd never considered herself wanton or fast. Much easier to resist if the object of her fascination wasn't so very scrumptious to gaze upon.

"I've been betrothed four times."

Oh, for mercy's sake. Just blurt it out, why don't you, Gwendolyn? You have the finesse of a hound in heat.

Dugall slowly turned his head, regarding her with his usual tranquil consideration that immediately calmed her jittery nerves.

"It be none of my business," he said, matter-of-fact. "As ye made clear last night."

She had, hadn't she? Most emphatically, too.

But she didn't want him thinking she was a flighty flibber-tigibbet that couldn't make up her mind. Or that she was defective in some manner, and men couldn't abide the notion of actually exchanging vows with her.

"I know." Lifting a shoulder, she transferred the reins to one gloved hand and scratched above her eye. "Still, I'd not have you think ill of me. I didn't call an end to any of the arrangements."

Did that make her sound more moral, or desperate to be married?

She didn't make commitments flippantly.

Why was she so set upon appearing in a good light to him? Did she seem as pathetic and anxious as she felt?

He angled his head, and his familiar smile worked one side of his mouth. "Just how shallow do you think me, lass?"

Oh, peach tarts and fried okra.

She'd insulted him again.

Disappointment more than anger or annoyance creased the fine lines around his hooded eyes.

Barehanded, his tan skin contrasting with his shirt's not-so-white cuff, he fingered his coat's only remaining button.

His face was much improved today. At least the swelling had decreased. But now, ugly purplish-green bruises and scabbed-over scratches marred his complexion on one side.

Still, the injuries couldn't hide what she'd suspected all along was a face too handsome for words.

Gwendolyn could unequivocally say, she'd never gazed upon a more beautiful man. He outshone her by far. Surpassed most everyone she knew.

A wonder he wasn't a conceited jackanape.

How do you know he isn't?

"I apologize if I offended you, Dugall. Honestly though, if our positions were reversed, I confess my interest would be greatly stirred."

Yes, but would any woman end a betrothal to him? Not unless she was a dafty thing and was missing chairs in her parlor.

He'd piqued more than Gwendolyn's interest, truth be known. Not that she wanted a catalog of his previous conquests. Horrid notion, that. She'd feel even more inferior, for she didn't doubt his list would contain more—*many more*—than four names.

Marigold pulled on the reins, and for at least the fifth or

sixth time, Gwendolyn guided the insistent mare away from Bran while giving Dugall a repentant smile.

Was Marigold's season close? Or did she simply find the stallion as tempting as Gwendolyn found his master?

"My wish," she said to steer her wayward thoughts from risky territory, "is that we proceed with our professional arrangement with the albatross of my troths out of the way. That is if you still want the position."

Something, she wasn't sure if it was annoyance or surprise, flashed in his keen gaze for a fleeting instant, then disappeared with the next blink of his thick-lashed eyes. "I'll no' desert ye or yer family. I'll stay as long as I'm able. Unless ye tell me otherwise."

Their small entourage emerged from the woods, and a stag bolted from the pines bordering the road. He darted behind the barouche, his sinewy muscles bunching and flexing as he flew past. Gwendolyn stood in her stirrups.

His magnificent canopy of antlers gleaming in the sunlight, he dashed down a grassy slope, gracefully loping to a stop where a bashful doe awaited.

Still standing, she shot Dugall a swift glance. "What kind of animal was that, Dugall? A deer of some sort? I've never seen the like."

Dugall's mouth skewed into a wide grin, and he rubbed his nose. "Aye. A red stag. They abound around here."

"He's beautiful." She sat once more and returned his smile. "I'm rather liking Scotland more than I anticipated I would."

"I'm glad, lass. And I do want to continue with our arrangements. I didna tell ye last night, but Hollingsworth was eavesdroppin' outside yer chamber. I don't know how much he might've seen or heard."

Heat, hotter than the gates of hell scorched her, immediately followed by a spine-rattling chill.

"Do you think he saw us?" She pinched the reins. All she needed was a scandal straightaway.

Dugall shrugged. "I honestly canna say."

"You've slipped into Scots again," she said with a droll smile.

"Habit, lass. It comes much more naturally to me."

"Then why not just talk that way? I'm from the south and I'd find it near on impossible to talk like a Northerner. Having to watch the pronunciation of every word. It seems unnatural." She gave him a cheeky grin. "I give you permission to speak Scots in my presence. But not Gaelic. I don't understand most of it."

"Thank ye." Brow elevated, he laughed, a rich, warm sound.

She drew in a bracing breath. "Now for that other matter."

Eleven

A wave of uncertainty snarled Gwendolyn's emotions. Trusting didn't come easily to her.

"Gwenny, ye dinna have to tell me. Ye dinna owe anyone an explanation about your betrothals." Kindness emanated from Dugall.

"Oh, I was referring to Hollingsworth listening to our conversation. How much do you think he heard, anyway?" Had she been aware of his existence before today, she'd have taken precautions to make sure he couldn't easily wrest the guardianship from her. Now it was too late.

Why hadn't Mr. Christie mentioned Hollingsworth? The other residents at Suttford House? Odd, that. Suspicious even, if a person were of a pessimistic bent. Which she wasn't. Until recently.

"I canna say, but I'll guarantee he's no' beyond usin' anythin' against ye if it gives him the slightest advantage."

No doubt Dugall meant the smile he turned on her to be heartening, but it transformed his face into pure masculine, highly distracting beauty. "Dinna fash yerself about it, though. I ken how to handle the likes of him."

Dugall's assurance made her happier than she had any right to be. Yet a tiny, intrusive voice whispered, *"Don't come to depend on him. Keep your distance. He'll only disappoint, and you know he must eventually leave."*

Well, naturally he must.

Straightening her spine, Gwendolyn notched her chin upward and told her pessimistic conscience to hush. More aptly, she quashed it beneath her booted heel, and then swept it into the dust bin and ordered it to stay there.

"I was betrothed the first time at seventeen to Tucker Lymon. The quintessence of a southern gentleman, he was one of the soldiers shot with William. They were the greatest of friends, and I'd known Tucker most of my life."

"Ye loved him?" Dugall, tall and relaxed in the saddle, seemed to be genuinely interested.

"I did. Very much. A young, starry-eyed girl's first love." She'd mourned Tucker deeply, and as young girls are wont to do, didn't believe she'd ever find love again.

"I was nearly twenty when I accepted the second proposal. Paul Haggens captained the *Sea Vixen*. Dashing and daring, he made me laugh and forget my grief for Tucker. Pirates attacked and sank his ship. Only a handful of men managed to escape in a dory. The rest were never heard from again and presumed dead."

She stretched her spine to dissipate the heaviness the old memories raised. Dugall needn't know all the ugly details. Needn't know the heartrending grief she suffered after Tucker, and then Paul's death had made her leery and guarded. Afraid to love again. Two blows of that magnitude did rather knock a person to their knees and left them reeling.

To keep suitors at bay, she'd worn black for three years after Paul's death, determined she'd never risk that kind of suffering again.

And she hadn't.

Prudence and sensible logic had governed her next choice.

And so she'd chosen a man whom she could respect; one she admired and had formed a comfortable friendship with, but still permitted her to protect her heart from further devastation.

"By the time I was five-and-twenty, I'd taken on much of the operation of Thistle Glen and had become friends with a business associate of Papa's."

His gaze indecipherable, Dugall held up three big fingers. "Betrothed number three?"

She nodded, giving a small closed-mouth smile at the antics of a red squirrel scampering up a trunk. From a branch overhanging the road, it swished its bushy tail and scolded them soundly.

"Yes. Benjamin Hampton also raised Thoroughbreds and was from a distinguished South Carolina family. Everyone proclaimed it a brilliant match between two prominent families."

"But it wisna?" Dugall angled his head, politely curious but not probing.

How had he perceived that? Had she given herself away in tone or manner?

"No. On the eve of our wedding, he eloped with my sister. There was a horrific carriage accident. They both died." As had the driver and the team.

Had Marilyn even breathed a hint she'd given her heart to Benjamin and he returned her sentiment, Gwendolyn would've called off the wedding. But having her affianced jilt her and sneak away with her sister in the dead of night had rendered a wound that had yet to heal completely.

Add the humiliation of enduring pity-filled glances and quickly shushed whispers whenever she entered a room or ventured into society—

A wonder Gwendolyn hadn't become a recluse.

"Although misplaced, and illogical, guilt plagues me. For if they hadn't eloped, I believe their lives would've been spared." Lips meshed, she tapped the fingertips of her free hand on her thigh. "I keep thinking there must've been signs. Hints that I missed."

"Och, Gwenny, I be verra sorry, but ye have to ken yer in nae way at fault." Such compassion laced Dugall's words, it made the hurt a trifle more bearable and her less inclined to scold him for overstepping the bounds by addressing her as Gwenny again.

With Marilyn's and Benjamin's betrayal, what remnant of vulnerability Gwendolyn had yet possessed had promptly and everlastingly been banished to the farthest reaches of her heart. And there it would remain until they became a fusty and mummified memory.

She inhaled a cleansing breath, made more so by the crisp autumn heather and pine scented air.

Only one more betrothal to explain.

"I agreed to Lance Eggleston's proposal a mere six months ago. His estate neighbored ours, and he'd asked me to marry him at least half a dozen times—the first when I was but seven and he eight."

Complete with a handful of bird feathers and wilted wild-flowers.

Eyes twinkling, Dugall cocked a raven brow. "Why did ye finally agree?"

"I didn't want to be a burden to my family." Scrunching her nose, she gave a small grimace. "And as we rubbed on fairly well together, I accepted, at last."

Pessimism deepened the fine lines fanning Dugall's eyes.

"Admirable, but are ye sure ye'd have been a burden?"

Eyeing the vehicle rumbling along before them, she lowered her voice. "I didn't want to end up a lonely old maid like Aunt Barbara." Gwendolyn lifted her shoulder an inch. "And I wanted children."

Of her own. Which she'd never have now.

And as much as she adored Julia and Jeremiah—was the only mother figure Julia had ever known—Gwendolyn wouldn't ever experience carrying a child in her womb. Feel it kick or hiccup or turn in her belly. She'd never suckle her baby at her breast or sing the infant to sleep.

And her spirit mourned that loss as keenly and profoundly as the many other losses she'd suffered these past years.

Such weren't the desires of all women, but since she'd been a little girl playing with her cherished dolls, she'd wanted to be a mother. Always assumed she would be one day.

Relinquishing the desire to marry for love had been brutal enough. But when she'd finally acknowledged she'd never cradle her child in her arms—

Enough.

She'd plowed that furrow clean down to the bedrock. Past time to put that mule to rest.

"Then yer other brother died?" Two creases furrowed Dugall's brow.

Her history did rather read like a tragedy.

"From an injury he received in a duel. My poor father was so distraught, he succumbed to a heart attack a mere fortnight later."

"So ye decided to call off yer betrothal?" He cut her a short, intense glance before perusing the road.

"No." She gave her head one short shake and adjusted her grip on the reins. "I told you. I didn't end any of them."

When the butler presented the neatly folded and sealed letter from Lance on a silver salver, she'd been curious, but not concerned. In three short lines, he'd ended their betrothal, though he didn't have the ballocks to tell her the real reason.

Poltroon.

He'd lied like a rug and claimed they weren't suited after all. The real truth soon became known, and it had jerked a knot in her tail, for certain.

"A beautiful French woman had recently moved to Raleigh and set her sights on him. Lance tossed me over. I sold him Thistle Glen, though. For a good price, too. He'd coveted the plantation for years, and since Jeremiah's future is in Scotland, there wasn't any reason to retain the estate."

A thoughtful expression warmed the corners of Dugall's face and eyes. "And now fate's brought ye across the ocean to God's country."

She wasn't so certain about the God's country bit, but Gwendolyn could've hugged him for not spouting some trite platitude that was intended to make her feel better but only added salt to an already nasty wound.

Dugall had heard and accepted the truth, and rather than toss the same dice again, he'd diverted their discussion to the present.

Either that, or he'd been so put off, he changed the subject to avoid further discussion.

She *had* been the one who'd insisted on spilling the fat into the fire. So it should be no surprise when the flames sizzled and exploded around her, and she received a stinging burn or two.

Julia thrust her head over the barouche's side. "How much further, Auntie Gwenny? I gotta make water."

The driver, Clacher, glanced over his shoulder at the conveyance's occupants. Not for the first time during the short journey either.

"Hush, chil'," Kandie gently chided, and shook her white-kerchiefed head.

"Well, I do, Kandie," Julia whined. "I'm fuller than a tick on a fat hog's arse."

Pinching her eyes closed, Gwendolyn crimped her mouth.

When would the children learn not to blurt everything that passed through their heads?

"Craiglocky is just around the next bend, but if her need is urgent, we can stop here. It's safe." Amusement crinkled the sides of Dugall's mouth as he regarded the equipage trundling before them. "Yer niece is a spirited lass, isnae she?"

"She'll be fine for a bit longer. And yes, she most certainly is spirited." A kind description. Most days, Julia was wilder than a March hare or a June bug in June. "So is Jeremiah, and honestly, there are days when I'm unsure I'll be able to do right by them." She sighed, then offered a rueful about-the-edges smile. "But what choice have any of us?"

"Ye've a generous heart, Gwenny, and ye love them. Dinna underestimate the power of either." Making a clicking sound in the back of his throat, he steered Bran away from Marigold. "Nae, lad. Mind yer business."

Yes, the mare most definitely was going into heat. That ought to make for an interesting ride home.

Dugall scratched his uninjured eyebrow and leveled her a penetrating look of acute consideration.

"What?" Did she have a smudge on her nose? Was there a bit of parsley stuck in her teeth from luncheon? "Why are you looking at me like that? Like you want to say something, but aren't sure you should?"

"Before we arrive at Craiglocky, lass, ye should ken that relationships between the McTavishes and McClintocks are somewhat strained."

"Strained? How so?" Why hadn't he told her this earlier? She'd never have agreed to go to Craiglocky. And what did strained mean? They'd had a falling out of some sort? A quarrel? Over what?

"Years ago, old McClintock wanted to marry my mither and conspired to abduct her."

Twelve

Dugall checked the laughter burbling in his chest.

Gwendolyn's flabbergasted countenance and sagging jaw might've earned a chuckle another time, but given her feisty nature, she might well turn her ill-humor on him.

Truth to tell, he deserved it.

He'd manipulated her, pure and simple. Had he told her of the feud, she'd never have agreed to go to Craiglocky. Likely, wouldn't have accepted his offer of help either.

However, for reasons he couldn't quite put his finger on, he was determined she should do both. His family wasn't the type to condemn someone because of a familial connection they had no control over.

One couldn't choose one's relations.

"And you're just now mentioning this bit of crucial information?" Green sparks shooting from her eyes and vexation flattening the line of her mouth, she drew the mare to a halt.

Jeremiah raised his head, his puzzled gaze shifting between his aunt and Dugall as Dugall reined Bran to a stop as well.

The barouche occupants needn't hear the squabble.

"It's nae as bad as all that. Over time, the dispute has

mellowed, and for the most part, the two families simply avoid one another." Dugall bent his mouth into his most charming grin. The one that generally caused the lasses to send him sultry smiles and even sultrier invitation-laden glances.

All the lasses except one with hair as fiery as her temper.

Gwendolyn narrowed her eyes into bottle-green slits, and shook a finger at him. "That trick won't work on me, Dugall Ferguson. I'm not a gullible miss who can be won over by a seductive smile and a smoldering turquoise gaze."

Och. She thought his smile seductive and his eyes smoldering? Masculine pride hammered a raucous, triumphant thrum through his veins, and he grinned wider yet.

From the horrified rounding of Gwendolyn's incredibly expressive eyes, and the *riddy* flush mounting her high cheekbones, she'd realized her stern putdown had turned into a compliment. More discomfited than he'd seen her, she flapped her hand at him as if to erase her carelessly uttered words.

"Don't get full of yourself." Her melodious retort was more amused reproof than cutting reposit. "You know full well what I meant."

"I do, indeed." He did chuckle then at the fuming glare she speared him, and the distinctly unladylike oath she muttered beneath her breath.

Didna ken ladies ever said that.

"There's Craiglocky." He pointed to the medieval stone castle grandly standing at attention on the horizon.

As he'd intended, he'd distracted Gwendolyn from her scold.

She swung her attention in the direction he pointed. "It looks very old."

"It is, and that's the second structure. The first Keep's charred remains are on the far side of Loch Arkaig. Perhaps another day ye'd like to explore them? They're quite fascinatin', as are the legendary tales about the residents who once lived and loved there."

She arched a disbelieving ginger brow. "I suppose you're going to tell me the ruins are haunted? Ghosts flitting about, moaning and the like?"

Dugall chuckled and shook his head. "Nae. Nae spirits of long-dead McTavishes lurk amongst the sooty relics." He winked. "At least, I've never seen or heard any. Others, however . . ."

"I'll pass then, thank you. I endure enough preternatural encounters with Kandie. Her grandmother practiced voodoo, and occasionally, the most peculiar things occur that are simply beyond human explanation."

She gave a little shudder. "Raises my hackles, it does."

Dugall considered her. "Did I mention my sister, Seonaid, had the second sight until she married?"

Done fussing with the fit of her gloves, Gwendolyn cast him a fascinated look. "Really? How intriguing. Did she truly know things before they happened?"

"Aye, though it wisna always for the best."

Her earlier pique seemed to have evaporated just as swiftly as it had come upon her.

Gwendolyn sighted the barouche, now a good quarter mile farther on. "Oh, we should catch up before they get too far ahead. Walk on." She clicked her tongue and urged her mount forward.

No sooner had Marigold taken a step, than a bang reverberated through the air.

Dugall jerked his head upward and Gwendolyn, her brows knitted, stared in the direction the sound had come from.

Another shot rang out, this one infinitely closer.

Releasing a terrified squeal, the mare reared onto her hind legs.

A skilled horsewoman, Gwendolyn managed to keep her

seat, though just barely. "*Shh*. Steady on, Marigold. There's a good girl."

Someone was being damned bloody careless.

As the frightened mare's front hooves slammed onto the earth, the jaunty black feather adoring Gwendolyn's hat fluttered to the ground. Almost omen-like.

Clacher drew the barouche to a stop and looked over his shoulder at them. Alarm lined his weathered face. Four wide-eyed faces peered behind the vehicle. No doubt they'd heard the rounds' echoes, too.

But where had they come from?

Face pale as alabaster, Gwendolyn sought his eyes. "Were those gunshots?"

"Aye. A rifle." Dugall nodded, raking his gaze over the surrounding area, seeking any sign of movement or a flash of steel to out the shooter.

Except for pinewoods to their left, and the aspen tree stand dividing half of the yonder field, nothing interrupted the open heather-strewn meadow.

He narrowed his eyes to slits.

The aspen grove, then.

More importantly, what—*or who*—was the target?

The stag they'd just seen?

Then someone was a hell of a poor aim.

The last ball had been far too near for his comfort, making it hard to credit such inaccuracy as accidental.

Dugall's spinal column fairly vibrated in warning, and his nape hair stood on end as if electrified.

Shite.

"Gwenny, bend low over yer horse's neck. This instant," he ordered, slicing her a sharp, do-as-I-say-now look.

She complied immediately, her face going impossibly whiter still.

"Clacher," Dugall bellowed. "To the Keep! Ye, in the carriage. Get onto the floor. Now!"

Kandie unceremoniously hauled Jeremiah from his perch and an instant later, no one was visible inside the conveyance.

Clacher didn't hesitate, but cracked the whip over the team's back and shouted them onward. They lurched forward, the horses' hooves tearing up the ground as they raced the last half-mile to Craiglocky.

Another rang out, and the mare squealed in pain.

Gwendolyn's terrified gasp seared Dugall straight to his core.

"Oh, my God! Dugall, she's been hit."

Eyes wide and luminous, Gwendolyn stared at the crimson streak marring Marigold's rump.

"Lass, we need to flee, and she canna carry ye." He whipped Bran to the mare's side. "Climb on behind me."

Gwendolyn hesitated, but then bit her lip and nodded.

A moment later, she settled onto Bran, and the moment she entwined her arms around Dugall's middle, he slapped the mare's uninjured hindquarter. She needed no further encouragement to charge off after the barouche.

"Hold on tight," Dugall all but growled.

He released a shattering whistle, and Bran's tense muscles bunched as his powerful form sprang frontward. Rather than pelt bent-for-hell down the road, Dugall guided the stallion into the woods.

They'd provide a degree of cover from the damnable blackguard shooting at them.

With each jarring of Bran's stride, Gwendolyn's breasts bounced into Dugall's back. Head buried between his shoulder blades, she clasped his waist as if her life depended upon it.

He feared it very well might.

Carelessness might've explained one volley, but multiple

blasts bespoke something much more sinister. It didn't escape him that Gwendolyn had apparently been the target and not the carriage's occupants.

A scare tactic or something more?

As worrisome was whether they dealt with a single gunman or multiple. Likely just the one since the time between shots indicated the cur had to reload.

"Will they make it to Craiglocky unharmed? Will the children and the others be safe?" Though her voice was steady, fear and worry tinged Gwendolyn's questions.

"I'm sure of it. Once beyond the bend, the road is open and there's naught but pastures and meadows. Nae place for an ambush. And as we're already on McTavish lands, I expect a patrol heard the gunshots. Even now, I'll wager clansmen are thunderin' in our direction."

Was Hollingsworth so desperate to retain his control at Suttford, he'd sunk to this? Had he truly become such a dreg of society? Such a cockscum, he would try to kill Gwendolyn?

So that he could attain Jeremiah's guardianship?

Or was it a ploy to frighten them so badly, they'd leave Scotland?

"What of Marigold?" Gwendolyn's face pressed into his back muffled her words. She clung to him as Bran pelted between the trees.

Dugall deliberately wove the horse back and forth, making them a more difficult target to hit.

Whoever had taken the shot at the mare couldn't have been terribly close, and chances were he and Gwendolyn had already moved beyond the range of the gun.

Amongst the trees' shadows they'd become more difficult to spot, too.

Nonetheless, he wasn't taking any chances.

"She was only nicked. She'll either make her way back to Suttford House or follow the road to Craiglocky, which is what I'm hopin'." Even if the injured mare didn't show up at the Keep, Clacher would raise the alarm in the unlikelihood the shots hadn't been heard.

In short order, the area would be crawling with McTavish clansmen.

"Where are we going?" Gwendolyn raised up so she could speak directly into his ear. Unfortunately, that pressed her marvelously full breasts even firmer to his back, and rocked her pelvis into him as well.

Desire pealed a boisterous chorus in Dugall's veins. God help him, even in the midst of this peril, he was consumed with the need to bed her.

The next few months would prove sheer torture; blast his gallantry to Hades.

Slowing the stallion and patting Bran's withers, Dugall scrutinized the area, looking for any hint of danger. Head cocked, he listened for clues that they'd been followed.

Nothing unusual resounded in the woods, nor was the forest silent.

Good signs, both.

The birds continued to sing and squirrels to chatter. If danger lurked nearby, silence would reign.

He relaxed an iota, though only just. "There be a cave a little farther along. On the other side of this wood. We'll wait there until the clan comes searchin' for us."

She nodded against his shoulder.

She trembled now, great shudders that shook her along the whole length of his back. He'd prefer she sat in front, where he could comfort her. But there'd been no time for such folly whilst fleeing from a madman's gunfire.

"I'm so worried about my family." Her quavering breath made him want to stop Bran—to hell with the danger—then take her in his arms and promise her they'd be fine.

Except he didn't dare.

They might've escaped danger this once, but an attack so soon after their arrival didn't bode well. The brazenness hadn't escaped Dugall either. The shooting was that of a desperate man.

Neither spoke as Bran carried them onward. The horse's breathing had returned to normal, but Dugall still felt like his heart had wedged permanently in his throat.

Such terror had gripped him when the last shot struck the mare. It easily could've been Gwendolyn, and the knowledge eviscerated him, leaving him vulnerable in a way he'd never experienced before.

Odin's toes, he didn't like the feeling.

The powerlessness. The utter vulnerability.

It didn't help that he carried no weapons on him either. Before they returned to Suttford House tonight, he'd be armed to his teeth.

Shortly, they arrived at the cave, more of a secluded over-hang nestled between the wood's edge and an outcrop, than an actual cavern.

He dismounted, then raised his hands to assist Gwendolyn down.

She regarded his upraised arms for an extended moment, then with a twitch of her pretty mouth, swung her leg over Bran and placed her hands on Dugall's shoulders.

Relishing the feel of her trim form in his arms, Dugall held her tightly to him as she slid off the horse. The top of her head almost reached his chin, and he indulged in a smug smile.

He'd known she'd be tall enough for him. A perfect fit. Like a coin; two sides of the same mold.

Aye, he was a churl for enjoying the moment despite their perilous circumstances. But he wouldn't regret the experience. Everything about this woman—from the endearing freckles dotting her nose, to her eyes so green, Highland grass paled in comparison—enthralled him.

Once standing, she crossed her arms and clapped her hands to her shoulders. She clinched her mouth against her chattering teeth.

Shock had set in.

Dugall gave her a reassuring smile, and after patting Bran —the stallion wouldn't budge unless Dugall told him to—he grasped Gwendolyn's arm. Bending over, he guided her under the overhang. "Watch yer head. The ceilin' be low."

A flat stone, much like a natural bench, partially ran along one wall, and he gently pushed her down upon its hard surface.

"Sit, Gwenny," he whispered. "Ye've sustained a considerable fright."

Hugging herself, she sank onto the granite and released a puff of air. She quaked from head to toe, like a late-season leaf during a windstorm.

Damn, he wished he had his flask. She could use a nip of whisky to bring the color back to her ashen face.

So could he, by God.

What he'd experienced when the blood spread across Marigold's flank, knowing Gwendolyn was mere inches away . . .

He gave a mental shake to dislodge the image.

Had the shooter been a better aim, the outcome might've been wholly different.

Dugall stepped to the entrance and, head canted, listened for any indication Ewan and the clan were nearby.

Or the shooter.

He whistled, an imitation of a bird; a signal the clan used to communicate in situations such as this.

No birdsong echoed a response.

He glanced over his shoulder.

Gwendolyn huddled on the rock, still shivering uncontrollably. She gave him a wobbly smile. "I'm unaccustomed to having my horse shot."

Should he tell her that she most likely was the target?

Nae.

Not until he had more evidence to support his suspicion. But this just made his staying at Suttford House all the more necessary. And perhaps a few McTavish clansmen ought to join him as well.

But what excuse would he concoct for their presence that she'd believe? He'd think of something feasible.

Dugall lowered himself onto the rock, and after stretching his legs before him and locking his ankles, gathered Gwendolyn to his side.

She came willingly, almost eagerly, and laid her head on his shoulder. She wrapped one arm across his chest and clung to him.

"Relax, *leannan.*" He kissed the crown of her head, breathing in her essence. Orange blossoms. And vanilla. And whatever that seductive floral aroma was. "I'll keep ye safe. I promise."

She tilted her head, and met his eyes for an instant before she dropped her focus to his chin. Tears pooled in her eyes, and she swallowed before rasping, "Coming here, to Scotland, was a mistake."

THIRTEEN

Gwendolyn couldn't stop shaking, and it peeved her to no end.

She wasn't an insipid female given to histrionics or waterworks.

No, by Juniper and June bugs.

She was the head of her family.

She should be brave and strong.

She knew how to shoot a gun—had seen and tended gruesome injuries.

And *she'd* been the one to wash and dress her mother, father, sister-in-law, and brothers before they were laid to rest one final time.

Yet she'd never felt more inadequate or insecure *or afraid* than she did at this precise moment.

What if—?

She could barely allow herself to form the terrifying idea. What if the shooting hadn't been accidental? What if she had been the target?

Foolish fabrications or a feasible possibility?

"I was lying to myself when I said I could do any of this." She fluttered her fingers in the air before wiping a curved knuckle across both eyes.

She sniffed and shook her head against the wall of Dugall's broad chest. If she didn't bring her emotions under control soon, he'd think her a complete water pot.

He continued to work his soothing magic, slowly and lightly caressing her spine, and every now and again pressing his lips to her head. Much the same way she did when comforting one of the children.

Only she wasn't a child, as her very womanly responses to his touch silently shouted. With each stroke, the urge to moan, to arch into him, and throw her leg over his trunk of a thigh grew stronger.

"Do what, lass?"

His query pulled her from her sensuous daze.

"Be the children's guardian. Move to a new country and start a life here. Equip Jeremiah to be a Lord of Parliament." She gave a watery chuckle and again swiped at the tears leaking from the corners of her eyes. "I don't even know what in creation the title means."

"It be the equivalent of an English barony." His warm, melodic baritone further lulled the fright from her. But not the feelings of inadequacy.

She never should've come to Scotland. Never should've agreed to visit Craiglocky.

He shifted and his pectoral muscles bunched beneath her hand.

Oh, the naughty, tempting things tripping across her mind.

By heavens, maybe she never should've permitted Dugall to hide them away in this hole in the ground either.

She gave a rueful shake of her head, wincing when her hair

caught on his coat. "If leather were brains, I don't possess enough to saddle a grasshopper when it comes to honorifics."

The rich timbre of his chuckle rumbled beneath her ear.

"Ye're too hard on yerself, lass." He gave her shoulders a squeeze and dared to kiss her temple. Like a sweetheart would. "Ye love those children as if they be yer own. Ye put Hollingsworth in his place with a finesse few possess."

He tilted her chin, then gave a charmingly rakish wink. "And ye saved my life and even stitched my handsome face."

"Hardly saved your life, conceited beast." She chuckled again and slapped his chest. His wonderfully wide, sculpted chest, straining at his shirt's lucky fabric.

She'd never met a more powerfully built man, and her feminine curiosity yearned for a glimpse of him shirtless. Maybe more than shirtless.

Not that such a thing could ever be permitted.

He cupped her face in his big palm, rubbing his thumb down her damp cheek. "Nae, not conceited. Just truthful."

And too confident for either of their good.

"I ken I be easy on the eye. I didna have any hand in it. 'Tis the guid Laird's doin', and I wilna be ashamed or falsely humble."

He ran his other strong hand up and down Gwendolyn's spine, the movement so natural and comforting, she wanted to crawl into his lap and wail her fears. To nestle closer and pretend for a few precious minutes that such a good and decent specimen of manhood was *her* mate, even if he was several years her junior.

She'd craved a man's touch for so long, and she feared, much like a tippler couldn't resist another drink of ale or a tot of whisky, she'd become addicted to Dugall Ferguson's practiced wiles far too easily.

More troublesome was the worry she mightn't be able to

resist him if he wanted to take their relationship to a different, more intimate level. She hadn't a doubt he knew the ways around a woman's body, that he'd introduce her to fleshly delights with a prowess borne of experience.

Her nipples puckered excitedly at the notion.

Praise heavens he couldn't see the traitorous things.

But she must resist. It was imperative. Too much depended upon it.

For her heart's sake as much as the children's wellbeing, she couldn't indulge in the enticement, no matter how tantalizing. No matter that she'd go to her grave a virgin. For if she lost the guardianship, she quite literally had nothing left.

Where would she go? What would she do?

What would happen to Aunt Barbara and Kandie? How traumatic for Julia and Jeremiah, too. Julia had known no other mother besides Gwendolyn, and Jeremiah could barely remember Jenny anymore.

No, Gwendolyn mustn't be selfish. She must think of the others who depended upon her. Put aside her personal wants. Surely these physical cravings could be controlled.

But then Dugall's rapt gaze twined with hers, and she could no more haul hers away than snatch the stars from the heavens.

He dipped his head and touched her lips with his. A fleeting, butterfly-wing-soft brush. And every last vestige of self-recriminations disintegrated. Floated away like a dandelion's fragile down on a windy day.

She arched into him, eagerly accepting his tongue into her mouth, welcoming his hands cupping her buttocks, pressing her to the hard mound at his groin.

She'd been half-crazed with want for him since he opened his eyes and stared into her soul. And even though this was rash and impetuous, even while her logical self shouted for her to stop this idiocy, she couldn't.

And that frightened her as much, in an entirely different way, than Marigold being shot.

"Dugall," she breathed as he feathered scorching kisses across her eyebrow, down her jaw, and then touched his tongue to the sensitive spot behind her ear.

A throaty moan escaped her, so wanton, if she hadn't been completely enthralled, she might've blushed.

Another sound penetrated her passion-induced daze.

A bird warbled, and Dugall tensed, lifting his head, the planes and angles of his face alert and cautious.

"What—?" Renewed fear pranced along Gwendolyn's spine; its sharp claws drawing blood with each cautious step.

He put a finger to his lips. "*Shh, leannan.*"

Twice he'd called her that. What did it mean?

The bird chirruped again, and he levered to his feet. Even bent at the waist as he sidled to the entrance, he radiated masculine grace with each sinewy movement.

The chatty bird continued to tweet, and a delighted smile crinkled his face before he echoed the call.

"The clan be here."

Bran snorted, shifting restlessly, and Dugall gripped the stallion's harness and spoke low into his ear. The horse moved his big head as if nodding in agreement.

The relationship between Dugall and Bran brought a new welling of emotion to Gwendolyn's throat—made her more homesick for South Carolina.

She missed her mare. Missed walking the stables each morning and greeting the horses. Missed the foals and fillies.

Missed the familiarity and comfort of knowing she was safe. That her family was safe.

Another melodious trill rent the air, and after Dugall answered the call, a relieved grin split his face. "That'd be my brother."

A few moments later, several brawny Scots, weapons

drawn, emerged from the woodlands, their movements silent and stealthy.

Gwendolyn shoved to her feet and made an attempt to repin the curls that had escaped the knot at the back of her head. The task was made more difficult by her lopsided hat.

She probably looked wretched and mussed.

Scared pissless, too.

Not how she'd imagined meeting Dugall's family the first time. Maybe this would diffuse the other issue between her family and the McTavishes.

With that optimistic thought emboldening her, she came to the cave's opening and clasped her hands before her. Inhaling deep, calming breaths into her lungs, she ordered her stuttering pulse to steady itself. She'd not meet Dugall's clan cowering and quaking like a spineless ninny.

A tall man, his hair and eye color a close match to Dugall's, strode to the entrance. He might've been ten years older than Dugall, and the half-circle scar on his cheek stood out starkly, a testament to his concern.

He hugged Dugall tight, then clasped his shoulders and looked him up and down. His gaze veered to her for an instant before traveling back to his brother. "What happened? Your note said you were attacked on your way home, and then minutes ago a barouche comes careening into the bailey, the occupants and driver in a complete dither."

His speech was refined, more a clipped British accent than Dugall's rolling brogue. Hadn't Dugall said his brother was an English viscount too? And their mother was French? Conversations ought to be mighty interesting at Craiglocky.

His attention still fixed on Dugall, the leader rubbed his nape. "You look like you've been run over by a team of Adaira's horses."

Adaira. She was one of their sisters, wasn't she?

"I was set upon two nights ago whilst returnin' home.

Miss McClintock was on her way to Suttford House with her family and came upon me. She assisted me. Even stitched my face. What do ye think?" He cocked his brows and pointed to his sutures.

Dugall's brother scarcely spared the neat seams a glance. "You're all right? Neither of you has been harmed? We were told shots were fired."

Dugall patted his brother's shoulder. "Aye. We be fine, Ewan. I've a crackin' headache. That be all."

He hadn't said a word, hadn't hinted he suffered. Maybe his earlier silence could be attributed to his thrumming head rather than last night's episode in her chamber.

Nonetheless, she'd have refused to permit him to ride to Craiglocky had she an inkling.

As if you had any such right.

Probably why he'd kept silent on the matter.

He motioned Gwendolyn forward. "Ewan, this is Miss Gwendolyn McClintock, newly of Suttford House. Gwendolyn, this is my brother, Laird Ewan McTavish, Viscount Sethwick."

What the hoppin' John and turnip greens was she to call him? Laird? Mister? My Lord?

Except for the minutest flicker in his keen turquoise gaze, the laird didn't register his surprise. He dipped his head politely. "Miss McClintock."

Head bowed, she sank into a graceful curtsy. Now that art, she had perfected. No southern belle's education was complete until she could curtsy with a stack of books atop her head. And deliver a cutting reposit without raising her voice or resorting to vulgarities.

"Sir. I'm honored to make your acquaintance."

Spur of the moment, she'd decided upon 'sir' until she could ask Dugall how to properly address his brother. Hopefully, she hadn't insulted the laird with her ignorance.

Actually, she, Aunt Barbara, even Kandie and the children could use a bit of tutelage in that regard.

Mayhap Dugall knew of someone who could help. Her schooling was sorely lacking in that arena. But then, in her defense, there hadn't been a great number of people bearing titles tootling around Raleigh and the surrounding area's ballrooms and parlors.

In fact, other than one Italian count, she couldn't recall any. And he'd turned out to be a charlatan. Nothing but a tailor who'd fallen on hard times and assumed a client's identity before fleeing to the colonies to escape his debtors.

As they spoke, the rest of the McTavish clan gathered near, forming a semi-circle of protection. Not a one of the battle-hardened men had lowered their weapons, nor relaxed their defensive stance.

They were a roughish lot, rugged and craggy. And though they exchanged curious glances, and more than one ill-tamed brow inched upward when Dugall had introduced her, they regarded her politely.

"Sir, did my family arrive safely at Craiglocky Keep?" She couldn't wait another moment to find out.

The corners of his eyes pleating, the laird gave her a kind smile.

"Yes, Miss McClintock. The children were bustled off to the kitchen for hot chocolate and shortbread, my three practically dancing circles around them."

Hopefully, Julia made straight for the necessary.

"And when I left, your aunt sat warming herself before a toasty fire while my wife, mother, and aunt plied her with a strong, hot toddy."

He winked then, reminding her of Dugall. "She might be a trifle foxed by the time we return."

Under the circumstances, Gwendolyn didn't blame Aunt

Barbara in the least. Right now, she wouldn't say *nae* to a toddy liberally dosed with brandy or whisky herself.

Dugall mounted Bran then scooted backward in the saddle. "Gwenny, you'll have to ride before me."

She flushed as his brother's astute gaze vacillated between them. Dugall really must leave off calling her by her pet name. He sounded far too familiar and possessive, and others might get the wrong impression about their relationship.

Still, she'd no choice but to comply, else she'd have to walk to Craiglocky.

In short order, Gwendolyn had been assisted onto Bran. One hand fisted in the horse's mane, she attempted to ignore the speculative looks and sideways slanted mouths directed toward her and Dugall.

Nonetheless, she was woman enough to admit, she quite liked Dugall's solid-as-oak arms cradling her. Liked the firm wall of his chest to rest against. Liked the way his breath warmed her scalp and tickled her ear when he dipped his head to speak to her.

"Lass, when the time comes, let me be the one to explain to my kin our agreement for me to aid ye at Suttford."

She angled her head, searching his face. It wasn't exactly unease framing his eyes, but by no stretch of her imagination could she claim he was excited about the telling.

"All right," she murmured just as quietly. "Do you think your family will object?"

"They mightn't be thrilled at the notion, but . . ." He hesitated and pulled his mouth into a stern ribbon-like line.

"But?" She flattened her palm on his chest and raised up to speak into his ear. "You've obviously something on your mind. You might as well tell me now. I'll hear it soon enough in any event, won't I?"

She sank back onto her bum.

Tenderness filled his eyes, and it warmed her to her chilled toes. "Aye. Ye should ken, though I dinna want ye to fash yerself."

She was past getting worked up or annoyed, and she wouldn't kick up a ruckus. What good would that do?

"I fear the ball that hit Marigold may have been meant for ye, *leannan*."

Fourteen

Dugall hadn't intended to reveal his suspicion yet, but after further deliberation, prudence decreed Gwendolyn ought to know. Especially since he intended to insist that when she or the rest of her family left Suttford House, armed guards should accompany them.

Until the shooter had been apprehended and questioned, they must tread warily.

Not a typical hospitable Scots welcome, for certain, but this situation had been irregular from the onset.

He glanced down at her burnished head. She had the most glorious, thick, curly hair. How long was it? He itched to run his hands through its shiny length.

Gwendolyn stared at the ground, her expression thoughtful and perhaps a mite melancholic. Was she further regretting her decision to come to Scotland?

She'd not like her comings and goings restricted. Not at all.

He might not know her well, but he'd already discerned her independent spirit and the importance of being considered capable.

"The thought crossed my mind, actually." Instead of denying the suggestion, she slowly nodded, one naughty curl teasing her ear with the motion.

He longed to grasp the strand between his thumb and forefinger and see if it was as silky as it appeared.

They both knew who stood to gain the most if she were disposed of.

She took the news far calmer than he'd expected. If what he suspected was true, someone had tried to kill her today. Or at the very least, frighten her into leaving Scotland.

He wouldn't blame her if she did precisely that. Yet he'd do his utmost to convince her otherwise. Not just because she intrigued him like no female ever had, but Jeremiah mustn't be denied his birthright.

They rode without speaking for a few moments, the gentle rocking of Bran's gait causing her to rhythmically sway into Dugall. With each slight nudge, her perfume wafted upwards, a subtle tantalizing scent, teasing his already aroused senses.

How she'd managed to burrow beneath his skin so swiftly was as disturbing as it was provocative. This feeling, this whatever-the-devil plagued him, was more than the urge to bed her.

Only the quiet murmurs of the other Scots and an occasional bird tweet rent the air. Had she noticed that the others had strategically surrounded Bran, forming a moving wall of plaid, leather, and horseflesh?

He surreptitiously watched her from beneath half-closed eyes.

As she stared at the passing landscape, a concert of emotions played across her smooth face, as readable as the pages of a newly bound book.

Helplessness. Apprehension. Bewilderment. Frustration. Shrewdness. And then resolve.

A determined expression settled on her face, and her eyes

pinched together the merest bit as she notched her chin upward in a silent challenge.

Brave lass.

"Well, no one's going to paint me green and call me a cucumber. I'm not tucking my tail and running," she declared. "I'll beat Hollingsworth at his own game, the no-good, pea-picking assling."

At her curse, momentary surprise widened his eyes, but she'd leaned over to stroke Bran's wither and murmur sweet compliments to the stallion and didn't notice.

Had she really just said assling?

As casually as if she'd called Hollingsworth a rapscallion or scallywag? Adaira was the only other woman, besides trulls, Dugall had ever heard swear.

He'd a hunch Gwendolyn would get on famously with his eldest sister. They both had a tendency to use colorful language and speak their minds.

"Paint ye green?" Dugall chuckled in remembrance.

A giggle escaped her. "Better than butter my bu—erm, behind and call me a biscuit."

His guffaw drew the inquisitive glances of the clansmen accompanying them. "I'd love to visit South Carolina just to listen to the people talk."

"That's oft' said of the Scots too, *ye ken*." Eyes sparkling, the dimple in her right cheek made an appearance. "Though I don't understand half of what they're saying."

She twitched a finger, indicating the other riders.

Because they were discussing her and her considerable attributes and beauty in Gaelic.

Mither vowed it was rude to speak another language when in the presence of someone who didn't understand it. Though, even she slipped into her native French on occasion when vexed with Father.

"I'm glad we are of the same mind about the incident." He

made sure to keep his voice low. He wasn't keen on being over-heard, yet with their heads so close together, Ewan was sure to get suspicious. "Ye won't object to me askin' Ewan to permit a dozen clansmen to accompany us back to Suttford House and stay until I deem the threat has passed?"

He slid her a questioning look, but she stared at the passing landscape, her profile grave.

"Gwenny?"

"*Hmm?*"

"The clansmen?" He jerked his head toward the Scots surrounding them. "Returnin' to Suttford with us?"

She shielded her eyes from the sun and twisted to look at him fully. "Surely there are servants, staff, and others there enough to keep a watchful eye."

"Aye." He arched a brow and slanted his head to indicate his doubt. "But can ye trust them? Ye dinna ken them, and ye dinna ken who they're loyal to yet."

She didn't know him either, and yet she'd trusted him.

"Fenella said the staff was happy that Jeremiah had inherit-ed." Toying with the lace edging her glove, she wrinkled her nose adorably. "And won't having McTavish clansmen lingering about stir old animosities?"

"I dinna doubt some of the staff are pleased to have ye there, but ye haven't had time to get to ken them." He gave her a slight nudge in the ribs with his left arm. "Do ye worry it will make ye look weak and incompetent?"

She flashed him a startled look. "You practically read my mind. That's precisely my worry."

"Understandable, but no one will fault ye once they learn what happened. If havin' a few extra swords at Suttford keeps ye and yer family safer, isnae it wise?"

He could almost hear the cogs grinding and churning away in her head. No one could accuse her of impulsive, rash decisions. She'd carefully, and logically considered everything he'd put to her.

"What of you, Dugall? Gratitude for a few sutures doesn't compel you to become a bodyguard. This is far more than you bargained for. I shan't hold you to the agreement if you—"

He tightened his arms about her and gave her a firm squeeze. "Wheesht. I dinna want to hear any more of that prattle. The shootin' be all the more reason I need to be with ye."

~

GWENDOLYN WOULD EAT FRIED OKRA—AND she loathed okra—before she admitted it, but something more than relief and appreciation sang along her veins.

A handful of minutes later, they clattered across Craiglocky Keep's drawbridge. Trying not to gape, she took in the medieval castle's gatehouse and bailey.

Laughing children and panting dogs played amongst the wagons. Speckled chickens inspecting the cobblestones for tasty insects clucked their disapproval when they had to flee the small feet frolicking nearby.

The clang of metal striking metal identified the smithy, and through open dual gates on the bailey's far side, she spied stables and pastures where more of those unusual long-haired cattle, several enormous horses, and dozens of sheep milled about.

She grinned at Dugall. Stubble shadowed his granite jaw. She rather liked the scruffy look. Rather liked his whiskers scraping her face when they kissed, too.

"Would it be impolite to ask for a tour? Inside and out?" She gazed around again. "It's so different from Suttford House."

Dugall handed Bran's reins over to a footman. "Maybe a

short one inside today. To do Craiglocky justice we'd need several hours, and I dinna want to return to Suttford after dark. And until Ewan's men have searched the estate, ye shouldn't be wanderin' about."

He slid off his horse, then lifted his arms for her.

Aware she'd drawn the curious regard of many of the Scots in the bailey as well, she stepped away as soon as he'd set her on the ground.

As she passed Bran, he stretched his neck and bumped her shoulder. She paused to lean into him and give him a hug. "Thank you, my friend. You were superb, even with my extra weight."

Dugall chuckled and swiped the stallion's neck. "Fickle beast. And here I thought I held his affections."

Gwendolyn eyed him uncertainly. He didn't sound jealous, but a man's relationship with his horse was a very personal thing and one such as that which Dugall had with Bran, precious too.

Easing away from the stallion, she sent Dugall an apologetic smile. "Forgive me if I've overstepped with him. I've missed my horses far more than I'd realized."

"No' a bit of it." He cupped her elbow and whispered for her ears alone. "I can only admire his excellent taste."

A delighted flush infused her, but she refused to give in to the smile tugging the corners of her mouth. She must resist his charms, her logic admonished sternly.

Deuced hard when her womanly self hovered on the precipice of yielding.

"Are you coming? I'm sure your family is worried for you, Miss McClintock."

With a start, Gwendolyn realized Laird McTavish stood at the top of the gatehouse steps, awaiting them. His expression inscrutable, his astute gaze traveled between her and Dugall as it had numerous times since rescuing them.

Crayfish and chicken dumplings. He knows I'm taken with his brother.

Just a silly infatuation at being shown kindness and attention by a handsome man. That was all. Nothing more could come of it.

More's the pity.

Yes, well, be that as it may, if Gwendolyn didn't rein in her lustful musings and take her feminine responses in hand, she might very well forfeit everything. And it wasn't just her life that would be sorely impacted.

That thought served to sober her.

A flirtation, no matter how mild, wasn't worth the risk.

"Yes, of course." She grabbed her skirt in one hand as Dugall guided her to the risers, giving his brother a rather sardonic look.

"Dugall?" she whispered. "How do I address your brother and the rest of your family?"

He dipped his head slightly. "Ewan prefers his Scot's title, McTavish. Yvette be Lady McTavish. My father's a knight, so he's Sir Hugh. Mither be Lady Ferguson." He rubbed a hand across his bristly face. "Do ye want to ken the rest?"

"The *rest*?" A groan escaped her as she climbed the weathered stone steps. "I'm never going to remember. Why can't they simply be Mister and Missus?"

He squeezed her elbow. "Dinna fash yerself. They're no' like the snooty *haut ton*. Ye'll no' get cut for makin' a mistake."

Gwendolyn had scarcely stepped over the threshold when Jeremiah and Julia came tearing out of a carved set of double doors, each wearing a chocolaty mustache.

"Auntie Gwenny!"

Chattering elatedly and talking over each other, they launched themselves at her. She might've toppled, had Dugall not swiftly snaked his arm about her waist and pulled her to his side.

"Gracious, darlings." She hugged them to her waist and patted their heads as they clung to her. "*Shh*, now."

Several people, including Kandie, Aunt Barbara cradling a teacup—her cheeks flushed and eyes slightly bleary—as well as a trio of huge hounds, and three adorable children had appeared in the great hall's entrance.

McTavish made his way to a stunning blonde's side, and the smile they exchanged left no doubt they adored each other.

Quavering, Julia hugged Gwendolyn's leg and mumbled into her skirt. "I was afeared you'd die, too. Like Papa and Grandpapa. And we'd have no mama anymore."

Jeremiah clamped his trembling lower lip, and dashed at the tears filling his eyes. "Don't be a ninny, Julia. I told you Mr. Ferguson would save her. And I've told you before. She's our aunt. Not our mama. Our mama died."

He looked small and forlorn when he admonished his sister, an apology in his gaze when it skittered to Gwendolyn.

His words pricked, though she knew he hadn't intended to be unkind.

Serious little fellow, so grown up and stoic, Jeremiah thrust his hand out toward Dugall. "Thank you, sirrah for protecting our aunt. I am indebted to you."

Gwendolyn's eyes misted that her precocious nephew had transformed into such a perfect gentleman in a moment such as this. No doubt in five minutes, he'd be up to his starched— chocolate-stained neckcloth in mischief. But had he been her own son, she couldn't have been prouder.

Dugall clasped Jeremiah's hand, his great paw swallowing the child's, and solemnly shook it. "It be an honor, yer lordship. And I shall continue to protect ye and yer family as long as I'm able to. I give ye my word."

Jeremiah angled his head. "Is that what's called a vow?"

"Aye, lad." Dugall exchanged a meaningful glance with his brother.

Almost a challenge there.

Unease flared, skittering up Gwendolyn's arms to settle heavily on her shoulders. Foolish man, making such an impossible promise, even if he meant well and only wanted to reassure Jeremiah.

Didn't Dugall realize the children would take him at his word? They'd borne so much disappointment already, and when he left, as he must, they would be crushed.

Julia's eyes rounded until they consumed most of her face. She shoved the tendrils of unruly hair stuck to her damp cheek away and swung her head back and forth, her expression troubled. "A vow?"

Best to set matters straight at once before this situation became even more complex. "What Mr. Ferguson means, my dears, is—"

"Like marriage vows?" Julia asked, confusion puckering her features.

The striking dark-haired boy peering up at McTavish yanked on his father's hand. "Uncle Dugall is gettin' married? Am I goin' to have more cousins soon, then?"

Aunt Barbara tottered forward a pair of steps, still clutching the teacup like she held a sultan's most prized jewel. "Good heavenly days. A fifth proposal, Gwendolyn dear?"

Gwendolyn speared Dugall a mortified gaze, flames licking her cheek at his utterly stunned expression and slackened jaw.

The entry grew so silent, you could've heard a mouse pee on cotton.

Julia tugged at Dugall's tattered coat. "Does that mean you're going to marry my Aunt Gwenny?"

Fifteen

As they had every morning at dawn for the past month, Dugall and two McTavish clansmen rode out early, searching Suttford's nearest acreage for anything remotely suspicious.

Coronis hadn't joined them today. A first.

Perched on a stable rafter above Bran's stall, she'd cocked her head and gave him a perturbed glare with one beady eye before nuzzling her beak into her back feathers once more. She wasn't foregoing her comfortable roost for a blustery flight. Maybe, at long last, her infatuation with Dugall had paled.

He pulled his collar higher and his tam lower to prevent the steady, icy drizzle from creeping down his nape. The wetness amplified the pungent odors of damp wool, sweaty horseflesh, and dank earth wafting through the air.

Neither McLeon nor McKinnely, vigilant but at ease atop their mounts, seemed to mind the driving rain. Scots became accustomed to the Highland's surly weather as wee ones, else they lived a wretched, uncomfortable life.

But the Highlands boasted extraordinary beauty this time of year, too.

Autumn, in full fanfare, trumpeted her magnificent hues. A layer of thick frost the past five mornings testified to the cooler temperatures, and trees ablaze with riots of scarlet, yellow, purple, and russet revealed winter would soon shroud the Highlands.

Given the thick hair on the cattle's necks, the squirrels' bushier than normal tails, and the brighter than usual foliage, it looked to be a punishing winter, too.

He crooked his mouth sideways. At least, wintering would be more comfortable at Suttford than draft-prone Craiglocky.

If he stayed that long.

A missive could arrive from the Diplomatic Corps any day, though Dugall honestly didn't expect one just yet. Good thing, too, since Gwendolyn still needed him, and to leave now would seem like desertion. More so since the shooting culprit hadn't been caught.

Still, if summoned, he'd have no choice but to go.

Since as a young boy he'd heard the whispers about Ewan's intrigues and adventures, Dugall had been single-minded in his intent to follow in his brother's footsteps. Unthinkable he'd refuse the offer if—*when*—it came. With Ewan and his powerful friends backing him, Dugall held little doubt he'd be accepted into the elite service.

The wind whipped up, and rain pellets lashed the trio of riders with the vehemence of a maid beating a dirty rug.

Other than a place where the fence needed mending, probably as a result of a stag getting stuck, all looked as it should.

"I think we're good for today. Let's head back." Dugall jerked his head in the manor's direction, and chilly water streamed into his collar, soaking his neckcloth.

Hell's bells.

He'd have to change now.

Gwendolyn had asked him to be present for her meeting with Mr. Christie today. After cancelling two previous appointments, the solicitor was finally making a long-awaited appearance. He'd remain overnight as he claimed a round trip from Edinburgh was too arduous and distant for a man of his advanced eight-and-fifty years.

Rather impudent of the fellow to demand accommodations for the night. In fact, he'd had the nerve to dictate dinner, too. Seemed he couldn't abide vegetables or fish of any sort, most especially brown trout.

But Gwendolyn had said he'd hinted the old laird had always insisted Christie stay when he called for business and happily accommodated his appetites. More likely the man was an accomplished prevaricator and too pinch-penny to put up in an inn.

She'd also confided that she didn't entirely trust Christie and dreaded getting on his wrong side. The solicitor had failed to mention too many significant details for her peace of mind.

Dugall's too, actually.

A wily solicitor didn't bode well, either.

She'd chew nails before she admitted it to Dugall or anyone else, but the tightening around her mouth whenever she mentioned Christie revealed she still fretted he would find some excuse to wrest the children's guardianship from her.

As Dugall and the clansmen turned their mounts toward the great house, he scanned the area once more. Other than contented Highland cattle chewing their cud and a grouse taking to wing from a harvested oat field beyond a hedgerow, all was still on the tranquil gray-blanketed horizon.

What a difference a few miles made. Suttford's lands were less craggy and more accommodating for cereal crops than Craiglocky's rugged terrain. Barley and oats grew readily here.

So much so, that Dugall had proposed Gwendolyn consider a whisky distillery near Suttford Bourne, an excellent source for the water needed for such a venture.

He readily admitted the notion excited him. Not as much

as being an agent, but perfecting a signature scotch? Aye, a grand idea indeed.

"I'd prefer to invest in a cotton or linen factory." Gwendolyn had arched a starchy ginger brow, but hadn't said nae to the distillery. She'd mull over the idea, consider the advantages and disadvantages before offering an opinion.

He liked that about her.

Liked a lot more than that about her.

But dwelling on *those* attributes would have him shifting in the saddle uncomfortably for an entirely different reason than the sulky weather. Undeniably feminine in all the ways that counted, Gwendolyn also kept a firm rein on her emotions and possessed sensibleness and calm reasoning.

Once she mulled over the proposition, asked dozens of questions about the feasibility, she'd give him her answer. Her suggestion about a cotton or linen factory held great merit, too. Such an investment might prove very lucrative and would provide much needed jobs. Definitely notions worth considering and exploring further.

Even Hollingsworth had been amenable to the idea. If the man continued to be so agreeable, Dugall might send for the physician. Mayhap Hollingsworth suffered from a mind-altering ailment or had gone completely *aff* his *heid*.

Dugall couldn't help but speculate that Hollingsworth's about-change was artificial. Hopefully, he wasn't pulling the wool over Gwendolyn's eyes with his newly-found manners and gentlemanly comportment.

Since the shooting incident four weeks ago, nothing else untoward had occurred, and she'd relaxed a trifle. The more time that passed without any further incidents, the more it seemed perhaps it had been an accident after all.

Nevertheless, now wasn't the time to become slipshod.

Dugall couldn't relax entirely or shake the wariness plaguing him since that day. Nor could he discount that round-the-clock armed guards and regular surveillance of Suttford lands made another attempt on Gwendolyn's life much more difficult—*if* indeed that had been what occurred.

He'd feel more confident if the gunman had been caught and questioned, but though the area had been thoroughly searched, no clue as to his identity had been found.

Dugall had personally interrogated each member of Suttford's staff as well as Miss Dolina and the Whitworths who had returned unexpectedly from Edinburgh whilst he and the others had been at Craiglocky. To a person, everyone had been appalled but could offer no useful information.

A twinkle in her fading eyes that didn't completely dispel an impish glint, Miss Dolina had asked if one or two of the more handsome McTavish clansmen might be her personal bodyguards.

Poor McLeon, a striking, strapping fellow who dwarfed the petite lady, had taken to peeking around corners and eating his meals in the kitchen to avoid the elderly dame's teasing attention and appreciative ogling.

Hollingsworth, too, had been eliminated as the suspect. He'd been seen in the village, at The Tatties and Tankard pub when the shooting had occurred. That didn't mean he hadn't hired someone, however.

Cantering Bran back to the stables, Dugall spied the object of his musings speaking to the stable master. Bare-headed, his hair plastered to his head, Hollingsworth glanced up as the McTavishes filed by and offered Dugall a brief, but courteous nod.

In response Dugall inclined his head, still unable to reconcile this civil man with the selfish rakehell he'd known for so long. To be fair, he'd spent no time in Hollingsworth's company for years, but he had been his usual churlish self when they'd arrived at Suttford.

Since Gwendolyn interviewed Hollingsworth and agreed

to allow him to remain as steward, at least for a probationary period, Hollingsworth had demonstrated exemplary behavior. He'd become a most agreeable fellow these days, but, then again, he'd much to lose by being contrary.

In a shrewd move he couldn't help but applaud, Gwendolyn had appointed Dugall Suttford's agent. Prudent considering Jeremiah's inheritance consisted of different properties across the region and overseeing the vast estate meant regular visits to the other holdings.

Either Hollingsworth had become an accomplished actor, or he was truly trying to make a grand impression, for he hadn't balked at his demotion or having to answer to Dugall. By not banishing Hollingsworth's sorry arse from Suttford House, she'd made an ally of him.

Though Dugall didn't agree with her decision—trusting Hollingsworth went against everything in him—he'd kept silent. She had to establish her authority at Suttford, but Dugall had resolved to watch the man's every move. And when he wasn't here, McTavish men did so in his stead.

Once or twice a week, Dugall journeyed to the other, smaller properties. They, too, clipped along tidily thanks to Hollingsworth's previous efficiency. Dugall wasn't one to deny credit where it was due, and he could find very little to fault Hollingsworth in regard to his supervision of the estate's holdings.

Mayhap he'd truly changed since law school.

If so, then why did doubts yet niggle?

Dugall dismounted and, after stroking Bran, turned his damp collar down. He resisted the urge to scratch the healing cuts on his face. Gwendolyn had removed his sutures just over a week ago, but the purplish marks still itched like a flea-ridden hound.

Releasing a long breath of air, he rubbed a brow.

He both anticipated and dreaded seeing her. Since the

uncomfortable misunderstanding at Craiglocky when the children had jumped to the wrong conclusion, their encounters had become formal and stilted.

The undercurrent of sexual awareness hadn't lessened an iota. If anything, it had increased, simmering hotly beneath carefully schooled expressions and cool politesse.

A thread of irritation wended through him again when he recalled Ewan's reaction to the children's innocent mistake. Dugall's buffoon of a brother had guffawed like a lunatic until Yvette shushed him. Even she had sported an amused expression, as if she, too, found the notion absurd.

What was so damned funny about Dugall getting married?

He planned to. Someday.

However, the peal of wedding bells didn't fit into his plans for many, many years to come.

With finesse and diplomacy, her cheeks a delightful shade of pink, Gwendolyn had swiftly set things to right that day.

"Good gracious me. Mr. Ferguson and I most certainly are not getting married. He's simply promised to help us settle into Suttford House until I can hire an agent and steward."

At Gwendolyn's declaration, he'd writhed like a worm on a sun-warmed rock. His family's astonished countenances hadn't even summoned a pithy remark or cocky grin from him. So much for him telling them about his arrangement with her.

He couldn't be disgruntled with Gwendolyn, however. The children's disconcerting conjecture forced her to clarify, and there was only one ready explanation. The contrite smile she'd swept him soothed his discomfiture a hair.

He'd still had to explain his decision to aid her to his parents and Ewan a couple of days later when he'd ridden over for that express purpose.

They were hardly in a position to forbid him. But by thunder, he'd been thoroughly taken aback when they expressed more concern for Gwendolyn and her charges than they did for him being set upon during his journey home.

With a final sweep of his hand across Bran's glossy wither, he turned to Sam. "See that he's brushed down and dried well, please. He disna like bein' left wet."

"Aye, sir." Sam grinned, his weathered face folding in genuine joy. "He be a grand one, he be. He looks mighty fierce, but he be as sweet as yonder kittens."

Dugall glanced in the direction Sam tilted his head. Tucked beneath a bench, inside a crate padded with burlap bags a tabby, her eyes closed, purred contentedly as several wriggling kittens nursed.

The man had obviously not experienced Bran in a foul mood. "He's been ken to bite, so watch yerself."

Dugall paused at Marigold's stall, giving her wound a once-over. Thanks to a special salve Seonaid had sent when she heard about the mare's injury, the gash was healing nicely.

Marigold stuck her head over the door and nickered softly, looking for a treat.

"Sorry, lass. I didna have anythin' for ye today."

At the stable entrance, he raised his hand in acknowledgement of the several McTavish clansmen, then leaned a shoulder against the weathered frame and observed Hollingsworth. The rain had stopped, but given the sullen pewter clouds hanging low in the sky, not for long.

Hollingsworth gestured to the paddock and then pointed to the entrance. His expression thoughtful, the stable master cupped his neck and nodded.

Dugall straightened to continue on to the house when Hollingsworth gestured for him to wait. "Hold up, Ferguson."

Impatience nipped. Dugall needed to change before meeting with Gwendolyn and Christie. "Do ye mind walkin' with me to the house? I have an appointment I'm goin' to be late for."

Hollingsworth held out his arm for Dugall to proceed him. "With Christie?"

No surprise that he knew. Little could be kept secret with so many servants, and no one had attempted to hide the fact that the solicitor was expected today.

"Aye."

Hollingsworth cut Dugall a sideways glance. "I assume, I'm not invited? But ye are?"

The merest hint of resentment scraped the fringe of his words. Couldn't really blame him. He was kin, whereas Dugall was merely the man Gwendolyn relied on for advice.

"Gwendolyn didn't mention it one way or the other." Damn. He'd used her given name again. Dugall hurried onward, as if he hadn't blundered. "But I believe he's here to discuss the rest of the terms of old McClintock's will. And as the agent, she wants me abreast of any stipulations."

Hollingsworth released a rather pensive sigh as he checked his timepiece. "I fear we're all in for more unpleasant surprises."

Dugall had concluded the same thing, but Hollingsworth almost sounded as if he knew something the others didn't.

Dugall stopped and faced him. "What makes ye say that?"

A wry smile twisted Hollingsworth's mouth.

"Ferguson, yer family kens what a rotter McClintock could be. Young Jeremiah might've been the next in line to inherit the title and entailment, but would that selfish *batard* really leave everythin' else to an American? Someone he'd never met?" Hollingsworth gave a derisive snort. "Does that sound like the whoreson we both ken? He hated colonials, most expressly his kin for movin' there."

Interesting. He holds nae affection for his dead uncle.

But then again, many greedy sots only cared about what they could gain from their family. And that bit about McClintock hating his American relations—

Well, that added another shady and worrisome layer to this whole damnable thing.

Dugall dragged his sodden tam from his head with one hand and shoved his wet hair off his forehead with the other. "That's rather severe, comin' from someone who lived off his charity for a number of years."

A harsh, caustic laugh split the sodden air.

"Charity?" Hollingsworth scoffed. "Haven't ye seen with yer own eyes the state of Suttford and the other holdin's? Trust me. I've earned my keep these five years."

"Aye, ye have, at that." Dugall angled his head. What *wasn't* Hollingsworth saying? Why such bitterness if he was proud of his accomplishments? Something was too smoky by far.

Scorn curling one side of his mouth, Hollingsworth shook his head. "I freely admit I was an unmitigated arse as a young man, but there's much ye dinna ken about me. Even more neither ye nor Gwendolyn ken about Gerard McClintock. He was a connivin', manipulatin' scunner, and I'm glad he's dead. I only wish he'd stuck his spoon in the wall sooner."

He glanced at his pocket watch again.

Did he have someplace he needed to be? Then why waylay Dugall?

"For reasons I'll never understand, given he was as reluctant to part with a pence as he was to offer his foot to a hound to gnaw on, he paid a visit to my aunt when I was scarcely out of short pants." Hollingsworth scratched his forehead while gazing at the horizon. "McClintock insisted I be sent off to boardin' school, and later paid for me to attend university too, with the condition I work for him afterward."

"Why did you agree to the latter?" As a boy, Hollingsworth would've had no choice about boarding school. Strange for McClintock to take such a keen interest in a distant relative.

"Aunt Sibby had four bairns of her own to feed. She didna hesitate over McClintock's offer. She was my mither's sister and took me in when my da died in a dockyard accident. My mither had died birthin' me."

Dugall had learned more about Hollingsworth in the past couple of minutes than in all the years of their casual acquaintance. A tinge of compassion for the unwanted lad Hollingsworth had been pricked Dugall. To be separated from the only family you knew and sent to live with strangers at such a young age stirred his pity, too. And then to have McClintock dictating your every move.

Bloody awful.

"You needed to speak to me?" Dugall set aside his musings. He'd ponder the information when he had more time.

Hollingsworth gazed at him blankly for a moment. "Aye. I wanted to tell ye that I've spoken to some of the tenant farmers about growin' more barley." A thin, short-lived smile curved his mouth. "They're keen on the idea. Especially the notion of a distillery."

"Aye," Dugall chuckled while wiping his brow again. "Nothin' like fine whisky to put a spark in a Scot's eye, light a fire his belly, and flame his inspiration."

The path divided, the left fork leading to the big house and the other to the neat cottages stacked side by side like biscuit tins.

Hollingsworth swerved right. "I need to speak to the head gardener. I fear we're in for a wicked winter, and I want to make sure the greenhouses are in order."

A slight scowl wrinkling his forehead, he strode away.

The conversation left Dugall even more disturbed, for Hollingsworth's opinion of the old laird held more than a jot of truth. McClintock wasn't known for his generosity or benevolence.

Had he truly loathed his American kin?

Immersed in his thoughts, Dugall nearly plowed into the young woman dashing down the stairs, her head ducked against the angry wind. He instinctively seized her elbows to steady her and keep her from stumbling into the puddle dividing the trodden path.

"I beg your pardon, Miss Whitworth."

She blushed scarlet and wrenched her plaid shawl tighter over her shoulders and dark hair. "I'm just goin' for a short stroll. Mither and Dolina are nappin', and soon the weather will be so disagreeable I wilna have much opportunity." She darted a glance behind him, her guileless gray eyes crimping in pleasure at the corners before shyly dipping her head again. "The trees are glorious with color right now."

Plus, he'd be bound, she craved a break from her demanding mother and only found respite when the difficult woman slept. From what Dugall had observed, the timid thing could scarcely move without Mrs. Whitworth demanding she assist her, fetch some trivial item, or guide her about the house and grounds.

All of which Miss Whitworth did with a ready, long-suffering smile and a soft-spokenness her mother didn't deserve; even if the woman was blind. She treated Miss Whitworth like a hired companion rather than a beloved daughter.

"I fear yer walk may be cut short." He pointed his gaze to the sky. "Those clouds look ready to dump their contents."

"Aye. I may have to take refuge in the stables, but I dinna mind gettin' wet." She lifted a shoulder. "I'm Scottish after all."

"I've just come from there. There's a newborn litter of kittens."

Her eyes lit up. "Truly? I've wanted a kitten for so long, but Mither isnae fond of cats."

He released her, and with another bashful smile, she hurried on her way.

"Dugall, there you are." Gwendolyn, a vision in green silk, a knitted shawl about her shoulders and pearls at her throat and dangling from her ears, hovered just inside the entrance.

The bright smile she gifted the two front entrance guards didn't light her eyes.

As always, Dugall's breath faltered upon seeing her. He rejoiced, that despite her retreat into formality a month ago, she still addressed him by his given name.

A rush of lust sluiced through him. He'd never desired a woman for so long without bedding her. Hell, he'd never hungered after a woman with the intensity he did Gwendolyn. But she was off-limits, her bedchamber but a few short, torturous steps from his.

This might prove to be a deuced prickly winter after all.

Her gaze gravitated to Miss Whitworth's retreating form for an instant before swinging back to him, her eyes turbulent.

"Mr. Christie arrived while you were out. I've pacified him with refreshments, but he grows impatient. A bit petulant, too." Brows drawn tight, she wet her lower lip, then shuddered when a blast of wind pelted her. "It's peculiar, but he's bade Mr. Hollingsworth be present for the will's reading."

Sixteen

Another shiver juddered Gwendolyn as she stepped back inside the house, Dugall directly behind her.

Only October, and even wrapped in a woolen shawl, and fires burning hotly in the house's fireplaces, she'd been chilled all day.

Ordering warmer gowns was out of the question just yet, however. She'd have to make do with an extra chemise, long-sleeved gowns, and perhaps even a pair of crocheted, fingerless mitts.

"Thank you, Lowry." She spared the butler a swift, somewhat fatigued smile as he closed the door behind them. Sleeplessness had plagued her again last night.

Never at her best when tired, she didn't relish the forthcoming meeting with Mr. Christie. His bewildering request troubled her. Like as not, they were in for more surprises, probably not all pleasant.

She'd never much enjoyed surprises or being caught unawares, for instance; finding relatives entrenched at her new home or having her mare shot.

No, she preferred knowing what was to come in advance.

For some reason, she couldn't quite put her finger on why specifically—perhaps intuition or fear he'd fault her somehow —she'd chosen not to mention the shooting incident to the solicitor.

She could warn Dugall to keep silent on the matter, but how to make sure Cousin Lloyd did, too? Well, she'd simply distract Mr. Christie, and Dugall could discreetly advise her cousin to keep silent about the incident. But would he?

"I just spoke to Hollingsworth." Dugall passed his hat and drenched overcoat to Lowry who gingerly held the items at arm's length lest a droplet mar his immaculate uniform or his shiny-as-a-new-penny-shoes.

Windblown and soaked, how could Dugall still be as enticing as a pecan tart, her favorite dessert?

"He was headed to the gardener's," Dugall said. "In any event, Christie will have to wait a few minutes more. I need to change into dry clothes, and then I'll meet you in the—?"

Realizing she still gaped, Gwendolyn hauled her focus from Dugall's sculpted good looks. "Lowery has shown Mr. Christie to the study, and I've offered him the use of the desk."

The man likely snooped through every unlocked drawer and cabinet, which was why she requested the door be left open and a footman to stand just outside on the pretense of being available in an instant should Mr. Christie have need of anything.

Of its own traitorous accord, as unstoppable as the ocean's tides, her gaze hurtled back to Dugall.

She might've made it perfectly clear to their families what their positions were, but that didn't mean he wasn't still alluring as sin. With every sizzling gaze from his too-gorgeous-for-his-own-good eyes, and provocative tilt of his too-blessedly-perfect mouth, her resistance slipped further.

Honestly, even though he was younger—*four years wasn't so terribly much younger*—and a confirmed rapscallion of the sort to bed not wed, if any man might tempt her to toss prim and proper into the nearest rubbish bin and surrender to seduction, it was Dugall Ferguson.

And if she didn't have the responsibility of her niece and nephew, she might very well allow herself that indulgence. No strings attached. No expectations other than a few hours of mutually enjoyed passion.

Because, she'd finally admitted what she'd denied for so long; even though well on her way to being an old maid, she wanted to experience physical intimacy with a man.

Not with any man. With Dugall Ferguson.

None of her betrothed had ever had her floundering about in her bed, night after night, while her imagination tantalized her with risqué images of Dugall slumbering a few feet away. Why, she was as bad as Miss Dolina, lusting after a younger, sexy Scotsman.

"Lowery, please inform Mr. Christie of the unavoidable delay. Offer him a brandy, too. I think we can safely say, everyone will join him in under . . .?" She spared Dugall a questioning glance. "Thirty minutes?"

"Aye. That should suffice."

"I shall send a footman to find Mr. Hollingsworth at once." With a deferential slant of his head, Lowry trod down the passageway leading to below-stairs.

Lids heavy and eyes gritty, Gwendolyn yawned widely behind her hand. The nights of little sleep were catching up with her.

At the corridor's far end, the study door gaped open, and she eyed it warily. She wasn't a coward, but neither was she a martyr. She wasn't spending another second alone with Mr. Christie. Every time he looked at her, it felt like a horde of hairy spiders crawled across her skin on their cold, sharp little clawed feet.

A shiver scampered down her backbone.

Always before, she'd scoffed at such histrionics, but one glance from Mr. Christie's pale green reptilian eyes, and every inch of her exposed flesh had contracted and tried to scamper beneath her clothing or shawl.

It didn't take a whole lot of experience to recognize a degenerate when she met one. She'd already asked Lowry to have the female staff work in pairs, and if Mr. Christie required something, footmen were to do his bidding.

For Elspeth's safety, Gwendolyn needed to broach the unpleasantness with her. Surely as a resident of Suttford for some time, she must be aware of Mr. Christie's questionable character.

"I'll walk upstairs with you." She fell in step beside Dugall. "I have something I need to discuss, and it cannot wait."

He cocked a brow. "Is everythin' all right?"

"Yes." Gwendolyn nodded as they ascended the first riser. She glanced behind them, and then dropping her voice, sidled nearer. "I wonder if you could please ask the McTavish men to keep an eye on Mr. Christie while he's here. Especially tonight, after everyone's abed?"

Dugall's features hardened, and he paused mid-step, spearing a heated gaze in the study's direction. "He's done somethin'."

A statement, not a question.

The expression on his face suggested he'd like to throttle the solicitor. Or worse.

She was rather thrilled that Dugall was ready to champion her in an instant, before he even knew what had transpired. She quite looked forward to the average-sized solicitor meeting the strapping Highlander.

"No. No. Not exactly." Placing her hand on his forearm to calm him, she gave a little self-conscious laugh. "It's just he makes me uncomfortable. The way he leers at me. And the maids."

As if he could see beneath her garments with those cold, glittery snake eyes and caressed her bare flesh with his bony fingers, the fingernails unfashionably long.

Plainly put, the man was eerie.

"I cannot imagine that the previous laird actually invited him to stay over." She'd let her fear of offending Mr. Christie override good sense and her instinctive hesitancy. "I fear I've been misled and made a grievous error in providing him a chamber tonight."

Dugall's raven brows climbed his forehead.

Now she felt ridiculous, as if she'd overreacted. She'd fretted about Hollingsworth too, and after their initial awkward meeting, he'd done nothing untoward.

She wasn't becoming fanciful and fearful like Aunt Barbara, was she? The distasteful thought almost tripped Gwendolyn on the stair, but Dugall swiftly steadied her.

They'd made the upper floor, and rather than retrace her steps when Dugall and Mr. Hollingsworth would be several minutes longer, she decided to peek into Julia and Jeremiah's room. She'd probably find Miss Dolina in there again if she wasn't on one of her rambling walks or napping. The dear obviously adored children. She adored the Scot assigned to guard them too, poor McLeon.

Too bad she hadn't had any children of her own.

Gwendolyn really needed to hire a governess and tutor, but had hesitated to do so until she knew exactly where Suttford stood financially.

That was silly, too. The children must be educated, even if it meant using the funds from the plantation's sale. Gwendolyn wasn't about to tackle the task of educating them herself. She was their aunt, by Jingo, not a saint.

Another yawn threatened, and she placed two fingers to her mouth to stifle it.

Dugall hadn't responded to her speculations about Christie. He must agree she'd overreacted.

Botheration.

Chagrin and disappointment pinched her.

"Never mind, Dugall. I'm probably imagining things."

"Nae lass, ye aren't. I ken Christie's kind. Ye are wise nae to trust him. I suspect he's nae above cheatin' the lad and linin' his own pockets."

Dugall had unbuttoned his jacket as they marched down the corridor, and now strove to untie his neckcloth. Surely, that wasn't *de rigueur* even in Scotland. Why, he acted as if they were a married couple, and he was accustomed to dressing and undressing in front of her.

Probably is used to doing so with other women.

The notion miffed, sending a sickening jab to her ribs, even though she had no right to be peeved.

"I'll speak to the men. Ye can rest easy, Gwenny."

Rest easy? Hardly.

If she did, it would be the first night since arriving. This past week, she'd taken to slipping into the library when she couldn't sleep rather than stay in her bedchamber where her mind kept churning.

Thrice before, in the wee hours, she'd fallen asleep on the sofa and awoke when the housemaid came in to clean the fireplace.

Still she should acknowledge his promise. "Thank you. That's reassuring."

"Ye haven't been sleepin' well, have ye?" Dugall brushed her cheek with his fingertips, and she fisted her hands in the lamb's wool shawl to keep from sighing, closing her eyes, and pressing her face into his palm.

Had the purplish circles shadowing her eyes given her away? Yes, plus her repeated yawns and heavy-lidded blinking.

"I've been restless." Lest the longing that surely shone in her eyes give her away, Gwendolyn shifted her gaze.

"I have a foolproof cure for insomnia."

His tone made her glance back. He waggled his eyebrows and gave her one of his irresistible rakish, sideways grins as he shucked his coat.

She caught his meaning, and heat born of sensual awareness raced through every pore. Not an unpleasant experience at all.

"I'll just bet you do," she murmured, envying the fabric straining to hold his chiseled shoulders, chest, and arms.

Her mouth suddenly dry, she swallowed, but resisted the temptation to wet her lips. What that man did to her with a glance or a chuckle; made her knees feeble and tangled her insides.

She really must get a grip on this . . . whatever this was, before she made a complete and utter ass of herself.

They'd reached his chamber. He pushed down the latch, then leaned a shoulder into the door, giving it a forceful shove. "It catches and won't open or close without a push," he offered by way of explanation.

"Oh, you should've told me."

"It's a minor inconvenience, lass, and ye've enough on yer mind." His tender smile held a speck of something more.

Her resolve dipped another dangerous notch.

"Yes, well, I'll ask to have the door attended to at once." She swept a glance inside the tidy chamber. "Is everything else to your satisfaction?"

"Aye. I'm quite comfortable."

What a horrid hostess. She'd never inquired before. It hadn't even crossed her mind that he might have need of anything. She'd been so wrapped up in herself, the children, her consuming, distracting lust for him, that her basic manners had deserted her. And her hospitality was something she'd been proud of in South Carolina.

Dugall paused just inside his bedchamber. "I'll see ye in a few minutes, lass."

Lord, she adored it when he called her lass, but even more so when he said *leannan.*

Sweetheart.

She had put aside her embarrassment and asked Miss Dolina what the word meant. An enigmatic smile lit the dear's face as she'd answered. "Are ye and the lad contemplatin' marriage then?"

Gwendolyn had hastily reassured Aunt Dolina that wasn't the case at all.

"Um, of course," Gwendolyn said, retreating a pace. She couldn't very well follow Dugall into his room. More was the pity. "I'll just look in on the children and meet you downstairs."

Gwendolyn had meant it when she determined not to be alone with Mr. Christie. She wasn't about to enter the study unless it was on Dugall's massive arm. She'd taken no more than a dozen steps when she faltered to a stop.

Oh, horse feathers.

She'd forgotten to tell Dugall not to mention the shooting incident.

No help for it. She spun around and marched back to his bedchamber. The door stood slightly ajar, and she pushed it open and stepped inside. "Dugall, I forgot—"

Jaw slack, she stopped so swiftly, her slippers skidded on the parquet floor.

SEVENTEEN

U pon hearing a startled feminine gasp, Dugall froze, his hair snagging on a collar button.

Och, hell. Nae again.

He'd told Fenella nae at least a dozen times. He wasn't tupping the pretty maid. She'd gone too far entering his chamber without knocking after he'd warned her against doing so once already.

He tugged at his shirt, wincing when his hair pulled against his scalp. Devil it, he refused to play the gentleman and don the damp garment again.

He couldn't waste the precious minutes. He'd promised Gwendolyn he'd meet her below, and nothing this side of hell would detain him. He'd not risk her encountering Christie alone.

"Ye've nae right to enter my chamber without knockin'," Dugall said, his voice muffled by the fabric around his head. He'd threaten her with dismissal if need be. He managed to untangle his hair and then wrestle the clinging shirt off his arms.

"I'm out of patience with ye and yer forwardness. I dinna

167

mean to be unkind, but there can never be anythin' between us."

Irritated at her impudence and the delay she'd caused, he yanked the shirt the rest of the way off. Dugall tossed it onto the floor, then faced the door, prepared to put the lass in her place once and for all.

His heart tumbled to his toes and flopped there.

Lips parted, Gwendolyn stood statue-still three feet inside his room, the door yawning behind her. Her gorgeous eyes practically devoured him as her ravenous gaze skidded across his bare flesh.

Desire, immediate and overwhelming, pummeled him with the strength of a team of draft horses. He'd longed to see her look at him that way; the way a woman does when she wants a man.

But given the paleness of her porcelain skin, and that her refined features had shifted from rapt to stricken, she clearly heard his every word and believed he'd addressed her.

"I beg your pardon." She wrested her attention from his chest and focused it on the floor. "I . . ." She swallowed. "I remembered something important I needed to tell you. The door was ajar. I didn't think—"

"Gwendolyn." He extended an arm in entreaty and closed the distance between them. "I dinna ken it was ye."

If possible, the hasty glance she cut him from beneath her ginger-tipped lashes was even more aggrieved.

Ballocks.

She probably thought, and rightly so, he'd mistaken her for an eager-to-please servant. A lass whose advances he'd been rebuffing for weeks, but she couldn't know that.

"Forgive me." Face averted and poised to leave, she clutched her shawl tighter, chagrin radiating off her in wounded waves. "I can tell you later."

"But, Lloyd, ye promised me." Miss Whitworth's soft

voice echoed in the corridor. "Ye canna go back on yer word now."

"Circumstances have changed, Elspeth." Impatience riddled Hollingsworth's response. He'd certainly been found quickly.

"Why, because of *her*? Because ye've become a simperin' toady in an effort to please our pretty cousin?" That was the first hint of anything other than sweet compliance Dugall had heard from timid-as-a-mouse Miss Whitworth.

"Dinna be ridiculous," Hollingsworth said, near Dugall's doorway.

A crease pulling her brows together, Gwendolyn stared at the open door.

Just what she didn't need. To be caught in his chamber with him half-dressed.

In one swift movement, Dugall hauled her against his chest, and spun her away from the entrance as he kicked the door closed.

It banged loudly, reverberating against the door frame.

A small, alarmed squeal leached through the stout panel. He'd startled Miss Whitworth.

Better that and have them think he was in a temper of some sort than have Gwendolyn's reputation besmirched.

A firm knock jarred his door. "Ferguson. Is everythin' all right?" Hollingsworth asked.

Och, for the love of Guid.

Still pressed against his torso, Gwendolyn peered up at him, dread darkening her irises.

He put a finger to his lips and shook his head.

"Ferguson, are you in there?" Hollingsworth rapped again.

Damn the man's persistence.

"Aye. Just changin' out of my wet clothes. I've a window open and dinna realize my chamber door hadn't shut all the way again. The wind must've caught it and slammed it closed. I really must speak to Gwendolyn about that latch."

She narrowed her gaze and pinched her mouth into a thin, unamused line.

"I'll see ye below in a few minutes then. I must change my coat and neckcloth," Hollingsworth said, his tone suspiciously absent of any hint of gloating at being invited to the conference after all. In fact, if Dugall had to render a guess, he'd say trepidation tinged the man's words.

"You—"

Dugall put a finger on Gwendolyn's petal-soft lips and leaned down to whisper into her ear. "He might be listenin'."

She gave a short nod.

The aroma of orange blossoms met his nostrils and desire speared him. No other woman's scent could fan his desire into a scorching blaze so swiftly.

She relaxed, her soft curves melding with his hard angles. But her bowed head, and her breathing coming in short little puffs, revealed her tension.

Dugall didn't trespass easily or lightly, but to resist embracing her was futile. Holding her close, such contentment bathed him. If only they could remain thus forever.

"*Leannan*, I must explain to ye." He spoke into the soft cloud of her flaming hair.

"I believe I understand the gist of the situation. One of the female staff—I'd guess Fenella—has made herself available to you." Her crisp speech and imperious air revealed even more.

Och. He had the measure of her now. She was jealous.

Exhilaration buffeted him, and a chuckle rumbled forth.

A mistake.

She exhaled a vexed huff of air and looked ready to kelp him a good one. Deep lines scoring her forehead, she averted her eyes.

He lifted her chin with his forefinger, but her gaze glanced off his before she found something fascinating to stare at over his shoulder.

He kissed her forehead, and then her temple.

She trembled and sighed, but refused to meet his eyes.

"The lass is young and enamored of me." Another kiss to the sensitive spot where her jaw met her ear, caused a more powerful shudder to ripple through her. "But I've discouraged her interest, whilst tryin' to be kind."

"She should have more care," Gwendolyn muttered as she trailed her forefinger down his bicep. The flesh bunched in delicious anticipation as she traced his arm. "She told me she needs her position. I still might kick a mud hole in her hind end and stomp it dry."

"Pardon?" he managed around the grin splitting his face.

"Send her packing for her untoward behavior."

Daring to draw Gwendolyn indecently nearer, Dugall flattened one palm against the small of her back and cradled her jaw in the other. Feathering a series of short kisses from her delicate ear, across her soft cheek, and to her sweet mouth, he breathed, "Are ye jealous, Gwenny?"

She stiffened, all outraged femininity, then sagged against him, and nodded, her hair brushing his chest.

"Yes."

"Ye needn't be, *leannan.* The only lass I have any interest in kissin' is in my arms."

Her eyes went soft around the edges, and she sighed, as if she'd made a momentous decision. One she might regret but had determined to plow forward with anyway. She tilted her head and offered him her mouth.

He touched his tongue to one corner, just enough to inveigle, to entice. To make her crave more.

"Dugall?" Sliding her arms around his waist, she closed her eyes, her lashes a few shades darker than the freckles smattering her high cheekbones.

"Aye?"

"You're wasting what little time we have."

"Och," he said, before capturing her lower lip between his teeth. "But I thought ye wanted to keep our relationship strictly professional. Purely platonic."

He bit down gently, and she gasped.

A small sound of frustration escaping her, she moved her mouth hungrily against his.

"Nae flirtin'." He swept his tongue across the seam of her mouth. "Employer—employee. Completely professional."

"I haven't . . . paid you . . . any wages," she said breathlessly.

"Ye saved my life. Remember our bargain?" He pressed his lips against hers firmer, demanding a response.

She angled away and searched his face, her gaze amused and slightly resigned, too. "Fine. If you want to keep your position, do shut up and kiss me properly. Now."

A satisfied grin hauled his lips upward. Who was he to deny a direct order from his employer?

Shifting so she lay cuddled against one arm, he brought his mouth to hers in a reverent kiss.

She wasn't having it slow and gentle.

Clasping his face between her hands, she pressed her mouth to his hungrily. What he'd intended as a tender onslaught to satisfy her curiosity, instantly erupted into an uncontrollable inferno.

He cupped her buttocks and lifted her. Speaking against her mouth, he said, "Wrap yer legs around my waist."

Gripping his neck, she promptly did so, groaning when his groin melded into her softness as he pushed her spine against the paneling for leverage.

God help them both if Hollingsworth eavesdropped at the door. He'd get an earful, for certain.

Dugall would give Gwendolyn a taste of the passion she

sought, but only a taste. He'd no intention of ruining her. Besides, she didn't have time to repair her appearance before they were to meet with Christie.

Nuzzling her neck, he slipped two fingers inside her warm bodice in search of the lush mounds that had so mercilessly taunted him.

Finding a peak, he gently pinched the turgid nipple.

She jumped and moaned, arching into his hand.

Caught up in her passion, she ran her hands up and down his bare back, scraping her nails across the flesh in her fervor.

He'd suspected a fire simmered within Gwendolyn, but this goddess in his arms was on the cusp of igniting for want. He rocked his groin into the welcoming hollow of her hips, and she groaned.

The mantle clock chimed the hour.

If they had time, he'd bring her to completion, but they didn't. And he wouldn't be rushed in the act, even if it wasn't the joining his tortured body yearned for.

Had he ever been celibate this long before?

Mustering every ounce of self-control he possessed, and ignoring the painful pulsing in his trousers, Dugall gently lowered her to the floor.

"What?" she mumbled, still passion-befuddled.

"*Leannan*. Christie, and Hollingsworth too, no doubt await us below." Dugall brushed a knuckle across her flushed cheek. "And as much as I'd like to continue, I dinna think we should keep them waitin'."

That cooled her ardor faster than a dive into icy Loch Arkaig in January.

Licking her lower lip, she nodded. She swept the door a troubled glance. "Yes. Of course."

Once he was certain she could stand on her own, he swiftly retrieved a shirt from his wardrobe. He slid it over his head. "I'll make sure no one is loiterin' about in the corridor."

She'd retrieved her shawl from where it had fallen to the floor. Draping it across her shoulders, she pursed her mouth. "What if someone *is* out there?"

He winked. "I'll ask them to inform you that I'm runnin' a trifle late."

"And what happens when they cannot find me?" She furrowed her brow, obviously not convinced his plan would work.

"Ye worry too much, lass. It's a huge house, and they canna be in two places at once, can they? And we dinna even ken if anyone is out there." He carefully lowered the latch and cracked the door two inches, listening. Satisfied no one lurked nearby, he opened it further and stuck his head out.

Empty.

He glanced over his shoulder. "It's clear. I'll only be ten minutes more."

"You dress yourself? Even tie your neckcloth?" She swept into the hallway.

"Aye. I dinna like bein' fussed over, and I like to be self-sufficient." A boyish smile skewed his mouth. "Truthfully, when my last valet quit, claimin' I was a hopeless barbarian in need of shornin', I decided to eschew the practice."

"This was recent?"

He laughed and shook his head. "I was twelve."

"You're hopeless." Her mouth glowing from his kisses, she smiled. "I'm going to make sure there's nothing untoward about *my* appearance before I venture to the study. We don't need any speculation or gossip-mongering."

"Yer always exquisite, lass."

"Fiddle-dee-dee. Have done with you," she said, waving aside the compliment. Color saturated her face, but her delighted closed-lip smile belied her scold.

He tore his gaze away from the tempting sight. "Go on

with ye, then. Before I'm tempted to steal another kiss or two."

Her smile widened, revealing the neat row of her upper teeth. "I came to tell you not to mention the shooting incident to Mr. Christie."

Dugall glanced up and down the passageway and nodded. "Aye. If that's what ye want. Especially since we dinna ken anythin' more today about it than we did a month ago." He gave her a little shove and dipped his head toward her door. "Now go. To dawdle is to invite calamity."

She hastened the short distance to her chamber, and with another sweet smile, slipped inside.

Gwendolyn McClintock had caught him in her gilded snare, and he wasn't altogether certain he wanted to escape.

But what about the Diplomatic Corps? Yer appointment as a covert operative? Ye winna have another opportunity.

Why must the two things he most wanted in the world be incompatible?

Ewan had been an operative when he married Yvette.

For all of three weeks, and he'd already tendered his resignation.

Shaking his head to dispel his rueful reflections, Dugall stepped back into his chamber. As he closed his door, movement at the end of the corridor caught his eye.

Miss Whitworth's plaid shawl disappeared around the corner.

Eighteen

I *couldn't have heard correctly.*

But Gwendolyn had. *She had.* Saints preserve her and the children. Kandie and Aunt Barbara, too.

One hand resting atop the heavy desk, Mr. Christie, almost gloating in the power he commanded at the moment, relaxed into the chair, his mouth twisted in a satisfied—no, smug as the devil—smile.

The snake-eyed, double-crossing, backstabbing, whore-mongering...

The room remained uncannily silent as those present digested the news he'd gleefully revealed.

She'd check the legality, of course. Dugall might well know the truth of it. Lloyd, too. After all, they'd attended law school. Though given her new cousin's astounded expression, he was as staggered as she.

Or, he might be a damnable fine actor. At this juncture, it didn't matter which.

Wrath and despair burgeoned in her belly, and she clamped her jaw, curled her toes, and balled her fists so tightly her neatly trimmed nails cut into her palms. Through sheer doggedness, she dredged up a composed countenance. Madder than an ol' wet hen as Kandie would say, Gwendolyn struggled to inhale a calming breath.

"As I'm sure you've anticipated, I require that the documents and amendments be reviewed by another solicitor. One chosen at my discretion." She sent Dugall, sitting beside her, a rapid glance, and he gave an almost indiscernible nod.

Little good that would do.

Ire bubbled hotly beneath her poise.

Most likely every possible teeny tiny loophole had been considered and addressed. If Mr. Christie's satisfied expression were any indication, one of Scotland's plentiful midges couldn't find a gap big enough to poke an ant's antenna through.

If only the documents were forged.

"Certainly." Mr. Christie agreed, with such arrogant confidence she wanted to—?

What was that Scottish word?

Kelp him?

Clobbering him was the least of what she'd like to do to the wretch. Tarring and feathering might be a good start, however.

Lily-livered, deceitful, turd in the punchbowl.

"But I assure you, the codicils are perfectly legal," Mr. Christie droned while tapping his spindly fingertips on the papers, almost as a deliberate, taunting reminder of their devastating contents. "And as I've explained, as executor, I'm at liberty to use my professional discretion—"

Dugall's contemptuous snort cut him off. "Disna mean ye lose sight of common decency in the process."

"Precisely," Lloyd confirmed. "This should've been revealed prior to uprootin' Gwendolyn and her family."

She'd have thought he'd be pleased at the turn of events.

Mr. Christie cut him a superior glance. "It's all perspective, isnae it? My loyalty lay with Gerard McClintock, and toward that end, I carried out his dictates to the letter. He dinna ken all his male relatives except the child had expired. Had Gawyn saw fit to respond to his brother's correspondences over the years—"

"And what good would that have done?" Grandpapa had never, not once, mentioned Gerard. What had happened between the two men to cause such a divide that decades later, the elder brother felt compelled to exact revenge after his death? "You still failed to reveal critical information."

Rather than answering her, Mr. Christie quirked his thin lips. "Ye, Miss McClintock, are the one unforeseen variable he dinna factor in. And now I must decide what's to be done with ye."

Not what you want to do.

Gwendolyn longed to unleash her tongue. Instead, she pressed it to the back of her teeth. She'd give him nothing to use against her. If she'd been worried before that he'd wrest the guardianship from her, she was nearly frantic now.

But he'd never know.

He'd see it as a sign of weakness, and like a raptor preys on wounded or sick animals, Mr. Christie would sink his talons deep and tear her to shreds.

Women had minimal rights when it came to children, particularly if they weren't her own offspring. Single women had even fewer.

It had never occurred to her that the guardianship might be challenged in Scotland. The English didn't recognize many Scottish laws. Was the same true of Scotland upholding American decrees?

The oatmeal she'd eaten for breakfast lay like a lodestone in her gut.

Christie would challenge her position. He had everything

to gain by doing so. He controlled the funds, and if he managed to gain the guardianship, he'd control the heir, too.

Gwendolyn wasn't above fleeing with her family if that's what it took to keep the children, but if he succeeded, she'd be a criminal. And they couldn't leave Scotland, damn Gerard McClintock's crafty soul. Not if she wanted Jeremiah to claim his rightful inheritance.

Neither could they move someplace obscure and live unnoticed. She'd seen scarce few Negroes-truth to tell, only one other—since arriving in Scotland, and their southern accent acted like a glowing beacon to draw attention to her and her family.

Besides, the monies from Thistle Glen would only last so long. Perhaps she could obtain a position as a governess.

She tapped her chin with a fingertip.

Yes, indeed. That was a definite possibility. Educated alongside her brothers, she also could claim experience in managing the plantation and household. Surely the McTavishes had connections or knew of someone who might be seeking a governess.

That would only solve the monetary consideration, however. If she were married, her husband could assume the guardianship, and Mr. Christie would find it a deuce more difficult to seize the position.

Well, she wasn't.

She notched her chin higher and met Mr. Christie's gaze head on. She wasn't totally at his mercy. Might as well know now what he intended. "Do you mean to challenge my guardianship of the children?"

Something akin to admiration flickered in his pale eyes. "Ye're a spirited, intelligent lass, Miss McClintock. I'm sure we can come to an accord."

His gaze dipped lower, lingering on her bosom suggestively.

By her agreeing to become his mistress? Not as long as it rained in Scotland.

Only a blind person could've missed his meaning, and given the rough, muffled sound Dugall made, he'd hit upon the truth, too.

"Is there anything in there that specifically addresses any sort of guardianship?" She pointed at the papers. "Anything that would prevent me as a single woman from remaining the children's guardian?"

Worry scythed a jagged path across her shoulders. No one had witnessed Markus's laboriously written directive.

"McClintock assumed an adult would inherit," Mr. Christie finally said. "But if'n ye were married, yer husband would assume the role, and I wuldna see any reason to contest the arrangement."

"Because the courts would deny ye, and we all ken it," Dugall said.

Mr. Christie barely spared him a glance. "But ye aren't, lass, so the matter bears deliberatin'."

Gwendolyn couldn't prevent her small, jubilant smile.

"But as the executor, with sole discretionary rights, I can tell ye that I'm no' convinced a young, attractive, unmarried female is the best custodian for the children." He angled his head. "What can ye offer as a guarantee of yer fitness for the position?"

Alarm whisked the smile from her face.

His vapid gaze slowly roved over Gwendolyn, in such a leering manner, Dugall and Lloyd turned heated glowers on him.

It was nice to know she had two champions, even if her world had just been hurled teacup over ass.

"Have a care, Christie. Ye're no' above suspicion, and I suggest ye act accordin'ly," Dugall warned. "With Miss

McClintock's permission, I'll review those." He flicked a thick finger at the neat pile. "At once."

"I would like to as well. If ye dinna object, Gwendolyn," Lloyd said.

"You and Dugall can review them at the same time."

What was Lloyd's game? True concern or scheming? She didn't know him well enough to determine which. He'd been the epitome of congeniality and cooperation since she agreed to allow him to act as steward.

Did Gwendolyn dare trust him?

She'd started to, but in the last thirty minutes their circumstances had altered dramatically.

Pinning the solicitor with a disapproving scowl, she adjusted her shawl, taking care to cover her chest to her collarbone.

"You might've divulged this information prior to me selling our home and trundling my family across an ocean, Mr. Christie."

Now what was she to do?

She refused to meet Dugall's eyes for fear the pity there would undo her. This little toad of a man would not make her cry, nor would she be blackmailed into a scandalous liaison with him.

Fool! She'd been so stupid. So trusting. So desperate to flee her fourth botched betrothal. To prove being thrown over again hadn't mattered, because she could boast she had a new, more exciting life to pursue.

Truth be told, as much as she loved South Carolina, missed the culture and the people, the deaths of her brother and father combined with being jilted once more had taken a severe toll. And when the letter had arrived from Mr. Christie, she'd seized the opportunity to escape.

She could make all manner of excuses, justify her actions had been for the children's benefit, but deep in the recesses of her battered soul, the truth lingered. And every now and again, it bobbed to the surface, reminding her she'd been foolhardy and impulsive.

Still, had she known even a portion of what Mr. Christie had just revealed . . . "One has to wonder why you didn't divulge everything in your letters."

The solicitor lifted a sardonic brow, his smile growing even oilier. "I but carried out my client's wishes, Miss McClintock. He wanted his heir in Scotland. It's unfortunate if that excuse doesn't satisfy ye."

"I find excuses are rather like behinds, Mr. Christie. Everyone has one, and they usually stink." She shot Dugall a don't-you-dare-laugh glare.

To his credit, other than his lips twitching, he restrained himself.

Lloyd, on the other hand, gawped as if seeing her for the first time. A slow, appreciative smile bent his mouth as he shook his head and rubbed the side of his nose with his forefinger.

She'd never been able to control her tongue when thoroughly riled. And at the moment, a threatened eastern diamondback, coiled and fangs bared to strike, had nothing on her.

Christie had to have known how outraged she'd be, and he'd still inveigled an invitation to stay the night. Was the man slower than a bread wagon with biscuit wheels?

No, not a bit of it. That description was too kind and implied he couldn't help himself. He'd planned this, the manipulating blackguard.

But why?

Did he think to finagle his way into her bed?

That didn't make sense either. She might've been an aged, horse-faced tabby for all he knew.

A movement beyond the study's leaded glass windows caught her attention.

Jeremiah—jogging backward, gesturing wildly, and chattering like a magpie—and Kandie, holding Julia's hand, wandered toward the stables. No doubt they wanted to take a peek at the kittens.

They'd best hurry. The slate clouds looked about to spill their contents.

How was Gwendolyn to tell them that Jeremiah held the title of Lord of Parliament, but Christie controlled everything else?

Nineteen

Suttford wasn't entailed as she'd been led to believe. Everything, right down to those kittens, had been put in a trust, controlled by none other than Mr. Christie's firm. For which he no doubt received a tidy compensation.

An annual allowance would be provided for Jeremiah's care, education, and the operation of the properties, but Jeremiah—*Gwendolyn*—didn't have access to the funds until he was of age. And only if he remained in Scotland until then. If not, Mr. Christie was to disperse the properties and funds as detailed in yet another secret amendment.

For heaven's sake. How many were there?

The old laird certainly had been a mysterious, distrustful sort. And a manipulating cull. He neatly maneuvered her between a rock and a hard place. Had she decided not to move to Scotland, Jeremiah would've still inherited the title, but forfeited the rest.

But she hadn't known that. Hadn't been allowed to base her decision on all the facts.

Would it have made a difference?

Could she have denied Jeremiah his birthright?

Likely not, but she'd have demanded more information. Might have even required the troll to present himself at Thistle Glen.

Now she was faced with an impossible situation.

Because the rat of a solicitor hadn't told her, claiming he wasn't permitted to reveal that detail until Gerard's heir was actually at Suttford House.

As if she believed that. Mr. Christie's conditions changed as often as the wind's direction.

Just who was the recipient in the event Jeremiah left Scotland was to remain a secret—only to be revealed should that situation occur.

Awfully convenient that the solicitor was the only person privy to this critical information. She'd doubted she could trust Mr. Christie before. But now, she didn't believe a syllable he uttered.

The shooting episode of a few weeks ago lurched to the forefront of her mind, too. If someone had tried to scare her enough to make her leave Scotland, they'd no doubt assumed she'd take her nephew with her.

Perhaps she ought to bring up the incident after all and gauge his reaction.

No. No. She clenched her hands.

She wasn't going to say or do anything before thoroughly thinking through the consequences.

The will's other conditions created an additional pebble in her shoe, too. More like an elephant napping on her bed. The codicil specifically stipulated that for as long as Lloyd desired, the estate's agent position was his.

It seemed Lloyd wasn't old McClintock's great-nephew at all, but his illegitimate grandson.

Given his slack jaw and rounded eyes, she'd wager Lloyd hadn't known.

Or had he?

She considered him from beneath her lashes.

Was that why he'd said she couldn't so easily be rid of him?

All this speculating and suspicions had her scattered from hell to breakfast.

In any event, Dugall needn't remain at Suttford now. He'd have no authority as steward if Lloyd was the acting agent.

Such a profound wave of sorrow deluged her, Gwendolyn almost gasped aloud. Instead, she focused on breathing calmly and keeping her face expressionless.

After the wonderfulness in his chamber, a tiny flicker of hope had ignited. One she dared not fan into a full-on flame.

Besides, she'd already surmised he wasn't needed at Suttford except to educate her on the operations of a tenant estate.

Lloyd couldn't be faulted for his superb management of the old laird's holdings. So, until Jeremiah was of age, Lloyd would oversee the properties and Mr. Christie the monies.

Which left her precisely where? With no authority to even order food for the kitchen without permission.

Lord in heaven, the other ugliness the solicitor had disclosed! Good thing she'd been sitting, or she might've stumbled or fallen, so calculated and severe had that blow been.

Steeling her riotous emotions, Gwendolyn swallowed.

Was it possible to hate a man she'd never met? Even if he might've been her grandfather? Because, by jimble, she hated Gerard McClintock so passionately at this moment, her loathing sickened her.

The old reprobate had alleged Papa was *his* son, not Grandpapa Gaywn's.

No! It couldn't be true.

But how to prove otherwise?

There'd been nothing in all the documents she'd sorted through before selling Thistle Glen to validate or refute Christie's claim.

Truthfully, there'd been scant little in Grandpapa's or Grandma's possessions to suggest they'd ever lived in Scotland. Only a thistle brooch embedded with amethysts, a stack of ribbon-tied, faded, nearly illegible letters written in Gaelic, a couple of scribbled recipes, and a faded McClintock tartan. All lay tucked in the bottom of a trunk in her chamber.

Dugall spoke Gaelic, but did he read it, too? Mayhap she ought to ask and have him read the letters. The contents might be useful given this disturbing claim.

Christie rose and stretched his spine before rubbing his hands together in a satisfied manner. "I'm in the mood for a brisk walk about the grounds before dinner. I'd be honored if ye'd accompany me, Miss McClintock. We can discuss my suggestions about the best way to proceed."

Did he think she'd comply because he held all the cards at the moment? He might have a winning hand, but she wasn't ready to quit the field just yet.

Make that toss my cards onto the table.

He'd probably try to steal a kiss or grope her as soon as they were out of sight of the house, too.

"I've yet to arrange for your chamber, so I must decline your offer and do so at once." She rose and shook out her skirts. "Cook had a question for me regarding the menu as well."

Both lies rolled off her tongue as if she were given to fibbing on a regular basis.

Bewilderment lined Mr. Christie's ugly-as-an-old-potato face. "But I thought a footman took my bag upstairs when I first arrived."

"Quite possibly, but it's most likely on the landing or nearby." Another taradiddle.

Other than demand she heed his invitation, Mr. Christie had no choice but to yield. Mouth pressed into a peeved line, his lips like a goose's backside, he slanted his head. "Very well, but I must insist on discussin' how I'll require things to proceed henceforth."

Proceed henceforth all you want, you contemptuous wind-bag, but I'm not done in yet.

"And naturally, I shall insist my solicitor be present when we do." With as much poise as Gwendolyn could marshal, she nodded at Dugall and Lloyd before vacating the study and nearly plowing into the housekeeper outside the doorway.

Her ears red-tipped, Mrs. Norris suddenly applied herself to polishing the hall table with commendable vengeance, while Lowry just as studiously fussed with a fresh floral arrangement. For someone who'd never touched the apparatus before in her life, even Aunt Barbara wielded a feather duster with admirable finesse.

A trio of well-intended eavesdroppers.

How much had they heard?

Enough to fan the edges of their eyes with concern.

Movement drew Gwendolyn's attention to the upstairs landing. Elspeth and Miss Dolina, arms entwined and heads bent near, slowly approached the risers.

"Would you please accompany me to the kitchen?" Gwendolyn included all three in her request, knowing full well Mr. Christie was but a few steps behind her and wouldn't hesitate to intrude.

Fiddling with the feather duster, Aunt Barbara fell in step beside Gwendolyn, and the contrite butler and housekeeper followed. No one spoke, and their footsteps rang flatly on the parquet floor.

Gwendolyn ought to reprimand the servants for eavesdropping and Aunt Barbara for being a poor example, but for what she schemed, she'd need their cooperation. Besides, their lives were affected, too. No sense in pretending false affront when she might've done the same thing had she been in their positions.

As they descended the stairs to the kitchen, she glanced behind her.

"Mrs. Norris, I'm afraid Mr. Christie's current room is unsuitable." Gwendolyn swung her gaze to Lowry, not at all surprised to see his eyebrows inch upward. "His accommodations should be appropriate for someone of his station, should they not?"

Befuddlement notched deep grooves in Mrs. Norris's forehead, but she nodded, nonetheless.

"Though it poses an inconvenience," Gwendolyn said with an apologetic smile, "we'll need to move him to another chamber."

"Indeed, Miss, *I* quite understand." Lowry agreed, a distinct twinkle in his azure eyes. "I shall have the footmen move his possessions at once. Where might I ask to?"

"Perhaps . . . one of the bedchambers in the unused wings?" Understanding dawning, Mrs. Norris ventured tentatively. Growing bolder, she squared her shoulders. "The one popular with *uninvited* guests?"

Oh, well done you, Mrs. Norris. No dull nib, there.

Merriment cavorting in his eyes, Lowry smothered a chuckle.

"Precisely." It would be a goodly distance from the rest of the household too, although Gwendolyn would still have the McTavish men positioned to watch the bedchamber.

They reached the kitchen, and the delicious aromas of tonight's dinner swathed them. Hopefully, Cook wouldn't be too put upon with what Gwendolyn was about to request.

Aunt Barbara selected a sweetmeat from the dessert tray and eyed it thoughtfully. "Gwendolyn, sugah', don't *uninvited guests* have a particular fondness for sweets?" She held up the confection, and blinked innocently.

Ah, Aunt Barbara was on to her game as well.

Gwendolyn grinned. "They do indeed. Lowry, will you see

that an assortment of delicacies are left in the chamber Mrs. Norris selects for Mr. Christie?"

With any luck, the varmints would partake of the offerings whilst Mr. Christie was present. Ought to make him feel right at home, the oversized rodent.

"Oh, and Cook, you'll be pleased to know, the baked trout is back on the menu for tonight." Gwendolyn offered her most beguiling smile by way of an apology. "Perhaps you could manage salmon too? And even a vegetable dish? That scrumptious cabbage, potato, and onion one you served the other night—rumbledethumps, wasn't it?—would be simply marvelous."

Mr. Christie would find the hospitality so lacking at Sutfford House, he'd be eager to leave at morn's first light.

"But Mr. Christie dinna care for fish or vegetables." Holding a spoon coated in something green she'd been stirring in a large bowl, Cook's full brows wrestled each other.

"He doesn't." Gwendolyn accepted the shortbread Aunt Barbara offered.

Cook glanced between Lowry and Mrs. Norris before returning her attention to Gwendolyn. A slow smile framed her mouth as she nodded. "Aye, I can make rumbledethumps. Clapshot be neeps, tatties, and onions, and easy enough to prepare if'n ye like that too, lass."

Charming, how ready the staff was to ensure their guest didn't overstay his welcome.

Warming to the occasion, Cook wobbled the dripping spoon. "And I've peas ready for mushy peas."

Mushy peas? Sounded revolting, and from the thick greenish glops dropping from the spoon, disgusting enough to puke a dog off a gut wagon.

"Absolutely perfect." Gwendolyn bit into the light shortbread. This was one aspect of Scotland she quite liked. "As is this shortbread. Heavenly."

She winked at Cook and was rewarded with a toothy grin.

"Mrs. Norris," Gwendolyn said, "if you'll show me the chambers we discussed when I first arrived, we'll select the most fitting for Mr. Christie."

And then . . . Gwendolyn must have a word with Dugall about that other disconcerting matter.

TWENTY

Dugall handed the last parchment to Hollingsworth. "What do ye think?"

The original will, and at least a portion of the amendments, seemed authentic, but amongst the documents were pages that appeared newer. The papers were crisper, less yellowed, and the ink less faded.

Would Hollingsworth conclude the same? Especially since the agent appointment stipulation was detailed in a newer document?

Christie might explain the discrepancy away by claiming those were the final codicils McClintock added. Hard to disprove that, truth to tell. They'd need to know the last time Christie met with McClintock.

Hopefully, there'd be a record of some sort of Christie's appointments at his Edinburgh firm.

Hollingsworth set the final sheet down, then bowed his head and rubbed his nape. "I think we need an expert to examine the lot, Ferguson. I suspect Christie's added pages after my uncle's death." He pointed to a signature. "This signature isnae quite the same. See the G and M? Could be because my uncle was ailin', but . . ."

Interesting he hadn't referred to McClintock as his grand-father. That Hollingsworth acknowledged the amendments naming him agent were likely forged, made Dugall regard his old nemesis from a new perspective.

And Hollingsworth had also agreed about the signatures. Dugall had noticed the slight difference as well. Unfortunately, an accomplished liar like Christie could easily explain the discrepancy.

Nonetheless, nothing could've lifted Hollingsworth higher in Dugall's estimation, nor given him more cause to trust him, than that statement. Nevertheless, Dugall was no fool, and he wasn't ready to put his complete faith in Hollingsworth just yet.

Why, only an hour ago, his hushed conversation with Miss Whitworth in the corridor had raised Dugall's qualms.

What had Miss Whitworth meant when she'd said Hollingsworth promised her something? What, exactly? Why had circumstances changed?

And why was she lurking in the passageway afterward?

Spying for Hollingsworth? Or was she up to some other mischief?

Dugall needed to make Gwendolyn aware of that tidbit. She couldn't be too careful.

"So we're in agreement?" Dugall ruffled the edges of the stack. "Some of these are counterfeit?"

"Aye, though I have to be honest with ye. I dinna ken how we'll prove it. Unless there's an original hidden somewhere. And even then, it's not unusual to amend one copy and not the others." Hollingsworth scratched behind his ear. "We need a witness. A clerk perhaps who can testify to Christie's deceit."

Dugall wandered to the window, and after edging the crimson drape festooning the tall pane aside, nodded. "He might've written the amendments himself, but I'd be willin' to bet my stallion, a clerk filed the documents. Christie's kind thinks he's above menial tasks."

He touched his coat pocket where the letter he'd been awaiting lay tucked. He'd discovered it on his nightstand after Gwendolyn had left his chamber.

The news came as no surprise.

He was to report to the Diplomatic Corps' office within the week to complete the necessary documentation, and he'd start his training a fortnight later.

Oughtn't he be jubilant? His lifelong dream had come to fruition. He'd soon be an agent for the War Office. Perhaps more. Maybe eventually a spy as Ewan had been.

The timing couldn't be worse, however. For Gwendolyn, that was. How could Dugall leave her when fresh havoc had been wreaked upon her and things looked to become even more complicated?

No matter how many times he tried to tell himself she wasn't his responsibility, that he couldn't risk foregoing his career until she was in a safe position, he couldn't put aside his concern for her.

It's more than simple concern.

It couldn't be.

Too late.

From the moment he'd looked into her startling green eyes and she'd spoken in that irritating, endearing drawl, she'd burrowed her way beneath his skin and tunneled a path to his heart.

Nae, she had done more.

She'd touched his spirit. A man as experienced with carnal delights as he, recognized the rarity.

Such utter hopelessness had swept her delicate features when Christie announced he controlled the estate and monies. Not for herself, Dugall would be bound, but for what the news would do to her family. For the people whose lives she'd upended, only to discover they'd been falsely played.

And then the bravery she'd shown as the solicitor delivered blow after blow. She hadn't wilted under the onslaught, and neither had she dissolved into tears.

She possessed a Scot's fortitude.

Could old flinty McClintock really be her grandfather?

That made Hollingsworth her first cousin, the eldest heir, and in Scotland, even though illegitimate, he could inherit everything but the title itself. He could also petition for Jeremiah's custody, and the notion didn't sit well with Dugall despite his burgeoning trust and respect for Hollingsworth.

Swiping a hand across his face, Dugall sighed. Bloody fine kettle of smelly fish, all this.

He'd wanted to cheer Gwendolyn when she'd mustered her courage and gone on the offensive, challenging Christie about the guardianship. Her concern first and foremost was for the wellbeing of her wards. Not the estate or monies. Not even the title. And he bet she had no idea Hollingsworth could inherit or seek guardianship.

Christie had conveniently left those trifles off. This ridiculous stringing them along. Was that truly McClintock's doing or some perverse game of Christie's? No telling what sort of sculduddery the cur was capable of.

Come to think of it, might be worth digging into his past, too. Ewan would know someone Dugall could ask to poke around.

Something was off about the solicitor. Something Dugall couldn't quite put his finger on but which raised his nape hairs and sent his protective instincts into full gallop.

A naked trollop dancing in Roselyn Chapel was less conspicuous than Christie's hint—if Gwendolyn were agreeable, he might permit her to retain the guardianship.

Agreeable, as in becoming his mistress, the scunner.

Not bloody likely.

That affront had almost earned the scourge of humanity an affair of honor challenge.

Of course, Gwendolyn wouldn't accept Christie's proposal, and Dugall would make sure that no matter how frantic she became, she never considered such an unfathomable option. But even had she been so desperate, surely she knew Christie would then use that indignity to snatch the guardianship from her.

Would she remain at Suttford now?

She'd be under the solicitor's thumb if she did, and in another respect, Hollingsworth's, too. As long as she remained in Scotland she'd be subjected to Christie's whims, no matter what she did or where she went. If only she had a husband to protect her from Christie's meddling and manipulations.

The man was a crafty cull. Mayhap, he'd played old McClintock, too?

Now there was an interesting notion.

Just how long had Christie been McClintock's solicitor?

The oldest date on the documents was only five years ago.

Dugall made a mental note to investigate that detail as well. While nosing about, he might as well retain someone to delve into Hollingsworth's birth and that story about the aunt, too.

Dugall wasn't foolish enough to take Hollingsworth at his word, yet.

"What do ye suggest then, Ferguson? Gwendolyn and the children's situation be delicate, and I'm worried what Christie might do." Hollingsworth's statement rang with sincerity.

Dugall almost smiled at the incongruity that he and Lloyd Hollingsworth would ever agree on anything, let alone work together on solving something as important as forged documents.

With a final glance at the will, he brushed his hair off his cheek. "I've been summoned to London. I'll accompany Christie to Edinburgh when he departs tomorrow and spend a couple of days there before continuing on to England. I'll see what I can uncover."

He didn't like leaving Gwendolyn so soon, but he had no choice. The Diplomatic Corps wouldn't wait, and provided the perfect excuse for leaving with Christie. One that wouldn't raise the solicitor's suspicions or that he could object to.

No better time for Dugall to start using his sleuthing skills. He hoped to be able to persuade the Corps to permit him another couple of weeks or a month to help Gwendolyn decide on a course of action.

He needed to speak with her, and there wasn't time to waste. They must concoct a plan. Ideally, one she could start putting into effect tonight.

One that would put Christie off his pace.

As if thinking of the unpleasant man had conjured his presence, Christie sauntered up the path from the stables like he owned Suttford. Probably he wished he did, and with the control of the finances, he pretty much could do what he bloody well wanted.

In many respects, controlling the estate for the next dozen years granted him the same privileges as ownership. He'd not like relinquishing them when Jeremiah reached his majority.

"So, what do you two think?" Gwendolyn glided into the room, leaving the door partly open behind her. Other than two neat furrows lining her forehead as she stared at the documents causing her so much turmoil, she seemed collected.

Dugall and Hollingsworth exchanged a cautious glance.

"We think some of the will may be forged," Hollingsworth volunteered. "Ferguson's goin' to accompany Christie back to Edinburgh tomorrow and do a bit of detective work before he continues on to London."

Gwendolyn faltered to a stop and ducked her chin to her

chest. Though it was only for a fleeting moment, devastation and accusation had shadowed her eyes.

"Gwendolyn . . .?" Dugall had taken a half dozen steps her direction before he caught himself. Or rather, Hollingsworth's keen regard did.

Not how Dugall would've chosen to tell her, but Hollingsworth had no way of knowing there was something—*anything*—between him and Gwendolyn.

Even Dugall couldn't put a name to it.

Didn't know what to call it besides a compelling, unyielding attraction that grew with each passing day. He wasn't entirely convinced that had he bedded her, it would've disappeared either. Gwendolyn McClintock wasn't the type of woman a man dallied with and then went on about his life.

Not once she'd surrender to his seduction. Their souls would fuse. And that troubled him night after night as he lay awake staring at the flickering shadows on his bedchamber walls.

Nae. It scares the hell out of me.

Christie's annoying, nasal voice rang in the entry. "I wish to speak to Miss McClintock about postponin' my departure for a day or two. Perhaps as much as a week."

Och. Damned if he would.

"She's unavailable at present," Lowry said as the entry door clicked shut.

Gwendolyn's eyes widened, and she shook her bright head, the ringlets framing her face bouncing with her agitation. "Not on his life. I want that man gone first thing tomorrow morning. He's as unwelcome as the back side of a raised-tail skunk."

"Where did ye say she was?" Christie wasn't giving up easily, the boor.

"I didn't, sir." Distinct coolness had seeped into the butler's tone. "Permit me to show you to your chamber where refreshments have been provided for your enjoyment. Perhaps you wish a bath drawn?"

"Nae, but I would like to speak to the lass. It's verra important. I must insist." A mixture of rudeness and irritation tinted Christie's speech.

"Regretfully, that's impossible. Miss McClintock is otherwise engaged until dinner."

"Ye do realize who pays yer wages now . . .? What's yer name?" No surprise that Christie had abandoned any pretense of tact and resorted to threats.

"What a colossal arse," Hollingsworth muttered.

"It's Lowry." A glacier held more warmth than the butler's crisp voice. "And if I understand Scottish law, the estate of the Laird of Suttford pays my wages. And Master Jeremiah would be that laird."

That was the bottom and the top of it.

"And I've been appointed to control his funds until he's of age," Christie said, with such haughty arrogance, Gwendolyn pivoted toward the door, her fists clenched.

Boastful little piece of *shite*.

"Indeed." Lowry's drier-than-cold-ashes tone conveyed his utter disdain. "Your room, sir?"

"Nae need. I only brought the one suit with me," Christie said. "I'll have a brandy in the drawin' room instead. And when ye see yer mistress, inform her that I require a private audience this evenin'."

"I'm never going to be alone with that man," Gwendolyn whispered. Her mouth pulled into a taut ribbon, she closed her eyes and touched two fingers to the bridge of her nose. "In fact, if I didn't want to see his reaction to the revised dinner menu, I'd take a tray in my room to avoid any further contact with him."

"I'll see that Miss McClintock is informed." Lowry's tone clearly indicated he'd do so at his convenience.

"See to it that ye do. I do no' tolerate slackers or insubordination," Christie said. "How long have ye held yer position?"

Lowry's reply was lost as their footsteps faded down the passageway.

"I confess to utterly loathing that dung pile of a man." Gwendolyn glared at the opening, her eyes mere slits.

Dugall faced Hollingsworth. "Would ye excuse us?"

"By all means." Hollingsworth gave a crooked smile as he strode to the door. "I'll endeavor to entertain our guest. Should I get him foxed, Gwendolyn? Mayhap we'll be spared his company durin' dinner."

"No, because then he might plead an excuse not to depart on the morrow." A small smile played around the perimeter of her mouth. "Though after he sees his room, he may not want to stay tonight after all."

What had the minx been up to?

Hollingsworth slipped out, quietly closing the door behind him.

"You're leaving then?" She'd made her way to the sofa, and clasped the carved back. "I expected as much."

"Aye. I wanted to speak to ye about that." Dugall longed to kiss the wistfulness from her face. To tell her he'd always be there for her. "I received the letter I was expectin'."

She nodded as she brushed one hand along the sofa's carved back. "I understand. Just as well, since I've already decided I cannot stay here, and there's no reason why you should remain either."

Dugall's stomach dropped to the floor, leaving a horrid hollow feeling in his gut. "Where do ye intend to go?"

Please dinna say back to America.

He'd never see her again.

"I thought I'd ask your brother and Lady McTavish if they might know of a family in need of a governess or perhaps an elderly dame in need of a companion."

He released an extended, relieved breath. At least she wasn't leaving Scotland. Yet. He'd vow Christie would try to run her off though.

Perhaps he already had.

Clever of her to have already reached the conclusion she'd need income. To do so would lessen Christie's hold a touch, and self-sufficiency was essential if Hollingsworth decided to challenge the endowments as the eldest male heir.

A wise move on Gwendolyn's part, but had she considered where the children, their nanny, and her aunt would live? He couldn't conceive of any household taking in and boarding five people.

Except . . .

"Let me send a note 'round tonight. Ewan and Yvette mentioned they were contemplatin' retainin' a governess. And Craiglocky is so vast, ye and yer family could reside in yer own wing." If Dugall asked and explained the situation, Ewan and Yvette would agree.

They must.

A radiant smile blossomed across Gwendolyn's face and relief softened the fine lines pleating her eyes. "That would be marvelous. At least for the time being. Until I can decide on something permanent. I've no doubt Mr. Christie will do everything he is able to gain custody of the children. Or at least Jeremiah."

She veered him a frantic glance, her expression stricken. Her lower lip trembled the slightest bit before she stoically brought it under control. "He wouldn't separate the children, would he? He couldn't be that cruel."

Aye. He would. Dugall would gnaw his hand off before he told her as much.

"I'll think of something," she muttered as she slapped her palms onto the sofa, then with a ragged sigh, wandered to the window he'd been gazing out earlier.

At the notion of her living at Craiglocky, Dugall's heart had quickened. He'd rest easier knowing she was surrounded by his family, and that the McTavish clan protected her while he was away on assignments.

But she was right about Christie. The way he saw it, she had two options.

Get married or convince Hollingsworth to seek guardianship. Except if Hollingsworth sought and prevailed in a claim against McClintock's estate, the latter might prove as disastrous as if Christie gained the position. But the former—

Nae, it didn't bear contemplating. *His* fiery-haired, green-eyed lass marrying another.

You could ask her to marry you.

He trailed an adoring gaze over her.

If he didn't have to forsake the corps, he would before drawing his next breath.

His rational side objected to the impulse.

Impossible to make such an impetuous decision when he'd known her for such a brief period.

"I'll write Ewan now and send the missive this afternoon. We might even have an answer tonight," Dugall said, in an attempt to comfort her.

She turned from staring out the window into the gathering dusk. "That would relieve me greatly."

Quickly penning a note, Dugall also mentioned the change in the McClintocks' circumstances. He deliberately withheld that detail from Gwendolyn though. If Ewan and Yvette extended the proposition—and Dugall had every reason to believe they would—should Gwendolyn believe they offered her employment out of pity, she might refuse.

He couldn't risk that.

She couldn't risk that.

"Well, I should change my gown for dinner. And since I never did have a chance to see the children before meeting with Mr. Christie, I want to spend a few minutes with them. I won't mention we're to move again just yet. I'd appreciate if you'd keep my confidence in the matter, as well." Emotion, raw and tattered, pulled her mouth downward.

"Of course." Everyone would know soon enough anyway, but he understood her desire to shield her niece and nephew.

"I should think Lloyd will be pleased," she said. "After we're gone, things will be much as they were before we arrived."

She was wrong. About the latter, in any event.

Gwendolyn impacted her surroundings and people profoundly. The staff had already grown fond of her and her family. These McClintocks would be missed.

She angled her head, exposing the long column of her graceful throat. "I owe you much, Dugall. And I'm grateful for everything you've done on behalf of my family. We were strangers to you, and you've been nothing but kind and generous."

Shoulders slumped and head bowed, Gwendolyn looked so forlorn, Dugall had to comfort her. In a few long strides he made his way to her, then gathered her into his arms.

Ye've nae right.

He wasn't offering her forever. He couldn't even offer next week.

The battle raging inside threatened to rip him asunder. He didn't want to leave her. Especially not now. But he couldn't give up his lifelong dream either. Married men weren't recruited for the Corps, for obvious reasons.

Unattached men, free to come and go on minimal notice, whose minds were on their assignments rather than the wife and perhaps bairns who awaited them at home were the ilk of which the Corps was constructed.

He kissed her head, resting his face against the silky softness.

"I'll be back in a week, Gwenny."

She nodded against his chest. "But you'll leave again."

"Aye." No sense denying it.

"You must. I understand." She drew a long, wobbly breath and eased from his embrace. "But I'm not strong enough to fight my growing feelings for you. Even though I know nothing can come of them. And after what Mr. Christie revealed today, I need to focus all of my energy and attention on protecting and providing for my family."

"Perhaps in time I could—"

Could what?

Be verra careful about makin' promises ye dinna ken if ye can keep.

"If they offer it to me, I'll accept the position at Craiglocky. Until I know exactly what Mr. Christie's about, and I decide on something more permanent."

"Gwendolyn." Dugall grasped her hand and pressed a fervent kiss to her knuckles, the action conveying all he wanted to say.

The words, the promises, wouldn't come. Couldn't come. He couldn't give her false hope when he didn't know himself which he wanted more.

And he despised himself for his fecklessness.

"It's impossible. I know that." She touched the scar on his forehead, then brushed her fingertips along his jaw, tears glistening in her eyes. She smiled, a tiny, infinitely sad and fragile arcing of her rosebud mouth.

"So, no more touching, Dugall. No more kisses."

"Aye, lass. It will be as ye wish." A good thing he was leaving tomorrow, for after today, it would be torture to see her, hear her voice, smell her perfume and not sweep her into his arms.

"And, Dugall?"

"Aye, *leannan?*"

"If your brother and sister-in-law offer me a position, I'll only accept under one condition."

He caught one of her blazing curls between his thumb and forefinger. "Anythin' for ye, lass."

Almost anything.

Except what she most needed from him, selfish *batard.*

"Swear you'll stay away from me."

I canna, my heart.

His tall, strong, invincible Amazon made her way to the door, more fragile and defeated than Dugall had ever seen her.

She stepped through and, palm on the handle, looked over her shoulder.

"Leave me alone, Dugall."

TWENTY-ONE

A week later, as Gwendolyn wended her way through the original Keep's crumbled ruins, a wind gust slammed into her. For the third time, she seized her bonnet to prevent it from flying off her head.

Sapphire satin ribbons slapped her face as the curls she'd left dangling in front of her ears caught in her eyelashes.

The biting wind penetrated through her slate blue redingote and whipped her skirts around her half-boots. Still, as she pushed her hair from her eyes, she inhaled the crisp air, relishing her first sojourn outdoors since they'd arrived.

At least the clouds weren't dumping cartloads of rain onto the already saturated highlands.

Even Ewan and Yvette had taken advantage of the day's drier weather to look in on a newly widowed villager.

A shout of gleeful, boyish laughter rang out.

What had seemed like such a fun, educational outing on the first partially sunny day in over two weeks, had turned into a circus given the children's high spirits.

"Children, stay where I can see you. And please be careful. Absolutely no running. It's too dangerous. Remember your assignment. You're to try to find similarities between the old castle and the current one."

Not a one of them would do that.

Well, Iona might.

Truthfully, Gwendolyn had needed the exercise and fresh air as much as the boys and girls did. A chance to stretch her limbs and contemplate her future.

They couldn't remain at Craiglocky forever, even if Dugall continued to stay away. In any event, he wouldn't avoid the Keep indefinitely.

She missed him. Unbearably. She'd grown accustomed to the largeness of his presence, his baritone, and laughter like dark honey left in the sun to warm; of the half-seductive, half-roguish glint in his gorgeous blue-green eyes.

But this was for the best.

How could she have formed such a potent attachment in a few short weeks? How, when she'd forbade her heart to ever feel again. Seemed the imprudent organ wasn't in the business of taking sensible orders from her brain.

She hadn't seen him since that day she told him to leave her alone, her soul fragmenting with each bitter, gut-wrenching word.

Self-preservation—*panic that she'd be hurt again*—prompted her.

Well on her way to falling in love with him, she simply could not endure another loss. She might go mad from it, and she had two children and two women wholly dependent on her. Plain and simple, there was no room for unrequited love in her life.

Besides, Dugall had committed to a daring, adventurous life. She was sensible enough to know taking on a woman responsible for four others and the years of ongoing tumult that Christie would no doubt cause weren't nearly as appealing.

Or tempting at all, actually.

A yelp followed by a high-pitched giggle had her whipping her head in the direction of the mischievous sounds.

She would've accepted Kandie's offer to accompany them if the servant hadn't been suffering from a chest cold. Instead, Gwendolyn bravely—*or foolishly*—opted to attempt the venture on her own.

She hadn't seen the need to ask a clans member or two to twiddle their thumbs for an hour while the children scampered about like kittens, either.

McLeon had offered, even raised his dark brow as if he'd object when she'd refused an escort. She'd assured him they were within sight of the Keep, and if she needed help, she'd but call.

"Children. Did you hear me?" Gwendolyn shaded her eyes against the few, faint, but valiant sunbeams amid the ever-increasing clouds, and mentally ticked off a count of seven as she located each child.

Amid a chorus of ayes and yeses, seven tam or bonnet covered heads bobbed in affirmation.

Urging each other on, the boys, Broderick, Jeremiah, and Pedar, hopped from stone to stone. Iona and Julia, each holding one of the twins, Adelaide's and Adreanna's, hands examined what remained of a huge fireplace.

"Boys, that's not safe." Hands on her hips, Gwendolyn shook her head. "Those stones are not stable. If you cannot stay off them, we'll have to return to the Keep."

The lads grudgingly jumped to the ground.

In a moment, they spotted a mountain hare nervously twitching its black-tipped ears as it watched them from a grassy patch of heather.

Squatting, the boys conferred for a moment, and then, still crouching and looking very much like decrepit, bow-legged trolls, crept toward the petrified animal.

Nose quivering, it remained still for another instant before dashing into the forest.

The McTavish children were well-behaved—better than Julia and Jeremiah most of the time, truth be told—but like any youngster confined indoors for days on end, when given the opportunity to frolic about outdoors, attended to their play with a zeal only the young possessed.

Iona, the eldest at sixteen, proved a tremendous help, even in the schoolroom.

"Aunt Gwenny, can we look on the other side?" Julia pointed to a tumbled-down wall.

"As long as you watch your step, and don't climb on anything."

The worst of the rubble had long since been cleared away, and what remained must've fallen in recent months or years. Ewan and Yvette—as they'd insisted she call them—assured her the ruins were quite safe to explore.

Another powerful flurry whistled through the pines bordering the old Keep's grounds on one side. Their branches played nature's orchestra as the trees bowed and swayed.

Finding a flat place on what looked to have been a staircase at one time, Gwendolyn sat down. The children's laughter rang out every now and again as they chatted happily with each other.

She glanced toward the current Keep.

Did a clansman watch from an upper story mullioned window or the gatehouse tower?

The decision to come to Craiglocky had been a good one. At least for Julia's and Jeremiah's sake. The children all got on together famously. A tremendous blessing in the midst of so much turmoil.

However, Ewan McTavish resembled his brother far too much for Gwendolyn's peace of mind. Nevertheless, she'd been grateful for his generous offer.

The room and board alone for five people would've slowly corroded away the monies from Thistle Glen's sale. Ewan had insisted on paying her a generous wage as well. Actually, he and Yvette had extended an invitation for them to stay as long as Gwendolyn wished, as their guests.

Lloyd had offered the same. He'd tried to reassure her that if Christie did indeed petition for guardianship, he would apply as well. Surely a relative would find more favor with the court than the solicitor.

Politely, but firmly, she'd refused their offers.

The McClintocks weren't reduced to charity, yet.

She earned her salary, though. Every last penny. She'd never have believed how exhausting teaching seven children would be, especially a troupe this energetic.

Which was good.

It meant when she at last found her bed at night, she slept. Or rather, she fell asleep straightaway, but awoke in the early morning hours, yearning for Dugall.

That was when her thoughts spun all manner of frivolous what-ifs and fanciful, unrealistic maybes.

He'd written once to say he'd hired an investigator to look into Gerard McClintock's will as well as the old laird's association with Mr. Christie.

Reason dictated there wasn't likely to be anything of substance found. Nonetheless, she appreciated the gesture, and knowing she'd done everything she could to safeguard Jeremiah's birthright did bring her a small measure of peace.

Mr. Christie had threatened her, quite directly, before he'd left last week, demanding to be advised of all her comings and goings.

Gwendolyn had told him, *quite directly*, to go bugger himself, and that *she* wasn't accountable to him.

He'd left in a furious huff, and they'd moved to Craiglocky the next morning after receiving a letter inviting them and offering her a governess position. In the preceding days, she'd already grown fond of the pixyish and intelligent McTavish young'uns.

After stretching her legs in front of her, she crossed her ankles, closed her eyes, and lifted her face to the sky. Even the paltry, feeble rays struggling their way to earth between the dishwater-dirty clouds would freckle her nose.

She didn't care. It wasn't as if she needed to worry about her appearance.

Lloyd had insisted she and the children were welcome to stay at Suttford, but Mr. Christie had made it clear she had no authority or say there.

What was she to do all day?

Embroider? Knit? Polish the already gleaming furniture?

Before she departed, however, she had directed Mrs. Norris to clean the neglected suites before the infestation of vermin spread to the rest of the house. Surprising they hadn't already, but that might be attributed to the three tabbies prowling the other wings.

"Burn the mattresses, bedding, carpets, and anything else that the mice and rats have gotten to," Gwendolyn had directed.

She chuckled a trifle wickedly.

Already in a foul mood because of the dinner menu, Mr. Christie's encounter with a "rat the size of a fox" had resulted in him brandishing the fire poker like a claymore and destroying two chairs, a nightstand, and a small table in an attempt to thwack the terrified creature.

The solicitor had spent the rest of the night in the library, curled on a short settee, clutching the poker.

Her grin vanished as well-deserved chagrin prodded her.

Not well done of her.

She'd resorted to petty and vindictive behavior, putting him in that chamber. And worse, she'd involved the staff in her unkindness. She'd apologized to Mrs. Norris, Lowry, and Cook before she left, and though she detected no judgement from them, disappointment in her behavior yet plagued her.

Gwendolyn opened her eyes, and did a quick head count again. The sky had darkened, and in the distance thunder grumbled.

Yes, all seven were in view.

She'd permit them another five minutes of play then scuttle the children back before the tempest was upon them. Thunderstorms in the Highlands proved entertaining, but wickedly powerful.

Returning to her ruminations, she crinkled her nose the merest bit. She truly couldn't have stayed at Suttford. Mr. Christie might pop in unannounced, and she didn't harbor the slightest doubt he'd try to compromise her, then blackmail her into doing his bidding.

At Craiglocky, she was safe from his unwanted advances and she had something to occupy her time. At least here she kept herself busy, which meant her muddled musings drifted toward Dugall a trifle less often.

Not likely.

His rakish smiles, his playful winks, his melodious brogue . . . they seeped into her thoughts and commandeered her dreams.

There I go again.

She gave an unladylike snort, then quickly looked about to make sure the children hadn't heard. In the schoolroom, almost daily, she had to render a discourse on inappropriate body noises.

How the boys managed to burp or pass wind, practically at will, still baffled her. But each time one did, the other two promptly joined in. Then the girls held their noses and giggled, and all except Iona, attempted their own rendition of belches and burps.

Gwendolyn quite drew the line yesterday, when so exuberant in their efforts had the boys become, that she had to open the windows and schoolroom door, while covering her nose with her handkerchief.

Thunder growled angrily again, this time closer. The girls squealed and clutched each other, then giggled in self-conscious relief.

Shaking her head, Gwendolyn smiled to herself, recalling happier times when she and Marilyn would scamper to the window seat and watch nature light up the sky. Kandie always said thunder was nothing more fearsome than the Good Lord rearranging his furniture.

Gwendolyn still hadn't made a final decision about what to do. Her position at Craiglocky was a temporary solution. How could she keep her family together and away from Mr. Christie's control and yet not compromise Jeremiah's inheritance? It seemed rather impossible.

She sighed and straightened.

They'd best be getting back. The twins' piano lessons were this afternoon and Yvette had said she'd be back from Craigcutty in time for the instruction. A gifted pianist, Yvette gave each child lessons twice a week.

Lightening ripped a jagged blue path across the sky.

Botheration. Gwendolyn had tarried too long.

"Children, it's time to head back. At once, now." She stood and clapped her hands to get their attention. Little good it did wearing gloves.

One, two, three, four, five, six, seven.

For at least the twentieth time she counted the children. "Come along. Don't dawdle," she admonished. "I fear we won't make the castle before the storm is upon us."

His cap clamped in one hand, Jeremiah trotted to her side, his cheeks glowing red and a wide grin exposing his newest lost tooth.

"Did you see the hare?" he asked, breathless and panting.

"I did." She bobbed her head toward his as she ruffled his hair. "Put your cap back on. It grows chilly, and I don't want you catching Kandie's sickness."

"Uncle Dugall!"

At Broderick's joy-filled exclamation, she slowly turned around. Her heart, ridiculous fickle thing, kicked into a swifter beat upon spying him, flanked by four rather fierce-faced clansmen.

The wind caught his unbound hair as he stood gazing at her, such tenderness etched upon his face, her insides went all soft and squishy.

Faithful Coronis, who'd been noticeably scarce till now, circled overhead, cawing joyfully.

Gwendolyn well understood the bird's glee for she couldn't contain her welcoming smile. "Dugall . . ."

Rolling thunder crashed again, this time so piercing and loud, her ears rang. She jerked and gasped as fire lanced her upper arm.

The girls shrieked, and the boys cried out in fear.

"Aunt Gwenny!" Jeremiah cried, staring at her arm, his eyes wide and horror-filled.

Good heavenly days. Had she been struck by lightning?

Burning heat radiated just below her shoulder, and she rotated her arm to examine the area. Curious, the mark was smaller than she'd have guessed from a lightning strike. She touched the damp patch, her fingertips coming away bloody.

Haziness engulfed her, made worse by the muffled roaring in her ears, and when she tried to blink away the peculiar smoky blurriness, her eyelids felt leaden.

A zap by lightening did rather stun one.

She swayed, and Jeremiah threw his arms around her waist, bracing her.

"Gwendolyn!" Dugall shouted, sprinting toward her.

Twenty-Two

The next afternoon, Dugall paced back and forth at the foot of Gwendolyn's bed. His hands clasped behind his back, his gaze remained fixed on Gwendolyn as Dr. Paterson examined her arm.

Amusement arcing her coppery brows, and her hair a cascade of fire falling past her shoulders, she regarded Dugall over the doctor's shoulder.

How he longed to gather those blazing tresses in his hands, and bury his face in their glorious, sunset-hued ribbons.

An ivory and poppy-red counterpane, a shade more crimson than her hair, covered Gwendolyn to her waist, and someone—probably Yvette—had loaned her a tartan shawl to wrap around her shoulders and provide an additional layer of modesty over her sleeveless nightgown.

"Dugall, do sit down. You look about to topple over from exhaustion." Gwendolyn slanted those striking emerald eyes to one of two dainty armchairs situated on either side of the cheery fire.

His buttocks instantly rebelled at the notion.

He'd spent a decidedly uncomfortable night perched in

that very chair while Gwendolyn, dosed with laudanum for her pain and to help her sleep, had slumbered. He'd not willingly subject his posterior to such torture again so soon. As it was, he might have a permanent groove in his left buttock from the chair's edge.

As she slept, Gwendolyn had snored softly, though she'd likely be mortified to know it. But the slight rasp had been a blessing, for with each breath, he knew she yet lived.

True, last night Doctor Paterson had assured Dugall that she'd only suffered a superficial wound—nothing at all life-threatening. But she'd been so ghastly still, her skin pale as death, he'd still feared the worst.

Doctors misdiagnosed patients sometimes.

"I'd rather stand if ye dinna object." His unhappy buttocks relaxed a fraction. Not so, his taut-as-a-violin-string shoulders. Until Dr. Paterson guaranteed Gwendolyn would absolutely make a full recovery, he'd not inhale a regular breath.

Yvette and Gwendolyn's aunt, Miss Standish, stood on the bed's other side, utterly calm. *Ridiculously calm if you ask me.* As if his dearest *leannan* hadn't come within a hand's breadth of being killed yesterday.

Why were they smiling as if everything were right in the world?

How could it be?

His Gwendolyn had been shot and might yet die.

What if an infection set in?

She might begin bleeding again.

No matter how hard he tried, he couldn't unravel the snarl in his stomach. Dread dug her talons into his spine, scything deep grooves across his already knotted shoulders.

There'd been so much blood.

He'd seen wounds before, some ghastly and fatal. But

when it was the person you adored most in the world whose life was in peril—

By God, that had nearly unhinged his knees.

He shut his eyes and swallowed the thickness clogging his throat.

At first, he'd thought she'd taken a ball in her side, and in that instant, desperate fear like nothing he'd ever experienced prior or ever wanted to feel again had stabbed him to his core.

Gwendolyn had fainted, and Jeremiah, his face contorted in exertion and determination, had valiantly kept his aunt from slamming to the ground until Dugall reached her and swept her limp form into his arms.

Without asking, three of the clansmen, weapons drawn, had fearlessly torn into the woods in pursuit of the gunman. Gregor, Ewan's cousin and a healer in his own right, had sprinted to Gwendolyn, sacrificing his neckcloth as a makeshift bandage to stem the flow of blood.

She'd been so pale, her eyelashes miniature auburn fans against her alabaster cheeks.

The urge to charge into the pines and put an end to the shooter's life had paled in comparison to Dugall's need to get her to safety.

And there were the children to consider, too. Seven moon-eyed, traumatized countenances sought his assurance, desperate to know Gwendolyn would be all right.

Not convinced the danger had passed, he ordered the children home as fast as their feet would carry them. They trotted before him as he carried Gwendolyn, his legs eating up the ground in his haste to get her inside, out of harm's way.

A gentle touch on his arm stirred him from his gloomy reverie, and he opened his eyes.

"Why don't you get some sleep now, Dugall?" Yvette's blue-eyed gaze searched his face, fine lines of concern edging hers. "You were up all night."

"Nae. I dinna want to leave yet." He never wanted to leave his Gwendolyn again.

A sympathetic smile tipped Yvette's mouth. "Then how about a pot of strong coffee? I know you favor the brew over tea. But I must insist on a toddy for Gwendolyn with a spoonful of heather honey. It's a mite bold-flavored for tea, but the honey helps fight infection."

Could some be smeared on Gwendolyn's wound then, too?

Patting his forearm, Yvette glanced to Miss Standish. "Would you care to help, Barbara? I know you wanted to see how cock-a-leekie soup is prepared. I asked Sorcha to make a pot this morning. There's nothing better for speeding healing in all of Scotland."

Miss Standish's intelligent gaze flickered between Yvette and Dugall before she nodded regally. "Yes, Sugah, I did. Quite the tastiest chicken soup I've ever had the pleasure of eatin'."

Yvette raised up onto her toes and kissed his cheek. "She's going to be fine, Dugall," she whispered in his ear.

She kens.

Knew what he'd only admitted to himself last night.

Och, he'd known there was something unique about Gwendolyn from the onset. Knew he'd ached to take her to his bed for just as long. But he hadn't known what to call the unsettling, niggling feeling that beleaguered him.

He needed to protect her, not that she'd ever admit to any such need. He wanted to help her raise Julia and Jeremiah. He longed to see her belly swell with his child.

And he yearned to make this fascinating woman his wife far more than he wanted to become a covert operative for England.

He loved Gwendolyn.

Loved her enough to hurl everything else aside, because while he could contemplate the end of his life drawing near without ever having been an agent, living his life without her was unfathomable.

That had become clear as fine glass last night as he watched her sleep and realized how close he'd come to losing her. Had she not had her arm raised, tousling Jeremiah's hair, the ball might've struck near her heart.

Or struck Jeremiah in the head.

As the demented fiend had intended.

"Ye'll barely have a scar, lass." Doctor Paterson winked and straightened after tying off the bandage. "Ye're verra lucky the ball only grazed ye. I dinna want ye usin' yer arm for at least a week, though."

He wiped his hands on a cloth then pointed at the blue laudanum bottle. "Dinna be afraid to take yer doses. Sufferin' never hurried anyone's healin'."

"Thank you, Doctor." Drawing the plaid over her bare shoulder, she winced. "Other than aching and feeling a bit stiff, it's not that uncomfortable."

"Ye still have the effects of yer last laudanum dose in ye, Miss McClintock." He joggled his wiry brows. "So mind my words. Take yer medicine."

"I shall if I need to." The slightly crinkled corners of Gwendolyn's eyes and the stubborn angle of her jaw said otherwise. But unless you knew her well, had watched her expressions, you'd not recognize her subtle defiance.

Not wishing to be on the receiving end of one of her lethal glares, Dugall constrained his grin.

After a couple of attempts, the doctor's well-worn bag's clasp finally closed with a crisp snap. He held it up and cocked a grizzled brow. "I ought to get me a new one, I ken. But I've had this bag for nigh on thirty years now. I canna just toss her in the rubbish because she's showin' her age."

He scratched his chin and considered Dugall. "Ye look like

ye wrestled with Black Donald all night, mon. I agree with Lady McTavish. Seek yer bed for a wee spell."

Dugall *had* grappled with the devil, all right.

His conscience.

And he'd made a decision.

Fatigued as he was, peace encompassed him.

It was the right conclusion.

Now all he had to do was convince Gwendolyn. Leaving her alone was the last thing he intended to do from now on.

"I've gone without sleep longer than this." He swallowed his yawn. Actually, he hadn't slept in almost eight-and-fifty hours. He'd been eager to tell Gwendolyn what he'd uncovered in Edinburgh.

"Suit yerself. I'll call back tomorrow mornin', lass. Make sure yer still abed." Hunching a shoulder, the doctor waved his hand in the air as he departed.

"You should get some sleep, Dugall." Fidgeting with the counterpane's crocheted edge, she produced a weary smile. "I need a nap myself. The doctor said blood loss would leave me tired and weak, and I am feeling the after-effects."

Unbuttoning his rumpled coat, Dugall crossed to the bed, and without an invitation, scooted onto the other side. He extended his legs, careful not to jar Gwendolyn's injured arm.

She eyed him warily, then cast a troubled gaze to the open door. "This is most improper. What if someone comes in? My reputation will suffer."

No one at Craiglocky would spread tales, but it mattered not in any event.

He gave her a conspiratorial wink as he gathered her to his side and gently pressed her head to his shoulder. "Then I'll tell them they're intrudin' on a newly betrothed couple."

TWENTY-THREE

Gwendolyn snapped her head up so swiftly, her crown cracked against Dugall's chin. Accusation sparked in her eyes.

"Ouch," they said at the same time.

Idiot. Now ye've upset her.

"Dugall, that's not amusing." Rubbing her head, she presented him with her aristocratic profile. She tried to shove away, flinching when her injured arm objected to the movement. Voice low and thick, she mumbled, "In fact, it's most unkind and not worthy of you. I don't require a pretend betrothal to keep Mr. Christie at bay, I assure you."

Och, she assumed he jested.

His fault for the piss-poor proposal.

That was what came of impulsiveness. He ought to have waited until she'd healed and then done the pretty. Went down on one knee and all of that twaddle.

Nae, she'd been through that folderol four times before.

This time ought to have been exceptional. Spectacular.

And like a ham-fisted baboon, he'd botched it.

"Gwenny, forgive me for speakin' out of turn."

He'd waited this long. A little while longer would give him time to contrive something truly special when he proposed again.

"*Hmph*." Gwendolyn pointed her nose ceilingward and made a discomfited sound in her throat.

She'd not forgive his recklessness so readily. He'd trod upon previously bruised territory.

"I wanted to tell ye straightaway, that the man I hired to poke around Christie's office was able to bribe a clerk to search through Christie's records."

The chap was only too eager to accept the offered purse in exchange for information, which he promised to deliver as soon as he had the evidence. He'd volunteered to testify in court too, if it came to that.

Apparently the fellow felt no loyalty toward his employer. From what the investigator revealed, Christie was a contemptible arse to his staff. A real pinch-penny.

A glint of hope sparked in her eyes. "I pray he uncovers something that proves Mr. Christie's duplicity. If not . . ."

Dugall lifted her hand and pressed his mouth to the knuckles. He'd much rather kiss the frown from her lips. Instead, he pressed her palm to his cheek.

"You need a shave." She gave him a you're-overstepping-the-bounds-again look but stopped trying to escape his embrace. Before he could proceed with a proper proposal, she asked, "Did they catch the shooter this time?"

He rubbed his thumb across the back of her hand, mindful he couldn't do much else with the door gaping open. Or with her arm freshly stitched.

"Aye."

Reluctant to trundle down that path just yet, he laid his head against her hair and shut his eyes for a blessed moment.

A not so gentle poke to his ribs conveyed her impatience, and he sighed and opened an eye.

"And?" Exasperation crinkled her nose adorably. "Aren't you going to tell me who tried to kill me?"

For all of her bravado, her voice quivered the merest bit.

"It was Miss Dolina."

"Well, hush my mouth!"

Dugall couldn't prevent his amused grin at the unusual expression.

Astonishment rounded Gwendolyn's eyes and slackened her jaw. "Surely you jest. She's a frail old woman. What motive could she possibly have?"

"Revenge."

Almost ominous in its timing, a log exploded in the fireplace. The bevy of sparks churned upward, the glowing chaos similar to the incandescent golden flecks in Gwendolyn's tumultuous eyes.

She shook her head, the silky cloud of her red hair billowing around them. "I just cannot fathom it."

Dugall couldn't resist gathering a handful of her hair and threading his fingers through the shimmering length. "She wisna the only one less than keen to learn an American inherited the estate. She considered Lloyd the son she never had and was livid he'd been cheated."

"But that's not even rational." Gwendolyn pressed her fingertips between her eyes.

Did she have a headache? He ought to have waited to discuss this with her.

A wry grin threatened.

Not a chance of that when Gwendolyn set her mind to something. "Fenella did say Dolina was dotty, but I assumed she meant eccentric. Not mad as a kettle of frogs."

"Gwenny, there's more." He'd spare her this, but she must know. "The first time, she hoped to scare ye enough that ye'd take the children and leave Scotland. Yesterday . . ." He tightened his embrace. "Jeremiah was the target."

"Oh, my God! If I hadn't . . . My God . . ."

Her voice caught, and she buried her face in Dugall's chest. Shoulders quivering, she cried softly, not loud rasping sobs, but the hushed weeping of someone practiced at concealing her sorrow from others.

"*Shh*, my love." He caressed her spine and shoulders, kneading the tenseness from her muscles. "She canna hurt ye or the bairns anymore."

"How could she try to kill a child?" Gwendolyn shook her head against his chest, then turned her luminous tear-filled eyes to him.

He waded into those mesmerizing verdant pools, knowing full well he could drown in their depths.

"That's more than greed and frustration. That's pure evilness." Outrage sharpened her voice and transformed her features.

Dugall handed her a handkerchief from the night stand, and waited until she'd dabbed her eyes and dried her cheeks. Even with a rosy nose and red-rimmed eyes, she was still the most exquisite female he'd ever set eyes on.

Once she'd tended to her face, he took the sodden scrap of linen and tossed it onto the floor.

"Dolina despised yer grandparents. Absolutely despised them. Her words, no' mine." Yesterday when McLean had hauled her, cursing and struggling, into Craiglocky's great hall, she'd ranted and raged, spittle flying from her mouth like a mad woman.

"But why?" Gwendolyn scratched her neck, and the fire popped again. "Grandpapa left Scotland when he was barely nineteen. What could've possibly occurred to fester that kind of hatred for decades?"

After tucking a hank of her hair behind her ear, he cupped her pale cheek. Despite the cheery blaze, her skin felt cool.

The tale rather resembled a Shakespearean tragedy, and

this part of the story paralleled Gwendolyn's misfortunes too closely. What she'd learn might forever taint her memories of her grandparents.

"Dugall, I can see you don't want to tell me, but isn't it better I hear it from you than someone else?" Such trust she placed in him.

"It seems as a child, yer grandmother was betrothed to Gerard. The McClintocks coveted her title and the wealth that accompanied it. Had counted on it."

"Poor Grandmother." Gwendolyn pursed her mouth into a disapproving line. "Barbaric practice, forcing unions between children. What happened to make Dolina so bitter?"

"When your grandparents skedaddled off to the colonies, the family blamed her for leaving them alone during a Hogmanay celebration while she indulged in a *tête-à-tête* with her soon-to-be husband."

"But it wasn't her fault. Surely the family realized my grandparents had already planned their elopement and simply seized the opportunity." Face drawn, Gwendolyn stared at the canopy overhead.

Had the similarity between her grandparents' elopement and her sister and fiancé number three sparked painful memories?

"True, but her father didna see it that way." Miss Dolina had spewed her venomous tale to him and Ewan, so altered from the sweet-tempered dafty dame he'd come to know, Dugall could scarce believe she was the same person.

"Her father confined her to her room for a month and afterward, refused to let her entertain any company or leave the house. He even terminated her betrothal, which turned out to be disastrous when she was found to be with child."

Gwendolyn lifted her head, amazement etching her features. "She has a child then?"

"Nae, the bairn died soon after birth." He rubbed a hand across his eyes and stifled a yawn.

"How awful," Gwendolyn murmured, idly playing with the buttons on his coat. "And all these years, she's blamed my grandparents. The bitterness had to have been incapacitating."

"True, and it drove her to madness." Dugall could barely keep his eyes open. He might very well nod off where he lay if he wasn't careful.

"Given what you've told me and the degree of the hatred she held for us, I'm beyond grateful that there weren't more attempts on our lives." She shuddered, and clutched the blankets higher. "To think, we lived beneath the same roof, and the whole while she plotted against us."

"Ye can thank the diligence of the McTavish guards for yer safety." Thank God Dugall had ordered round-the-clock surveillance. Dolina must've been frustrated beyond reason.

"Do you suppose she's been sneaking out daily, looking for just such an opportunity as I stupidly provided her yesterday?"

Dugall considered her question carefully. "That's somethin' we'll look into."

Gwendolyn slumped into the curve of his ribs, all soft feminine roundness. "Has she been arrested, then?"

"Aye, but because of her age and ailments, she's being temporarily held under guard at Suttford. Ewan and I both agreed she couldn't be imprisoned here. No' with the children present."

Lashes spikey from her earlier tears, she blinked drowsily, covering her mouth as she yawned. "And you're positive she won't escape?"

Eyeing his boots, Dugall crossed his ankles. Mither would scold him for putting his feet on the bed. "No' with McTavish guards posted. By the way, Hollingsworth didn't ken anythin' about this. He's offered to leave Suttford house. Permanently."

A miniscule smile pulled one side of her mouth up. "He's not quite the ogre you made him out to be."

Dugall acknowledged the truth of his prejudice. "He's proof that a mon can change. I confess, I think I could like him given time."

"I'm cold and tired." Gwendolyn yawned again and scooted lower.

He pulled the counterpane over her shoulders, and kissed her forehead. "Go to sleep."

"You should too."

"I'll find my mattress in a few minutes."

The pillow's softness, Gwendolyn resting in his arms, and nearly three days without rest lulled him. He shut his eyes and relaxed into the mattress. He'd get up in a minute and add a log to the fire, but right now, he wanted to savor this moment.

"Gwenny?"

"*Hmm*?" She was half asleep already.

"Did ye ken yer grandmither was older than yer grandfather?"

TWENTY-FOUR

Was she really?

Gwendolyn's arm barely pained her, and snuggled in Dugall's strong embrace, she'd almost drifted off when footsteps and the clanking of dishes roused her.

"Dugall, a messenger arrived, and Ewan has news of some importance he wishes to speak with you . . ." Yvette's word trailed off in amusement, and she chuckled softly. "Well, if this isn't a fine kettle of fish."

Gwendolyn struggled to open her heavy lids. But she was so comfortable.

And tired. So very tired.

Just a few seconds more, and she'd rouse herself and tell Yvette she wasn't asleep.

However, from the rhythmic breathing below her cheek, Dugall was. Had he truly slept in that dreadfully uncomfortable chair all night, refusing to leave her? Sweet, sultry heat, like thick hot chocolate seeped into her bones. This was how it would be if they were married.

Cocooned together as they slept.

Her heart had stopped for an instant when he jested about

them being betrothed. He'd meant well, but hope clashed with hurt at his carelessly flung words.

"Are they both asleep, poor lambs?" Aunt Barbara whispered from the bed's other side.

"Yes, I fear so." Dishes and silverware clattered again, this time near the table before the window. Yvette must've put the tray down. "Though I'm loathe to wake Dugall—he's utterly exhausted—it's most improper for him to be in Gwendolyn's bed with her."

"Who's to know but us, Sugah? We could close the door and take turns sittin' in attendance to make sure that no compromising behavior takes place." Had entirely proper Aunt Barbara suggested something so beyond the pale? And what, pray tell, did her modest maiden aunt know of compromising behavior?

"I assure ye, I'm awake and have heard yer every word. Compromisin' and all."

Dugall stirred, and Gwendolyn opened her eyelids, her gaze crashing into his penetrating turquoise eyes. Neither moved for a hypnotic moment.

"*Ahem.*" Her cheeks glowing rosy, Aunt Barbara cleared her throat and pretended absorption in the serving tray. Her censured gaze cut sideways to the bed several times.

Was this the same woman, who but seconds ago had scandalously suggested Gwendolyn and Dugall be permitted to sleep while she kept watch? Perhaps, now that they were awake and still lying entwined, neither making any attempt to put a proper distance between them, her finer sensibilities were offended.

"I do declare, these are quite the most temptin' scones I've ever eaten. Gwendolyn darlin', you must try some of these topped with marmalade. Why, I almost think I've died and gone to heaven." She lifted a golden pastry.

She didn't exaggerate. Sorcha made the most scrumptious scones.

"Dugall," Yvette admonished, not unkindly but with firm expectation, "remove yourself from Gwendolyn's bed before a passing servant sees you. I trust our staff's discretion, but even so, there's no sense tempting the devil. And Ewan is waiting for you. He says it's important."

Her intense look conveyed a silent message, and Dugall nodded.

With some effort, Gwendolyn levered herself upright as he heaved a sigh and swung his long legs off the bed's side.

He scraped a hand through his hair, disheveling it even more.

She quite liked his untamed appearance. "Dugall?"

"Aye?" Fastening his coat, he swung his gaze to her.

"If the news pertains to Mr. Christie, I should like to be party to the conversation." Cupping her injured arm, she held it to her chest. Thank goodness it wasn't her dominant hand.

His eyebrows climbed high on his forehead before he gave a grudging nod. "Ye've the right, I ken. I just dinna want ye further troubled."

Deep lines of fatigue furrowed his handsome face, and with his unkempt hair and dark beard shadowing his face, he resembled a fierce buccaneer or a wild Highland warrior.

When she'd first met him, she'd had a similar, less complimentary thought. Now she'd grown to prefer the rough and rugged Scot to the polished, refined southern gentlemen she'd once admired.

"Ewan's in the study, I presume?" Dugall helped himself to a scone and took a hungry bite before washing it down with a gulp of coffee.

Had he eaten since this ordeal began?

"He is." Yvette placed a brown paper-wrapped rectangle on the nightstand beside Gwendolyn, a piece of foolscap folded and tucked into the string securing it. "Gwendolyn, this just arrived for you from Suttford House."

Had she forgotten something? Perhaps. They'd packed in such haste. Couldn't have been important, or she'd have missed it by now.

After setting the lap tray across Gwendolyn's thighs, Aunt Barbara balanced on the edge of the bed. "Sugah, the young'uns are ever so worried about you. Might they visit later?"

How terrifying it must've been for the children. Of course they must.

Gwendolyn took a sip of the strong tea, its heavy heat trailing clear to her belly. Heaven above. Was that whisky she tasted? She took a discreet sniff, and then a longer sip.

Yes, indeed. She'd never partaken of strong spirits, except that one swig when suturing Dugall's arm, but Grandpa had a penchant for scotch, and she recognized the aroma.

Before she realized it, she'd drained the cup and a second, which Aunt Barbara had been suspiciously quick to pour. A comforting, languid feeling, much like being wrapped in a fire-warmed blanket and tucked into bed, encompassed her.

She quite liked Scottish toddies.

Aunt Barbara had asked her something. What was it?

Oh, yes, the children. "Of course, the children are welcome."

Dugall shook his head, his loose raven hair skimming his shoulders. "No' until after ye've rested. Ye need to regain yer strength."

"Thank you for your concern, Dugall, but I'm not so inca-pacitated that I cannot answer for myself." Her tart response earned a quickly concealed smile from Yvette and a what-did-I-do-wrong befuddled look from him.

Why must she be so prickly all of a sudden? He'd meant well.

Propping a pillow beneath her injured arm, which despite the whisky throbbed with the devil's own vengeance now, she said, "I confess, you're right. I'm quite done in—*and perhaps a trifle foxed*—and could use a short rest once I've learned Ewan's news. However, afterward, please bring them 'round."

She checked a grimace when Aunt Barbara jostled the bed.

A barely detectable, satisfied smile kicked the edges of Dugall's mouth upward, making her concession worthwhile. He'd noticed her discomfort, however. "Is yer arm painin' ye?"

"Just a mite, but I don't want any laudanum before seeing the children." Didn't want it at all, truth be known. Besides tasting the way the backside of a mule looked, it muddled her thoughts and made her tongue as thick as if she'd stuffed fleece into her mouth.

And after two cups of tasty whisky-laced tea, she'd be drugged senseless if she took laudanum, too.

Not really hungry after the toddies, but also not wishing to worry or offend Yvette or Aunt Barbara, Gwendolyn dutifully picked up the spoon and took a bite of the delicious soup.

Dugall finished his second scone, then brushed the crumbs from his coat front. "If it's regardin' Christie, I promise I'll return shortly with Ewan."

"I'll go with you." Yvette drew the drapes partway before crossing to the door. "Gwendolyn, I'll send a maid up to let you know if the matter pertains to something else. That way you can take your nap directly."

Aunt Barbara rose, then kissed Gwendolyn's cheek. "I need to rest my eyes a few moments myself." She patted Gwendolyn's shoulder. "I'm so grateful you're not seriously injured, darlin'." She blinked, her eyes glistening.

"With such diligent care, I'll be right as rain in a day or two." Gwendolyn dabbed her mouth with the serviette. She'd managed to eat half the soup and even a couple bites of the scone and cheese. "Would you be so kind as to take the tray too, Aunt Barbara?"

The others had scarcely left the chamber before curiosity overcame her, and Gwendolyn lifted the bundle to her lap. She slid the paper out from beneath the string and unfolded the foolscap.

Written in neat, tidy strokes was a single paragraph.

~

MISS MCCLINTOCK,

Whilst cleaning the chambers at your behest, I found this journal beneath the wardrobe. Since everything at Suttford House belongs to the young laird, and you are his guardian, I thought it best to send it directly to you.

Your Faithful Servant,

Mrs. Morag Norris

~

WHY WOULD someone hide a journal beneath a wardrobe? How long had it been there? Unless . . .

Could it be Heather Abernathy's?

Gwendolyn unwrapped the old, rather decrepit diary. Frowning, she turned the slightly musty, nibbled-about-the-edges, deep-blue leather-bound journal over.

The letters *H A* embossed in gold script, stood out boldly.

She stared at the initials, curious and yet reluctant to intrude upon something as personal and private as someone's journal.

Biting her lip, she gingerly opened the cover.

~

To my darling daughter on her sixteenth birthday.

Heather, may these pages be filled with your happiest memories.

With love, Papa

~

18 October 1773

Did Mr. Abernathy know what had become of his cherished daughter?

Gwendolyn traced her fingertips over the faded writing and hesitated only a moment more before flipping to the first page.

By the time Dugall and Ewan knocked on her door twenty minutes later, she'd read the last of the few, sporadic, increasingly shorter and more distraught entries.

Short until she reached the last one, that was.

Tears blurred her eyes as she stared at the final entry.

~

3 August 1774

At long last, after almost nine agonizing months, I shall escape this hellish gilded prison!

My beloved Lloyd has arranged it with the help of his sister and Miss Dolina. No one suspects them. Deizi has acted as my maid these long months but has proven to be a true and dear friend, and Dolina despises McClintock as much as I do, though she's never revealed why.

We've practiced the escape over and over, and now we are ready. I'm giddy in anticipation of being free! Of never having to endure McClintock's vulgar attentions again.

May God condemn his black soul to hell.

I care not that Lloyd's a simple sheep farmer. I love him, and would rather live in poverty than enjoy the luxuries McClintock showers upon me.

My greatest sorrow is that I am now certain I carry McClintock's bairn. He must never know, or he'd force me to marry him, and I'd never be free of that monster.

Lloyd doesn't care, and I adore him all the more for it.

~

THE WRITING SMEARED HERE, as if tears had splattered the foolscap.

~

PAPA, *I forgive you.*

McClintock cheated you at cards that night. He told me so himself, boasting how gullible you'd been. I hated you at first for sacrificing me to save our home and keep Mama and the other children from the workhouse.

It's time. I must go—

~

A STREAK of ink dripped down the page from the last word.

Why hadn't Heather taken her journal? Had she left it behind accidentally? Was she still alive?

Possibly.

Gwendolyn's Cousin Lloyd—named for his grandfather?—would know.

But how had Gerard learned of Lloyd's existence if Heather hadn't told him of her pregnancy?

A soft knock disturbed her reverie, and with a sad, closed-lip smile, Gwendolyn shut the diary. Lloyd ought to have it. After all, the journal was his grandmother's.

"Come in," she called, setting the book and note on the nightstand.

Dugall stepped into the room, followed by Ewan. Arig, one of the humongous gray-blue boarhounds, accompanied them. Though they had different fathers, with their coal-black hair and vibrant blue-green eyes, the men greatly resembled each other.

At the moment, they both wore concerned smiles.

Her stomach quivered.

Bad news, then.

"I thought perhaps ye'd fallen asleep after all, and I didna want to wake ye if'n ye had." Dugall gave the journal a cursory glance, and bold as freshly polished brass buttons, sat on the bed.

A flush heated her face, and she veered Ewan a swift, embarrassed glance. What must he think?

His expression remained kindly as he made his way to the armchairs flanking the fireplace. He gestured toward one. "May I?"

Truth be told, she wouldn't object to another log on the fire. The chamber had grown chillier, despite the cavorting and crackling fire in the hearth. A quick glance to the windows revealed low-hanging pewter clouds. She'd bet her boot buttons the puffy gray masses portended an early snow.

"Of course." Gwendolyn nodded while covertly assuring she was modestly covered. Once satisfied, she drew the bedcoverings higher, too acutely aware of the impropriety of entertaining gentlemen in her bedchamber. "If you'll pardon me, Dugall, I'm a trifle cold."

He lifted his hip to allow the blankets to shift upward.

Only then did Ewan's mouth twist into a droll smile, and he pointedly looked between his brother and the other chair. The dog turned in three circles before settling onto the floor before the fire and released a contented groan.

Dugall grinned, and rather than heed Ewan's broad hint, took her hand in his.

Because he wanted to touch her as much as she longed to touch him, or as a gesture of defiance? Or perhaps, what he and Ewan had come to discuss she'd find distressing, and he sought to lend her strength and comfort.

Suddenly nervous and uncertain, and not wanting to bring Ewan's censure down upon her and risk losing her governess position, she withdrew her hand and pointed to the journal. "That proves Lloyd is Gerard McClintock's grandson."

Across the bridge of their noses, Dugall's and Ewan's midnight brows crashed together.

"We have proof he isnae." A hint of apology or perhaps pacification fringed Dugall's denial.

Gwendolyn jerked her head upward from her drowsy contemplation of his strong hand lying atop his preposterously masculine thigh. "Pardon?"

Ewan casually laid an arm across the back of his chair and hooked a booted ankle across his knee. "Dugall asked that I have a man prod around Hollingsworth's background. It's true he was taken in by an aunt when his father died, but his father wasn't Gerard McClintock's by-blow."

"But it says, right there in her own writing," Gwendolyn pointed at the diary again, "that Heather Abernathy carried Gerard's child."

Taking her hand once more, Dugall gave her fingers a little squeeze. "The aunt lied. She's still alive and confessed all. Desperate for funds with a drunkard for a husband, she wrote McClintock claiming Lloyd was his grandson. Seems her sister had shared a tale about her mother-in-law, Heather Abernathy Hollingsworth, and how she'd fled old McClintock's in the middle of the night after a maid drugged his ale."

"She did flee. It's the last entry. And she also says she's

expecting Gerard's child. It's a horrid, sad tale." Weariness and sorrow weighted Gwendolyn's eyelids. Sorrow for the young woman who'd suffered so at Gerard's hands but also for Lloyd.

"Aye, she was with child, but she lost that bairn." Ewan stood and took a poker to the fire, encouraging the flames higher. "She kept another journal afterward and it documents everything. She didn't bear Lloyd's father until almost a year after fleeing. The birth is recorded at the Church of the Holy Rude."

What did that mean for Gwendolyn's new cousin? Would Christie permit Lloyd to stay at Suttford when he learned the truth? She cradled her arm. "Lloyd needs to be told. Is he even related to Gerard?"

Dugall and Ewan exchanged a guarded look, but Dugall answered. "Nae. It dinna look like it."

"Unfortunate man." How utterly unfair. She'd been so prepared to dislike Lloyd—he had been rather a rotten turnip when they'd first met—but after she'd gotten to know him, she'd come to admire her cousin.

Cousin.

But he wasn't a cousin, and that meant he couldn't petition for Jeremiah's guardianship.

How could she be simultaneously relieved and troubled?

Suspicion trotted up her spine when instead of preparing to leave, Ewan resumed his seat. He needn't have accompanied Dugall here in the first place. Dugall could've easily relayed this information. Perhaps Yvette, concerned for propriety, had encouraged her husband to act as chaperone.

That must be it. They didn't want their governess in a compromising position. And neither could she afford to lose the post.

"There's something else." Not a question.

Gwendolyn could see vexation in Dugall's eyes. Something

had put thunder on his face, and trepidation sent her pulse frolicking.

"Aye." The great dog raised its massive head, and Ewan scratched behind his charcoal-colored pointed ears. "Miss Dolina escaped her chamber last night. She drugged the footman assigned to guard her room. Stupid fool. She claimed she wasna hungry and offered him her mutton stew dosed with laudanum."

Fear stabbed Gwendolyn, the icy tendrils coiling around her ribs, and she jerked upright. "Where are the children? Are clansmen guarding them?"

Dugall answered. "The children are perfectly safe."

"I expect the guard was reprimanded for his carelessness?" She pressed her palm to her forehead to calm her tumultuous thoughts. It would be difficult for Dolina to sneak into Craigcutty. Nevertheless, Gwendolyn would insist on a watch round the clock. "She's being pursued, of course?"

"The contrite footman roused soon after and alerted the others. They found her in the bogs." Dugall tapped his fingers on his thigh, the lines of his face gone stern. "Whether by accident or deliberate intent, she drowned in a bog pool."

"Better that than wasting away in a prison, I should think," Ewan offered.

"I should feel pity for her, but at this moment, I cannot dredge any sympathy. Her crimes are too fresh in my mind." Prior to this, Gwendolyn had always been quick to forgive, but she couldn't get beyond the evilness of Dolina targeting Jeremiah.

"There's something else you should know." Ewan leaned forward, resting his elbows on his knees and steepling his fingers. "Citing unethical practices, McClintock discharged Christie two years prior to his death. Dugall's man unearthed that information."

"I'd say forgin' documents and namin' himself executor or

representative for a number of deceased clients qualifies as corrupt." Dugall shoved a hank of his midnight hair behind his ear, his exhaustion tangible.

Gwendolyn yearned to brush the lines of fatigue from his face. No, she wanted to put her arms—well, her good arm—around him, pull him down beside her, and for them both to sleep until tomorrow. For a few hours, forget all of this ugliness and pretend that they had a future together.

After she'd so firmly forbade her heart not to succumb to Dugall's dashing manliness, the imprudent organ had ignored her sage and learned advice and done precisely that. And despite the rash impossibility of it all, she'd seize every moment she could with him.

"My intuition told me not to trust that man, and now I know why." She swallowed a yawn and, fingertips pressed to her lips, shook her head. "Surely he had to have known he'd eventually be caught. Why would he take such a risk? Can't he go to prison for this?"

"After he succeeded the first couple of times, he became careless. The cull has a gamblin' problem and debts up to his beady eyeballs," Dugall informed her. "A few years ago he faced debtor's prison. Then suddenly, clients started appointin' him executor and, *voilà*," he snapped his fingers. "Christie paid all his vowels off in a matter of months."

"He'll spend a long while in prison now, or if he's fortunate, he'll spend the remainder of his life in a penal colony." Ewan bounced his foot lightly upon his knee. "The authorities have been advised, and I shouldn't be surprised if he hasn't already been detained."

Waves of pain riddled Gwendolyn's arm, and it took great effort not to let on how much it hurt. She might yet succumb to the laudanum. Or another toddy. "So how do we know what part of the will is legitimate and what's not?"

Dugall grinned, the flecks in his eyes glittering with

delight. "That's the beauty of it. McClintock retained another solicitor—Cyrel Pinfield—and Pinfield possesses McClintock's most recent Last Will and Testament."

Gwendolyn's relief was almost dizzying. Of course, that might be the whisky, too.

He withdrew a letter from his coat pocket and passed it to her. "He wrote ye," Dugall said.

Laying the letter aside to read at her leisure without two pairs of curious eyes regarding her, she asked, "Why haven't I heard from him prior to this?"

"He returned from America just this week. He'd personally gone to find Suttford House's heir. I ken the mon." Dugall yawned behind his hand. "Met him in law school. A good sort. So straight-laced, he'd sooner bite off his own tongue than tell an untruth."

Full of questions and more than a bit befuddled, Gwendolyn shook her head. "Why didn't Mr. Pinfield just send a letter to Thistle Glen? And why the delay? It's been months."

"He was in India recoverin' from a severe case of malaria, and Christie took advantage of his absence. In fact, Pinfield, upon hearin' of McClintock's death, was quite frantic to contact ye, lass."

Christie probably hoped Mr. Pinfield would die and no one would be any wiser.

"He wrote ye straightaway, but he either had the wrong address, or his letter and yer passage to England intersected on the Atlantic." Dugall picked up the journal and after a moment, thumbed through the pages. "Why do ye suppose she left this behind?" He raised the volume chest-high.

"I'm not sure." Gwendolyn lifted her good shoulder. "Perhaps she dropped it in her haste." She peered between Dugall and Ewan. "So precisely where does this new information leave my family and me?"

Arig lifted his great head, then stood. After yawning and stretching, he padded over to the bed. The size of a small pony, he laid his muzzle on her lap.

"Greedy laddie, begging for pets," Dugall admonished even as he leaned over and ran a big hand across Arig's neck.

Gwendolyn, always fond of dogs, played her fingers through the boarhound's short fur.

"I'd guess exactly back where you were when you arrived. You'll know more after you meet with Pinfield. He's expected here tomorrow, unless the weather turns waffy." Ewan smiled and slapped his hands on the chair's arms. "And this likely means, you'll no longer need to remain as governess. My children will be disappointed, and even more so that their new friends are leaving so soon. We'll all miss your company at Craiglocky."

"Let's no' get ahead of ourselves." Dugall scowled at his brother. "Best to wait and see what Pinfield has to say. There still may be stipulations we're no' aware of." He cut her a mollifying look. "I'm sure ye'll agree, lass."

"That does seem wise." She loathed carting the children back to Suttford prematurely. "At least we know now that Lloyd's fully capable of overseeing Suttford, so the estate will trot along quite well."

"Aye, he's done a commendable job," Dugall agreed.

All this turmoil to come full circle. Still, better to be at Suttford as soon as possible where everything didn't remind her of him—of what could never be. She managed a cheerful smile. "You must be very excited to start your training. When do you return to London?"

"That depends on ye, lass." Dugall leveled Ewan a speaking glance.

Ballocks and bluebells.

Had he delayed his departure because of her injury? Would his superiors reprimand him? He'd only been here one day, so she hardly believed they'd kick up too much of a dust. Would a missive from her help at all?

"And that's my cue to leave." Ewan slapped his thigh, and at once Arig lumbered to his side.

The door slid closed much quieter than one would expect on the centuries-old hinges.

"I apologize if my recuperation has hindered your plans, Dugall." Steeling herself, Gwendolyn raised her bandaged arm. "I must be up and about tomorrow to receive Mr. Pinfield in any event. You needn't postpone leaving on my account."

No one would be coming or going from Craiglocky if the portly clouds released their flaky burdens.

"Wheesht, sweet Gwenny."

Dugall gave her one of those stomach-tumbling sideways smiles, making it ever so difficult to be curt or cross with him for telling her to shush as if she were a rambunctious toddler.

She tilted her head and after raising her eyebrows gave him an extended, expectant look.

He cupped her jaw, rubbing his big thumb over her cheekbone. "I meant, my leavin' for London depends on whether ye say yay or nae to marryin' me."

Twenty-Five

Dugall wasn't certain exactly what Gwendolyn's reaction might be to his second impromptu proposal in just over an hour, but a fit of nervous giggles hadn't topped the list of possibilities, even if the musical mirth caused an answering twitch of his own mouth.

Truth to tell, hilarity hadn't been on the list at all.

Tears of joy?

Aye.

Peppering his face with excited kisses?

Aye.

An exuberant hug?

Aye.

Declarations of love?

He had hope for such.

Each had crossed his mind as well as surprise or astonishment that he was indeed serious about wedding her.

More serious than about anything else in his life.

Her giggles finally subsided, and still wearing a large grin, she swiped at the corners of her eyes with the edge of the sheet.

"Please forgive me. I fear Yvette liberally dosed the tea with whisky, and I quite forgot myself."

Her face and eyes did have a spirit-born glow, as did her bemused smile.

"Marry you," she muttered. "That'd make five betrothals. Surely that's a record somewhere."

Verra well could be, but this time she'd actually find herself wed.

Gwendolyn Ferguson.

Aye, the name had a lovely ring to it.

She hiccupped and slapped a hand over her mouth while giving him a chagrined peek.

Just *how* much whisky had the toddies contained?

Dugall didn't have any flowers, or sweets, nor had he composed an ode or sonnet. Hell, he didn't even have a ring. He'd rather botched the second proposal too, so much so, she'd not taken him at his word once more.

Still, no time like the present.

Clasping Gwendolyn's uninjured hand, Dugall sank to one knee beside the bed. "Gwendolyn McClintock, I've loved ye since I awoke in that cart and looked into yer magnificent eyes. I'd be honored above all men if ye'd consent to be my wife."

Gwendolyn's jaw went slack for an instant before she recovered herself and tugged her hand loose.

Blast and damn.

Too short? Not romantic enough?

He ought to have waited until he could gather a few posies, although where he was supposed to find blossoms this time of year was beyond him. Even the heather was done for the season.

Probably should've made a trip to Edinburgh. He could've purchased a few sentimental tokens, done something to make the moment more memorable.

Normally, he was quite the romantic. So why had his usual adeptness vanished like steam wafting from a teacup?

"Are you daft, Dugall? You cannot marry me. And there's no need for such a sacrifice now in any event, though I do heartily appreciate the chivalry behind the gesture."

Chivalry be hanged.

There wasn't a blasted thing noble about asking her to be his wife. He wanted her at his side for the remainder of his days. Purely selfish motivation promoted him, and he'd neither deny it nor paint it pretty.

Quite simply, he needed her far more than she needed him.

Despite her chirpy rejection, Dugall detected the merest gleam of something in her eyes, and her gracious smile seemed forced at the corners.

He rose and rather than take his former seat on the bed, crossed his arms and rested a shoulder against the heavy, carved posts.

"Lass, 'tis nae sacrifice, I assure ye."

She pinched her lips together, then opened her mouth but snapped it shut again without uttering a sound. Darting a glance his way, she gave a slight shake of her head, sending the curls caressing her shoulders to pirouetting. Inhaling, the whole while tormenting the lace-edged counterpane, she sat up a bit straighter, and met his gaze.

"Dugall, answer me one question, if you will. Does the Diplomatic Corps countenance married agents?"

"Nae." Hadn't he already told her that? Mayhap not. Ewan might've mentioned it, too. "They dinna want their operatives distracted."

"Well, there you have it." She threw both her hands up and promptly flinched and clutched at her sore arm. "What kind of woman would I be to selfishly accept your offer? You'd be giving up what you've most desired, and I cannot help but think in time, you'd come to begrudge your choice. You mustn't forfeit this opportunity, the likes of which will never come along again."

Och. Gwendolyn hadn't said she *didn't* want to accept. Only gave her reason for *not* doing so. Two vastly different things. A selfless excuse. And one that gave him hope and filled him with unfamiliar giddiness.

He chuckled, earning him a decidedly peeved glare, her eyes all but shooting green sparks.

"Forgive my naiveté, but what is humorous about what I just said?"

Wise man that he was, he didn't remind her that but moments before, she'd laughed until tears leaked from her eyes.

Dugall did sit then, and clutched her hand to his chest. "Ye are what I most desire, lass." He flattened her palm over his chest. "Do ye feel my heart beatin'?"

Eyes wide and uncertain, she gave a cautious nod.

"Every beat, *leannan,* is for ye. Ye twist my thoughts, keep me awake at night. And when I do sleep, ye invade my dreams. Ye've melded with my spirit to such an extent, that I dinna ken where I end and ye begin. I'm no' whole without ye."

The temptation to take her in his arms and show her just how much he loved her, hummed through his veins, channeling its way to his heart.

Unmoving, except for the shallow rise and fall of her chest, she stared at him for so long, the flicker of hope he'd harbored faded bit by bit.

"How can you forsake something so important to you? You told me yourself you'd yearned for this very thing like nothing else since you were a wee lad. Becoming an agent is your lifelong goal." Peering deeply into his eyes, she gripped his forearm. "You cannot, must not, give up your dream."

"I think I ken my own mind."

She crossed her arms, as much as she was able to given her

wound, and notched her pert chin up at a mutinous angle. "I won't permit it. The guilt would haunt me all my days."

He reclaimed her hand, linking her long, delicate fingers between his thick, roughened digits.

"Sometimes, we strive for somethin', believin' with our whole being that if'n we can achieve that elusive thing, that we'll be content. And many times that might be so, unless ye're as blessed as I've been to have somethin'—*someone*—even more special and important cross my path."

Or be run down by her carriage.

He'd go to his grave, grateful for her driver's cowardice.

"And then the former passion loses its luster and appeal. Because *she* is so glorious, so perfect right down to the adorable freckles pepperin' her nose, nothin' else matters."

He placed a quick peck on that upturned nub.

"You think my freckles are adorable?" She touched her nose, wonder shining in her eyes. "Really?"

Out of all that pretty speech, it was his love of her freckles that won her over?

"Aye, lass. Especially that tantalizing one just below yer left ear." He touched the love mark, wishing she wasn't injured and he could yield to the impulse to place his lips where his finger had just been.

She searched his face, a mixture of hesitation and yearning swirling in her eyes. She was afraid. Frightened of taking a chance, of being disappointed and rejected again.

He could see it clearly, in the shadow that shaded her eyes, reshaping her countenance from happy to troubled.

"Gwendolyn, I love ye."

A timorous smile curved her mouth as she blinked back tears. "You'd have regrets."

"Aye, if'n I didna persuade ye to marry me, and let me help ye raise those two hellions." He winked. "That alone ought to have ye callin' for the reverend before the day's end."

A watery chuckle escaped her, and she brushed a tear away with her bent knuckle. "I'll admit, *that* tempts me mightily. But what will you do instead of working for the Corps? I rather hoped to allow Lloyd to stay on as Suttford House's agent. Especially now that he isn't kin to McClintock. He'll need a position. And once Jeremiah's of age, he'll take over what responsibilities I'll carry. I actually expect he'll be ready before his majority."

Dugall winked again and waggled his eyebrows. He leaned forward and whispered, "The whisky distillery has great appeal. And I think yer linen factory suggestion is brilliant, too. Why no' try both?"

"But I don't have funds for—"

"*Shh.*" Placing two fingers across her lips, he quieted her objection. "I have a tidy sum set aside, and I've nae doubt Ewan would want to invest, too."

She tapped her chin with her forefinger. "And I could invest a portion of Julia's and Jeremiah's funds from the plantation also. If overseen diligently, they might see a handsome profit."

Excitement danced in her eyes as the first fluffy snowflakes sifted from the sky outside.

He laid his palm against her satiny cheek. "Say aye. Marry me, *mo chroi. Tha goal agam ort.*"

My darling. I love you.

Her eyes widened, pleasure flushing her cheeks as she recognized the Gaelic.

"Are you sure, Dugall? Absolutely, without a single doubt or speck of hesitation?" She cupped his hand framing her face and closed her eyes, her voice the merest thread. "For I love you too, and 'tis better to reject you now than for us to wed, and I have to watch remorse and disenchantment transform your love to something I couldn't bear."

Turning her face so that but an inch separated their

mouths, he placed a tender kiss on her lips. "As positive as that's snow fallin' from yonder sky."

Dugall wrapped his arms around Gwendolyn, mindful of her wound, and drew her near.

Her pulse beat frantically at the base of her throat, but her eyes held a woman's invitation, before her lashes fluttered closed.

He lowered his head once more, eager to drink deeply of the nectar of her mouth. Without hesitation, she opened, her tongue jousting with his, and the hunger he'd kept in check burst free of its boundaries.

A child's giggle interrupted the blissful moment, and Dugall raised his head as Gwendolyn gasped and jerked away.

Julia's elfin face, one hand covering her mouth, peered around the edge of the door. She glanced over her shoulder, saying, "I was right! I told you, you donkey's behind. Aunt Gwenny *is too* gonna marry Mr. Dugall. She's kissing his face off right now."

"Good heavenly days, that child will be the death of me yet," Gwendolyn murmured, her lips dewy from his kisses, and color flaring across her cheeks.

Passion-induced or embarrassment?

Both, perhaps.

Dugall chuckled and moved to a more discreet position. None too soon either.

A moment later, the door swung open all the way, and seven eager-faced children swarmed into the room, all talking at once as they clambered toward the bed.

A grin wide enough to park a coach split Kandie's face as she trundled in behind her wards. Her rich laughter filled the room. "Fo' certain, the chil' be right, dis time."

Dugall swung Julia onto his lap and pulled Jeremiah near his side. "What say ye? Would ye like me to marry yer aunt?"

"Oh, yes. It's the most romantiestest of things," Julia breathed.

Jeremiah nodded, and said, "She means romantic."

Not to be outdone, the other five chorused their approval as well.

"What say ye, Gwendolyn, my love?"

Eyes shining, her gaze touched on everyone before settling on him. "How soon?"

Och. She didn't want to rush into the union. He shoved aside his disappointment. Looked like he'd be visiting Loch Arkaig until he took her delectable form to bed. "We can wait for as long as ye like, Gwenny."

His groin gave a disgruntled twitch.

Too bad for ye, laddie. I'm no' about to rush the lass.

She smiled, a decidedly impish gleam in her green eyes. "How long will it take for a cleric to get here?"

EPILOGUE

Suttford House, Scottish Highlands

June 21, 1826

For the umpteenth time, Gwendolyn leaned on the balustrade and gazed at the tranquil scene before her. Twilight had settled on the Highlands, and the noise and bustle of the builders didn't intrude upon the peaceful moment.

The buildings under construction paralleled Suttford Bourne: the distillery to the left and the linen factory to the right. Even from here she could smell the fresh wood.

Dugall had proven brilliant when it came to both endeavors, and as he'd predicted, Ewan had been keen to invest. Lloyd had surprised them with his eagerness to help as well.

A movement below her window caught her eye, and she bent over the handrail, her loose hair brushing the railing. Dugall preferred that she sleep with the mass unbound, which gave her a devil of a time brushing it in the morning. But he so adored her hair, she couldn't refuse him.

"Working late again, Lloyd?"

He turned and peered up at her, and even in the dim light, his teeth flashed in a broad smile. "I wanted to check on the new foal."

He didn't know it yet, his birthday wasn't until next month, but the filly was his if he wanted her, and given he'd spent hours with the sweet-faced darling, he'd be overjoyed.

Jeremiah's knickers might twist a trifle. He'd repeatedly hinted that as the laird, he was old enough to have a horse. Dugall had wisely assigned him stable duties.

"Until the lad learns what goes into carin' for a horse, he's got nae call demandin' one of his own, even if he be the laird."

Lloyd had proven his worth over and over, and though they weren't actually kin, she'd grown to think of him as her cousin.

Not so much the Whitworths, both of which Gwendolyn had learned by way of Fenella's eavesdropping, had subtly fed Dolina's hatred. Oh, nothing as brazen as actually encouraging her to shoot anyone, but a constant string of grumbles, complaints, and grievances, inflaming her anger.

They'd steadily stoked Dolina's fury, and when confronted about their part, their first concern had been whether they'd be permitted to remain at Suttford House.

Those two had threated Fenella with dismissal, and with her mother ill, and Fenella the only source of income, she'd been terrified to come forward with the truth.

Especially after the attempts on Gwendolyn's life. She thought she'd be blamed. But after Dolina's death, Fenella could keep her silence no longer. She fretted about the new laird's safety if he returned to Suttford and the Whitworths still lived there.

Good thing Lloyd had already promised Elspeth she could marry her innkeeper—because once Gwendolyn learned of the Whitworths' subterfuge, she ordered them from Suttford.

Made them pack that very instant, and they were on their way within the hour.

That was what Elspeth had been whining about that day in the corridor. She'd wanted her mother to remain at Suttford House, and Lloyd had told her circumstances had changed. So, Elspeth had married her lover. But dear Mama had gone with her, much to Elspeth's new husband's chagrin.

Dugall wandered out onto the balcony, one of the letters Gwendolyn had found in her grandparents' things in one hand. "I'm surprised ye didna have me read these sooner, *leannan*."

Glancing over her shoulder, she shrugged. "I honestly forgot about them. I did have an inclination along those lines when we first arrived, but things became as chaotic as coons in a cupboard, and I plumb forgot until today."

She turned around and, leaning against the rail, pointed at it. "What do they say?"

"They're love letters yer grandfather wrote yer grand-mother while at university. From what I gleaned, they'd been in love for years. He hadn't wanted to betray his brother, but their love was too strong."

"Like Marilyn and Benjamin."

"Aye. The difference bein', I think, is that ye would've understood, and though perhaps ye'd have been hurt, ye'd have called off yer betrothal and allowed them to wed. Gerard McClintock would've never done somethin' as unselfish. So in the end, he forced their elopement."

A light breeze grabbed several strands of her hair and toyed with them. She caught the tresses and twisted them into a rope. "Does he say anything about . . .? What I mean is, is there any reference to Gerard being my grandfather?"

Dugall folded the crumpled letter and then reaching inside the balcony doors, set it on a table. "Aye." He crossed to her and after kissing her forehead, bent over and kissed her rounded belly.

"Hello there, laddie."

Gwendolyn laced her hands in his hair and gently forced his head upward. "Or lassie."

He grinned up at her before kissing her tummy again. "Wee bairn, yer mither and I canna wait to see ye."

Who'd have thought this brawny, strong-as-a-plow-ox Highlander would be so sentimental over his wife's expecting their child?

Softly boxing his ears, she asked, "Are you going to tell me, or do I have to fret even longer about the possibility that Gerard McClintock's blood runs in my veins?"

Dugall grinned and straightened. "Yer grandfather was quite the romantic, and one poetic letter to his darlin' leaves nae doubt as to who sired yer father." He puffed his chest out and patted his pectoral muscles. "We Scots are mighty proud in that way."

"You no more than any other randy man," she admonished with a soft chuckle. "I'm relieved. I know it seems silly, but the notion of that foul man being my grandfather, our child's great-grandfather, made my head hurt."

Dugall suddenly bent and scooped her into his embrace, and with a tiny startled yelp, Gwendolyn flung her arms around his neck.

"What are you about, you daft man?"

That naughty grin she'd come to associate with his rising desire tipped his mouth up at one corner. "I have the perfect cure for yer headache, my darlin'."

Dugall laid her on their great bed, and in moments had stripped away both their clothing. He lay beside her, resting his palm on the small mound of her stomach. He captured her mouth in a ravenous kiss and played his hand lower. Then lower still.

With a sigh, Gwendolyn entwined her arms about his neck and surrendered to his skillful seduction.

~

I hope you enjoyed
WISHES AND WONDER
If you'd like to leave a review, I would be grateful.

~

Keep reading for a free preview of
A YULETIDE HIGHLANDER
Book 10
Highland Heather Romancing a Scott: Castle Brides
Series...

~

A Yuletide Highlander
Highland Heather Romancing a Scot: Castle Brides
Book 10

East India Docks, London England

December 1826

The oak entry to Stapleton Shipping and Supplies flew open, and a wet young man bolted inside, his chest rising and falling as he gasped for breath. Panic pinched his thin face as he swiftly shut the door behind him. He grasped a small blade wedged into the worn leather belt encircling his navy bridge coat as his frightened gaze careened from corner to corner of Gregor McTavish's office.

Gregor had seen that same terrified look in the ebony eyes of a fox caught in a snare. Still grasping the quill hovering over his account books, while gripping the dirk he'd yanked from his boot when the youth dashed inside, he relaxed his tense posture.

This scared spitless waif, his back angled toward him while peeking at the pier around the window sash, wasn't a threat. Scrutinizing the dreary, water-soaked gray docks, Gregor lowered the quill while slipping his blade back into his boot.

Rain pelted a trio of burly, unkempt thugs heatedly arguing several yards away. Wrath contorted their apparent leader's face, and he flung a stocky arm toward a narrow alley a block farther along the wharf.

The largest of the other men shook his head, and the brute drove his open hand into the man's chest then smacked the shorter, swarthy-skinned sailor on the side of the head with enough force to send him stumbling backward a few steps.

Fists balled, the other man took a menacing step forward, but the bully puffed out his chest and yelled something. Whatever he said stalled the other man mid-step. After a slight pause and exchanging infuriated glances, his two companions thundered off.

Where to, and why did every instinct suggest the lad would know? Gregor veered a swift, hooded glance toward the boy before refocusing his regard on the sailor.

Only three buildings opened directly onto this section of docks. Was his uninvited visitor fleeing those thugs?

His hands on his hips, a fierce scowl pulling the corners of his eyes and mouth downward, the remaining sailor rotated slowly to the left and then to the right. He obviously searched for something. *Or someone.* His acute gaze swept past Stapleton Shipping and Supplies then slowly gravitated back.

Even from his seat, Gregor recognized the shrewdness quirking the sailor's mouth and gleaming in his narrowed eyes fixated on his office.

His nape prickled.

Danger.

He stood, pushing his unfashionably long hair over his shoulder. In the Highlands, he seldom tied it back, and he oft' forgot to do so in the morning since moving to London almost a year ago. He rather enjoyed the shocked expressions his blond mane caused the stuffy upper echelons of society.

The boy's narrow shoulders and back quaked. From cold or fear?

"Can I help ye?"

The lad spun to face him, his frightened gaze ricocheting about the office once more.

Nae, no' a laddie. A lass. A comely one at that.

"I'm Gregor McTavish." He introduced himself, careful to keep his tone calm and soothing in the hopes he might alleviate some of her fright. "My cousin's wife owns these buildin's and this establishment."

"Those men attempted to abduct me." Still breathing hard, she motioned toward the window. "Might I stay here for a few minutes until the last one leaves?"

"Aye, of course." Brutes, like those outside, had no honorable business with bonnie lasses.

At first glance, because of her height, bulky, dark blue overcoat, and sailor's cap, Gregor had mistaken her for a boy. She wasn't as young as he'd first believed either, though she certainly was not on the shelf. About the ages of his Ferguson step-cousins—somewhere in her early to mid-twenties, he'd guess.

Another inspection of the dock sent alarm, sparking up his spine.

The unsavory fellow tramped across the wooden walkway, straight for Stapleton Shipping.

Damnation.

"Quick, lass. Come here. He's comin'." Gregor made an urgent gesture. "Hide beneath my desk. *Now.*"

In a blink, she dashed across the room, and he stepped back to allow her to crawl into the kneehole.

No sooner had Gregor resumed his seat and dipped his

quill in the inkwell than the office door sprang open again. With deliberate intent, he took his time and finished the entry. His mind on the terrified woman crouched inches from his knees, he almost swore upon realizing he'd recorded two hundred and fifty barrels of molasses instead of twenty-five.

The sailor blocking the entry roughly cleared his throat and angrily stamped his feet. The wind blasted rain into the entrance, yet the man made no effort to shut the door.

The blighter earned himself a longer wait. Gregor suppressed a grin and dipped the nib into the ink again.

"Give me a moment," he muttered, taking far longer than a child's first attempt to form the letters of each word. After scribbling a few more lines—he might've ordered more flour than the whole village of Craigcutty could consume in a year—he finished and set the quill aside.

Twisting his mouth into a thin, hard smile, he rested a forearm on the desk and took the blackguard's measure from greasy brown hair, unshaven face and stained clothing, to his even filthier boots. The man's rank odor wafted across the room, and despite the open entry, Gregor's nostrils twitched in protest.

"Come to apply for one of the crew openin's, have ye?" He nonchalantly cradled his jaw in his palm. "Have ye any experience?"

Upon hearing Gregor's Scot's brogue, a sneer curled the man's upper lip. "No. I'm lookin' for a fugitive. She stole a large purse from my employer and was last seen runnin' in this direction."

"Och," Gregor murmured with mock understanding.

The sailor's astute, accusing eyes searched every inch of the office, lingering for a long moment on the half-open door leading to the stairwell and Gregor's apartment. Suspicion flared the man's nostrils before he tore his distrustful scrutiny away.

"I can assure ye, nae lawless lassies have entered this buildin' today." He leaned back and flung a casual look about the tidy office. "As ye can see for yerself," he waved a languid hand, "there's naebody here but Cat and me."

Upon hearing his name, the long-haired white and orange tabby opened his citrine green eyes and yawned, then arched his back before padding over to Gregor and hopping onto the desk. Purring, and with complete disregard for the ledger he stood upon, he pushed his head beneath Gregor's hand, demanding he be petted.

Gregor sliced a pointed look to the open doorway, water dripping from the overhang and wetting the floor.

"If ye'll excuse me." He tapped the ledger with the fingers of his other hand. "I've much work to do. Monthly reports, ye ken. Inventory to take. Supplies to order."

Lasses to protect.

"Receipts to record."

Riddin' my office of stinkin' horses' arses.

"Och, my employer is most demandin'," he rattled on, giving a woeful shake of his head and wholly enjoying the impatience creasing the sea tar's weather-worn face.

Cat, now sprawled full-length across the register, his eyes half-closed in lazy contentment, made a mockery of Gregor's claim he'd work to attend.

He'd rescued the starving kitten from the hard life of a wharf cat after he first arrived in London. Loneliness had compelled him, though he'd never admitted as much to a soul. For the first time in his life, there wasn't the pleasant chaos of a dozen or more people around at any given moment.

The spoiled beast didn't hesitate to show his gratitude. Although at times, his affection embarrassed Gregor. Cat lazily lifted a paw and patted his hand as if to say, "I require your attention. A belly scratch, if you please."

"Nae, I'll no' be rubbin' yer belly." He gathered the cat,

frowning at the smudged entries, and placed the ball of sharp-clawed fluff on the floor.

With a dismissive flick of his impossibly long tail, and a few fresh ebony ink stains accenting his silky coat, Cat sauntered to the stairs.

When the man continued to lurk in the doorway, Gregor summoned his most formidable look. The one that usually sent men scuttling away.

"Yer sure I canna talk ye into applyin' for a position? I have a ship sailin' to Africa in a fortnight that needs hands." He scratched the back of his head, raking his gaze up and down the man's form. "Can ye cook?"

The sailor's mouth skewed into another wide sneer, revealing missing, broken, and yellowed teeth. He folded dirty fingers, one by one, around the bone knife hilt protruding from his belt and, spreading his legs, ticked his chin upward as brutes of his ilk were wont to do when bent on threatening others.

"You best be tellin' me the truth, you bloody Scot." He settled another doubtful look on the stairs.

Bloody Scot?

Was the man a lackwit that he dared come in here and hurl insults? This Sassenach piece of horse shite had just tipped the scales from patience to annoyance.

The sailor wasn't a puny weakling, but Gregor and his twin had been called giants on more than a few occasions. And for good reason. Standing well over six and a half feet and massively built, even at three and thirty, no man had ever bettered him in a physical challenge—except for his twin.

Only because of the terrified young woman huddled beneath his desk had he kept a tight rein on his temper and tongue. Otherwise, this codpiece would've already found himself sprawled on the dock—unconscious and arse up.

"Cap'n Santano doesn't take kindly to people interferin' in his business," the blighter pressed.

Why wasn't Gregor surprised to learn this sod worked for Santano?

The captain's nefarious reputation preceded him, and six months ago, Stapleton Shipping and Supplies had refused his request to enter into a commercial relationship. Infuriated and full of his own self-importance, Santano had taken his business elsewhere.

Leisurely rising, and wholly unrepentant, Gregor used his immense size to intimidate the churl. He spoke slowly and deliberately as if addressing a simpleton. "If I tell ye nae thief entered this establishment, then nae thief is here." He made a show of lifting his clenched fists waist-high. "Do ye ken?"

The shady fellow's eyes shifted back and forth several times, and he nervously fingered his scraggy tobacco-stained beard with one hand while the other flexed upon his knife handle. He gave a grudging nod, his bluster disappearing in the face of someone capable of pounding his ugly face into pulp.

"Well, if you do see a tall, skinny blonde wearin' a peacoat, notify the cap'n at once." He half-turned and examined the pier. "While in port, he's usually aboard the *Mary Elizabeth*, at the Seven Seas Alehouse or," a lewd smile curved his mouth. "Madam Mionnet's."

Ah, the infamous brothel. No man valuing his ballocks sampled those whores. Most were fraught with disease.

"The chit usually has a scrawny, crippled whelp with her, about this tall." Santano's henchmen raised his hand midriff high. "You'd best take care, or she and that street rat will pick your pockets clean."

Gregor remained silent as he maneuvered around the corner of the desk. In about thirty seconds, he'd toss the bloody bugger out the door. Mustering what scant patience he had left, he managed to keep his annoyance from showing. "What's yer name, sailor, in case I needed to reach ye?"

"Yeates." After spearing him another hostile glare, he left, not bothering to shut the door behind him.

"Bloody rotter." Gregor closed the door, and though it was only just after two in the afternoon, turned the key in the lock and slid the bolt home, as well.

Rustling alerted him to his fugitive's intention.

"Stay where ye are. He's still watchin' the buildin'. I'm nae sure he believed me when I said ye weren't here, lass."

Her sharp intake of breath revealed she believed her appearance had fooled him into thinking she was a male. Hadn't she glanced in a looking glass of late?

He made a pretense of adjusting the three model ships displayed in the bay window then rearranged a telescope and a couple of maps before turning away.

"Have you a back entrance?" Refinement, but not the haughty cold tone of privileged nobles, colored her voice.

"Aye, but I think ye should stay here for an hour or two."

Or longer.

Gregor placed a sextant atop one of the maps and then, for good measure, added an open compass, positioned just so. Standing back, hands on his hips, he admired his handiwork. *No' bad.*

"You don't understand. My brother's out there. Alone and scared." On all fours, she peeked 'round the side of his desk, a few fair tendrils dangling on either side of her face.

Cleaned up and with a bit of meat on her bones, she'd be a right bonnie lassie.

He bent and flicked a couple of dead flies from the windowsill. Brushing his hands on his trousers, he casually turned halfway around. "Where is he?"

"I left him hiding amongst some barrels outside the cooper's." She jerked her head in that direction. "I attracted those ruffians' attention to lure them away."

One eye on the marina, Gregor ran a hand over his jaw. "I dinna believe ye stole anythin', so why are they after ye?"

At once, a shuttered expression masked her pale face. She pulled her soft mouth into a tight line and fixed her attention on the floor, her gold-tipped lashes fanning her hollow cheeks. Her short nails dug into the floor said what she feared to.

She didn't trust him.

Gregor couldn't blame her, and compassion welled behind his ribs. Survival on London's unforgiving streets meant never trusting anyone.

He eyed her covertly from beneath half-closed eyes. What dire circumstances had forced her and her brother to this life? He hadn't a doubt she'd not been born into it. Everything about her so far suggested she came from a genteel background.

There were few things he liked more than solving a challenging mystery, and this young woman was a puzzle, to be sure. Och...a good fight was always enjoyable, but on occasion, he preferred using his brains rather than brute strength. Only on occasion, mind you.

On hands and knees, the lass edged to the room's farthest corner before scrambling to her feet. Wise on her part. No one outside could see her in the lengthening shadows.

Since becoming his cousin-in-law Yvette McTavish's manager for her London warehouses, his life had been nothing short of mind-numbingly dull. He'd only accepted the position because he was ready—*och, bloody damn desperate*—to do something, anything, different than continuing at Craiglocky Keep, his cousin's castle.

Until just short of a year ago, Craiglocky was the only place Gregor had ever lived, and his sole purpose had been to serve his laird, Ewan McTavish. He'd loved both, still did, but discontentment ate away at him, growing and growing and growing...

Except for him, everyone at the Keep had married. And truthfully, he left as much to escape his extended family's matchmaking attempts as to try his hand at something new. At one time, he thought to become a doctor, and he still dabbled in the healing arts from time to time when called upon to do so. But there hadn't been any real need for his services after Yvette commissioned the building of a local hospital.

Gregor had also believed he'd marry Lily Ellsworth, but several years ago, she'd fallen in love with another. He hadn't been altogether shocked to realize he wasn't heartbroken. She'd been too young for him, in any event. Feeling much older than he was, he'd decided to leave the Highlands for a time.

Someday, he'd return. Scotland was as much a part of him as the blood tunneling through his veins at this very moment. He missed the fragrant heather, the craggy rocks, the hairy cattle, and the bright green meadows. He even preferred the Highland's harsh, unforgiving weather to London's perpetual stench and coal-laden skies.

"Mr. McTavish, I must find my brother right away. He'll be frightened." A tinge of fear peppered her impatience.

"Aye, lass, of course ye do. I'm just thinkin'." Not about rescuing her brother, but what he'd chosen to leave behind. Those musings were a waste of time, and before him was an opportunity to relieve the tedium his life had become as well as to help someone in desperate need. "We canna be too careful with the likes of those blackguards."

She muttered something unintelligible but which sounded distinctly unflattering.

One hand on his hip, he pulled his ear, trying to read her. He'd likely regret becoming involved, but if it brought a dose of excitement into his existence, well, damn it, it'd be worth it. "Ye can wait upstairs and have yerself somethin' to eat while I fetch yer brother."

Arms folded, she eyed him warily. "Why should I trust you?"

~

***I hope you enjoyed this free preview of
A YULETIDE HIGHLANDER
Book 10
Highland Heather Romancing a Scott: Castle Brides
Series.***

~

From the Desk of Collette Cameron®

Dearest Reader,

Gwendolyn and Dugall's story is one of my favorites. An American convinced she'll never marry after several broken betrothals, Gwendolyn decides a change of scenery is just what she needs. She didn't count on running down a burly Scot—by accident, of course—nor did she plan on falling in love with a younger man. I adored that element of their romance.

Dugall's a cock-sure confident charmer who knows exactly what he wants from life—until Gwendolyn comes along and turns his world head over tail. She's a wounded, wary spinster a few years older than him whose given up on her hopes and dreams. Their road to happily ever after is bumpy but worth the journey. I hope their romance makes you smile as you journey back into a simpler era where chivalry reigned.

Many of the characters in Highland Heather Romancing a Scot: Castle Brides series also appear in The Honorable Rogues® series. You can read the first chapters of all my books for free at **collettecameronbooks.com**.

Hugs,
Collette Cameron®

If you haven't joined Collette's exclusive mailing list click on QR image to sign up! You'll get access to exclusive content, sneak peeks, contests, giveaways, and more...

(P.S. No spam!)

https://collettecameronbooks.com/freegift

**Collette loves to hear from readers.
You can contact her via her website: collettecameron-books.com.
Or email her directly at collette@collettecameron-books.com.**

**You can also follow Collette on social media:
Facebook:** https://www.-facebook.com/ColletteCameronNovels/
Instagram: https://instagram.com/collettecameronauthor/
Goodreads: https://www.goodreads.com/collettecameron
Book Bub: https://www.bookbub.com/authors/collette-cameron

Giggles are Guaranteed
Collette's Cheris Reader Group

https://www.facebook.com/groups/CollettesCheris/

If you love to chat about all things romance-book related and enjoy taking part in fun and engaging live events, contests, and giveaways join **Collette's Chèris VIP Reader Group, https://www.facebook.com/groups/CollettesCheris/,** my exclusive private book group on Facebook.

Giggles are guaranteed!

Hope to see you there,
Collette Cameron®

COLLETTE CAMERON®

USA Today Bestselling author Collette Cameron® is renowned for her captivating, humorous, and heartwarming Scottish and Regency historical romance novels. With over 65 published titles, over 1.6 million books sold around the world, and multiple writing awards to her credit, Collette is a well-known author in the world of historical romance.

Readers love her witty and relatable characters including daring rogues, dashing scoundrels, and the strong and spirited heroines who capture their hearts. From the rugged highlands to the refined drawing rooms of Regency England, Collette's novels will transport you to another time and place, where love and adventure are just a page away.

Collette's Sweet-to-Spicy Timeless Romances® are the perfect escape for readers looking for romantic escape, poignant inspiration, engaging humor, and entertaining stories.

Based in the Pacific Northwest, Collette is surrounded by the lush greenery and rainy skies that inspire her writing. She dreams of one day splitting her time between the Pacific Northwest and Scotland. In the meantime, she indulges in her love of all things cobalt blue, dachshunds, chocolate, and of course, crafting her next historical romance.

Blue Rose Romance® LLC
collette@collettecameronbooks.com
collettecameronbooks.com

SEDUCTIVE SCOUNDRELS
A Sensual Marriage of Convenience
Regency Historical Romance

A Diamond for a Duke — Book 1

Only a Duke Would Dare — Book 2

A December with a Duke — Book 3

What Would a Duke Do? — Book 4

Wooed by a Wicked Duke — Book 5

Duchess of His Heart — Book 6

Never Dance with a Duke — Book 7

Wedding Her Christmas Duke — Book 8

The Debutante and the Duke — Book 9

Loved by a Dangerous Duke — Book 10

How to Win a Duke's Heart — Book 11

When a Duke Desires a Lass — Book 12

My Dearest Duke — Book 13

~

FOR THE LOVE OF AN EARL (Wicked Earls' Club)
A Humorous Aristocrat and Wallflower
Regency Romance Adventure

Earl of Wainthorpe — Book 1

Earl of Scarborough — Book 2

Earl of Keyworth — Book 3

Earl of Renshaw — Book 4

~

HEART OF A SCOT

A Passionate Enemies to Lovers
Scottish Highlander Historical Mystery
Romance Adventure

To Love a Highland Laird — Book 1

To Redeem a Highland Rogue — Book 2

To Seduce a Highland Scoundrel — Book 3

To Woo a Highland Warrior — Book 4

To Enchant a Highland Earl — Book 5

To Defy a Highland Duke — Book 6

To Marry a Highland Marauder — Book 7

To Bargain with a Highland Buccaneer — Book 8

A Christmas Kiss for the Highlander — Book 9

~

HIGHLAND HEATHER ROMANCING A SCOT: CASTLE BRIDES

A Passionate Enemies to Lovers Second Chance
Scottish Highlander Mystery Romance

Heart of a Highlander — Prequel

The Viscount's Vow — Book 1

The Highlander's Heiress — Book 2

The Earl's Enticement — Book 3

Triumph and Treasure — Book 4

Virtue and Valor — Book 5

Heartbreak and Honor — Book

Scandal's Splendor — Book 7

**A Second Chance Redeemable Rogue
and Wallflower Regency Romance**